THE HEALING DRAGON

DIANA DENISSE

THE HEALING DRAGON

THE RED BOOK SERIES
BOOK TWO

DIANA DENISSE

Para mis Padres. Los quiero mucho. <3

HELIOS
NAHLA
IGNIS
PUERTO QUINN
PETRA
ISLA TIERRA
GALLALO
THE BLACK CASTLE
LUZES
FIERNO
DIVINA
PERLA
HUMAN LANDS
PAZ

CHAPTER ONE

JANELLE

The illusion of freedom is as borrowed as time. It's impressive what life can make out of us. I went from prey to hunter in a matter of days. The fate I was eager to escape came to find me where I hid. I'm under no illusion it won't find me again.

I hear the cracking of sticks as my target closes in.

"One," I count under my breath.

I look over my shoulder, leaning against a tree, shielding me from sight. The creature is unsuspecting of my presence, heading exactly where I set my trap.

Crack. "Two." *Crack.* "Three." *Crack.* "Four." *Crack.* I smile to myself and whisper, "five."

The snap of the trap echoes in the forest. The creature thrashes violently. It fights to no avail as it hangs upside down tied by its legs.

"It's not dead," Ulysses says from my side.

I nearly jump out of my skin. He seems to have materialized out of thin air. I give him a glare I exclusively use for him. I met him at the small town I took refuge in a couple of weeks ago. For some unknown reason, he has taken a liking to me despite my best efforts to avoid him. Like a bad smell, he seems to have clung to me and is nearly impossible to shake off. I've concluded that my persistence in keeping my distance might actually encourage him. So now I just hope he gets bored.

"The trap is not meant to kill it." I take a step forward and pull a knife from my thigh strap. I throw it at an angle and it hits its mark in a breath. "Now, it's dead," I say.

The creature drops, hanging limp in the trap.

Ulysses doesn't look impressed. Quite the opposite. I still have no idea what he does for a living. In my time in town, I've seen him everywhere but at a job. Yet, he has an endless amount of coins and time on his hands.

"Help me get it down?" I ask as I move to the creature.

Ulysses looks at the deer, then back to me. Disgust is clear in his expression.

"I am a vegetarian."

I roll my eyes. "Since when?"

"Since you asked me to help you carve that thing," he says with crossed arms.

"If you're not going to help then you can leave," I say.

"See you later, Janelle," Ulysses says.

I pull my knife back and wipe it clean. By the time I cut down the trap, he's gone and I'm alone again.

The fresh air of the forest chills the sweat on my skin. I look down at my bloody hands. Only more crimson will paint my nails before the Fates are done with me. I know it in my bones. No matter how far I run, what was written for me will always find me.

I want to believe it all started the night my father led an attack on the Black Castle, declaring war on our King. The King took mercy on me and let me go when he read through the minds of my father's men and found me ignorant of his plans.

But, that doesn't erase the blood that stained my hands that night. My inaction was just as much murder as if I had lit the match myself.

A little voice inside my head fears I pushed the first domino that started it all many months before the attack. I went to the Fate's temple and pleaded with them. I begged for them to intervene with my father's plan to marry me off to Brandon Oscuro. They accepted and I was punished. My soul was bound to a cruel man who saw me as nothing but a pawn. I committed my last heinous crime that night when my blade ended his life and forever freed me from his grasps in this world.

A sinking feeling tells me none of this is over. My father took the Red Book and his plans for it are a mystery to even myself. My role in this will only end where it started. The voices that haunt me in every dream remind me of it, like I could ever forget. *They are tattoos written across my skin in invisible ink, a color only my eyes can see.*

My time is coming.

CHAPTER TWO

JESSE

In for five, hold for five, out for five, repeat.

The five count helps me slow my breathing and settle my heart rate. This is how I have managed to get my bearings and regain control of my emotions for as long as I can remember. I've never been one to falter in high-pressure situations, but a few months ago, everything changed. The peaceful halls of the castle became oven walls that cooked up every soul unfortunate enough to come across one of the three dragons. My life's been nothing but stress ever since. Five counts help me stay at the bridge of sanity.

I watch the commotion in the room with little interest. Leaning against this wall in silence has become my routine whenever Brandon calls for leadership meetings. Advisors argue about potential plans of action, but I have nothing good to add, so all I do is observe. It has been two months, and we have gotten nowhere closer to finding the Red Book or the traitors that took it with them.

The Duelo family marched against the crown on the bloody night that painted the Black Castle crimson. Lord Duelo is the leader and coward who sent his own offspring to torment the innocents while he snuck up on my grandfather and stole the Red Book. The all powerful book that controls all the magic in our kingdom is now in the hands of the rebels. We lost more than our King and loved ones that night. He stole our peace and the safety of our home.

Something died inside me that night. I held my grandfather in my arms, unmoving, knowing I could do nothing to stop the third attacker. I knew no matter how much anger ran through my veins I could never be the one to take down Janelle like I did her brother.

The woman I once held as my most esteemed friend is now the enemy. She earned that title in blood. Despite her not leaving with her father and facing her own punishment instead, I could never forgive her participation. I would have done anything for her. I would have sold my own soul for her.

I can still feel the tears running down my face as I looked at my younger brother and begged him to do it for me. To kill Janelle. My weakness was too great to carry out what needed to be done for him, his crown, and our people. I let them down then.

I don't see in his eyes the same hatred I see in the mirror, but I fear it is only a matter of time. It's been months and we are nowhere closer to finding the traitors. It's not long before they will begin looking for the guilt inside our own walls and I, by far, have the most to repent.

"This is absolutely absurd!" Brandon bangs his fists on the table.

A few pieces of paper fly out. His patience has been running thin for too long. Bianca is still searching for her friend Matias after he never returned from his trip to Fierno. The trip was supposed to be a quick visit to drop off medicinal plants at a clinic in the City of Sin and pick their remaining personal items from their old home.

We first presumed him lucky to have missed the attack but after days went by and he didn't show Bianca grew concerned. Despite my brother's pleas she set out to search for Matias multiple times now, returning empty handed and broken hearted every time. Having her out of sight after the attack makes him irritable. Which is understandable considering the enemy could very well be hiding in the forest that surrounds us.

"How is it we have gone from one stretch to another and have yet to find a single clue about their whereabouts?" His voice lowers to a seething tone. "Where is Duelo?"

The room is full of advisers and Royal Force leaders. The always opinionated individuals who usually can't shut up have nothing to say now. What an inopportune moment to run out of words. As if the gray color of the wall has become the most interesting thing, they don't look his way. Looking at their king with nothing to say is admitting their failure.

They combed through each city in Puerto Quinn and the surrounding land, leaving no rock unturned, yet they found no sign of the Duelo family or their followers. They were successful in exonerating a significant number of locals in their community. Not even the most influential families were aware of Duelo's plans to take over. He did not trust many people. Including the majority in the city of Ignis.

"They are not in Puerto Quinn. We have checked every-where." Damien leans back on his chair. He is the youngest advisor in my brother's cabinet and by far the most sane one. "They must be hiding somewhere else."

Brandon clears his throat. "I will need you to be more specific. Where?"

Damien's eyes turn my way but he pauses before speaking.

His words are carefully picked as he asks in my direction, "What did the vendors in Fierno tell you, exactly?"

His question reminds me that they're not the only ones who failed my brother in this aspect. My efforts to infiltrate and search the City of Sin turned unfruitful. The main center of Fierno is run by what locals call vendors. The council-like group consists of older local business owners who prioritize one rule above all else. Respecting a deal.

"Their stand stays. As long as no one messes with their business or other's businesses, you are free to do as you please. Their order keepers decline knowing anything about Duelo or his movement," I say.

"Their order keepers are only called to neutralize disruptive individuals with lethal force," My brother, Roman, interjects.

His frown is firmly in place. Even his new relationship with Isabel has done nothing to change that.

"That's only the case in the main city. The outskirts are a completely different world." Damien shrugs. "They could be there."

Four organized crime families run the outskirts of Fierno. They conduct business in the center of Fierno alongside the vendors, but only dictate orders and impose taxes on their corresponding territories. Each person inside this room knows how they function and the perimeter of their territories.

"Each and everyone of those families has a price for information and we paid it to no avail," I say, pushing off the wall to stand straight. "They know nothing about Duelo that we didn't tell them ourselves. If they would've lied to me about it I would know." I tap my ear.

My gift to hear lies is the reason I've taken a front role in searching for the traitors. I can hear a ringing in my ears that signals when a person has spoken deceitfully or omits parts of the truth.

Brandon has held no reserve to find Duelo. Under any other circumstance we would never pay an informant in Fierno but time is running out along with his patience.

"Perhaps they are working around your gift. Duelo might've learned of it and now plans around it," another advisor says.

There's only one person who could have relayed that information to him.

"Maybe we need a new strategy." Roman scratches his head. He shoots me a look that has the hairs on the back of my neck rising. "Perhaps it's time we go into the mountains again."

At this, I chuckle. The noise that comes out of me is flat and cynical. The mountains connect us to Fierno. I spent three weeks of my life inside those mountains looking for a trace of the missing traitors. There was nothing to find.

I know I've been a hollow of a man these past two months. Losing my grandfather and friends has not been easy. I've yet to figure out how to put myself together again. But I do know how to do my job.

"Is there something funny?" Roman asks as he crosses his arms.

He's ready for a fight, and I have so much pent-up anger inside me I might just give him one.

"It's a stupid suggestion. We are going in circles. You think I didn't conduct my search thoroughly enough, brother?" I move away from the wall towards him.

Roman's eyes narrow, and a glimpse of something dark crosses his face. "Then why don't we find someone who can point us directly to the man we have been looking for." At the loud silence in the room, he clears his throat, doubling down.

"An idea I'm sure every person in this room has had, but doesn't dare say out loud as to not cross the walking dark cloud you've become, *brother*." The last word is spit out in a mocking tone.

I admit I have not acted like myself recently. I gaze across the room and see how several people avert their eyes.

"Roman," Brandon warns.

The big fool doesn't listen. If anything, his eyes show a flash of something that says he is done playing nice.

"How about we go find the one girl who probably knows exactly where the book is?" Roman asks.

The pounding in my heart is so loud it makes it hard to hear. I've been avoiding the topic of Janelle for months. I've tried to. The ghost of her haunts me in my sleep and every waking hour. I can't eat without wondering if she has food. I cannot shower without wondering if she has clean water, and sleep avoids me wondering if she is safe at night. Her memory brings a mixture of worry and guilt. It's quickly followed by revulsion at myself. Despite what she did, I can't stop caring for her. It will be my downfall.

"What makes you think she knows?" I ask.

I hate how the mention of her existence stabs at my chest and reopens a wound I wish to forget. Her betrayal has tattooed a brand of shame and hurt across my forehead. I see it in the eyes of every person who looks in my direction, including myself in the mirror.

"All she has to do is find her daddy. Duelo Senior will always take back what's his."

At the mention of her father getting her back under his control, I sneer.

Roman pauses long enough to clear his throat. His voice softens like he is trying to reason with my better judgment. "She was his most-prized possession. The way he used to parade that girl for all to see. Duelo must be trying to steer her back to himself if he hasn't already."

I shake my head.

There's no way we'll find Janelle and make her do anything. She has done and been through enough. She'll laugh at our faces for even suggesting the idea. That's *If* she is alive. The thought that she might not be clouds my mind. I can't even think straight.

"He hasn't," Brandon confirms.

The confidence in his statement tells me he knows exactly where she is. I have not allowed myself to fall into the temptation of searching for her even while I was out searching for her father and his followers. Am I really surprised to learn that my brother knows?

"No, we are not going to take that route," I say with determination to my brothers.

"Do you have any other suggestions?" Brandon's tone is sharp.

I shake my head. There are grunts of disapproval coming from several people around the room. Roman was right. They've all been thinking about it to some extent if they are so quick to shake their heads at me for turning the idea down.

Brandon tiresomely adds, "you used to have ideas, Jesse. This is when we need them the most."

"Leave her out of this." I breathe out each word with more rage than I've ever felt. "You took her magic and told her to stay away."

I don't even recognize my own voice.

"Watch your mouth." Brandon slams his fist on the table again. Making all in the room jump. "You're speaking to your King in this room. Not your brother." His words are slow and full of enmity.

We don't use rank amongst our closest team members and

absolutely never around family. The tension in the room triples. Those who were shooting me disapproving looks and shaking their heads are now finding the edge of the table incredibly interesting as they look down. Not one gaze meets mine as I look around.

"Count me out." I look him up and down. "*King* Oscuro."

I move towards the door without looking back, but his words freeze me in place.

"What if we make her a deal?"

I pause and face the King of Puerto Quinn.

"Suppose we were to propose a pardon and the restoration of her magic in exchange for the Red Book?" Brandon asks.

I shake my head, but Roman takes me by the shoulder and pleads with me. "Think about it, Jesse. This is her opportunity to prove herself. She gets a do-over. She brings the book back and will regain her magic."

I say nothing as I stand there. They both wait for me to react but I fight the urge to give them anything else.

"This will happen with or without you. It's your choice to partake in the events that will inevitably unfold." With those parting words, Brandon exits the room, giving no one else a second glance.

I walk straight out of the room with no destination in mind.

"Jesse," Roman reaches for me but I side step him. "I had no choice. She's the key to all this. I know it and if you were thinking clearly, you would know it too."

"Leave me alone." I let the door swing shut behind me.

I walk with purpose but without direction, or so I thought until I find myself in the middle of a forest opening. I don't stop there, instead I keep going deeper into the woods. My legs grow tired, but it doesn't slow my pace. My limbs finally pause before my brain can register that I'm standing outside the Fate's temple.

I walk into the opening, but before I can cross the threshold, I stop and backtrack. My hands brush through my hair and I fight the urge to pull the strands harder. Nothing makes sense now. I would've never imagined myself in this predicament. What am I even doing here?

I feel as if I lost Janelle twice. First when Ray became her soul bond. Then again after the attack. I look at the opening again and wonder if they knew. Have they chosen anything of what came?

If Janelle hadn't been paired up with Ray, none of this would have taken place. She wouldn't have helped her father commit such a horrible crime and my grandfather would be here now. The illogical, hopeful side of my brain would like to believe that. The anger that flows through my veins has no target and choosing to place it on Janelle is useless. Despite it all, I can't help myself from worrying for her wellbeing, however undeserving she is of that.

I turn to the temple and stare at the entrance. I want to see them, ask them questions and most of all share some words with them. I want them to explain themselves. It's crazy to think that I can ask the Fates for explanations but that's how out of my mind I feel. I know very well they don't allow just anyone to come inside the temple to speak to them. Even Brandon doesn't have free reign to go inside when he pleases. The Fates only allow those who they wish to speak with to come in.

With all the anger now redirected to the beings inside those walls, I march to the threshold with no intention of turning back around. They are going to hear me one way or another.

An invisible wall keeps me from crossing inside. I place my

palm on the force field that acts as a door to bar me from entrance and test my magic against it. The instant shock of electricity I get is a clear sign I'm not welcome.

This should be enough for me to walk away, but the anger in my body only intensifies, muddying my thoughts.

I take five steps back and look forward. If magic does not work, brute force might be my only alternative. I rush the doorway with all my might. I don't truly expect the barrier to give in to my force. Instead, I expect to tire myself out by throwing my body against it. However, when the barrier should stop my momentum, it does not, instead it allows me to cross the threshold, running full force into the first wall of the temple.

My body and head connect directly with the marble, making me grunt at the impact. I lose all strength in my legs and immediately find myself on the floor. My head aches and my arm shoots spikes of pain when I try to bend it.

I sit on the floor for a second before I notice a trail of blood going down my shirt. I instinctively reach for my face and locate the source on the upper right side. There's a slight cut running down my eyebrow.

"Are you okay?"

The voice comes from nowhere and everywhere all at once. This isn't the first time I've heard it. It haunts the recesses of my mind. The impossibility of her being here jolts me into the present. I get to my feet and look around, but my vision begins to darken.

25 years ago.

The sun's heat is beating at my skin relentlessly. I wipe my sweaty hands on my shirt, leaving a stain of dirt and blood. I scratch the stain with my finger and grunt when I realize it is really stuck in there. Mom won't be happy to see this. I can hardly feel the sting from the cut in my hand, but I do feel an ache in my head.

Mom might be more upset at my brothers for that than at me for the shirt.

My brothers and I often find ourselves in trouble during our summer stays at the lake, but today might have gone too far. We usually stay away from all forest creatures, but winning a double dare to steal a duende's floral crown from their door seemed worth it at the time. I didn't know the creature would chase me down its garden, making me run into the rose bushes.

"Are you okay?"

The question comes from a small voice standing behind me. I nearly jumped at the abrupt question. I can't even turn to check quickly, so I take a second to turn my whole body to face her.

The little girl must be a few years younger than me. Her blue dress flows around her, reminding me of an angel figurine my grandmother keeps in her winter solstice decorations. The image transforms into something else when I get to her hair. It's bright red. That is when I realized what family she must belong to. The royal families own the area, and only they and those they invite can access the lake during the summer. The only ones with red hair are the Duelo family.

"Janelle," I say, assuming it must be her.

There is only one girl in the Duelo family. She gives me a small nod in confirmation. Her eyes move to my injuries curiously. I expect her to be disgusted, but her eyes show something else.

"Do you need help?" She points at my hand.

"How can you possibly help me?" I ask, annoyed that she's bothering me.

Her smile quickly drops at the tone of my question. Her eyes narrow, and her lips pinch together. Without answering me, she takes my hand in hers and places her palm over my cut. I watch as a small and quick light flashes. When she removes her hand, the cut is gone—completely healed.

"Wow," I say in amazement. "Thanks," I add when she says nothing in return.

Janelle just gives me a small smile, lacking all the warmth the previous one had held.

"I got one here too." I point at the cut in my head. "I got it from a hanging branch on my escape route."

She steps closer into my space and lifts to her tiptoes. She holds her hand inches away from the cut and, just like the other one after a flash of light, it's gone.

I run my fingers over the healthy skin. "How do you do that?" I ask.

She's far too small to be this good at magic already. It also doesn't feel like magic. Her lips don't move when the flash comes. I'm older than her and even I have to say my spells out loud.

Her shoulder lifts to one side. "I just can." She looks down at her hands with furrowed brows. "Is it weird?"

"Cool-weird," I say with a smile.

Her smile returns at my comment. This time I can tell it's a real one.

Without saying another word, she climbs a few rocks down to the river's edge. I follow her and see her set up. No wonder she heard me but I didn't see her. She has a blanket on the ground with a backpack nearby. An open book and a box of snacks on the side. She doesn't turn back to look at me as she settles back.

I don't wait for an invitation as I sit beside her. The sun is behind us, and the rocks above provide the perfect amount of shade. We still have a perfect view of everything in the lake, and the sun is not in our eyes.

"You found the perfect spot," I say, looking around. "How did my brothers and I miss it?"

They will love this. I look down at the edge of the lake. We are still slightly higher than the water, but not by much. I would have to *investigate the water level here, but it would be perfect if it's high enough to jump.*

"I like to read here," she says in a soft tone. She doesn't look at me. "It's close enough to be here in a short walk, but out of sight enough that people walk above and never see me. It's my favorite place to be."

As I sit there listening to the water and the few people who pass above us, I realize how sacred it is. It's silently peaceful yet not secluded. I look at Janelle and decide I never want to take anything from her. I promise I'll never tell a soul of this place to keep it only ever hers.

CHAPTER THREE

JESSE

I stand up and lean back against a cold stone wall of the temple. I squint my eyes and touch my head. Thankfully, the headache is only a subtle ache now. I'm only a few feet inside the temple, but it feels like miles, as every step I take is shaky and unstable.

Finally, outside the temple, I sit on the steps and lean back. Rays of sun break through the tree branches, making me flinch at their directness. I focus on my breathing as I feel my breakfast coming back up. Something tells me the strength I used to run into the barrier wasn't enough to cause this level of damage. The Fates are teaching me a lesson.

"There you are," Roman says. He stops when he notices the state I'm in. His eyes move around us as if expecting someone or something to jump out unexpectedly. "Who the hell did that?"

I point behind me with my thumb. "I had a few choice words for them, but they denied me entry."

His eyes move from the temple to me. "Go on," he says.

"I tried to barrel my way in."

A burst of laughter rings from Roman. "You tried to force your way in?" He bellows louder. "You were looking for a fight, so they beat you black and blue."

"I look that bad?" I join in laughter at the absurdity of it all.

"Did you get what you were looking for?" Roman looks between me on the floor and the temple.

Slowly I tilt my head back to look at the structure. I don't think I needed to verbally express to the Fates what I wanted. The all-knowing creatures surely saw me and my rage coming. I look at my hands and wonder where the urgency for answers fled. The simmering anger that pushed me to seek answers is not gone but somehow calmed. Whether it was the beating that did it or her voice in the edges of my mind, I don't know.

"Something like that," I say, trying not to laugh.

"You look awful, but maybe this is what you needed to clear your mind." He looks out into the forest. "You need to realize that this plan has merit. If you don't want to go, you don't have to. I have two trusted soldiers in mind for the mission. They will not harm Janelle. They're willing to help her if required. We don't plan to send her to her death."

"That is exactly what she will walk into if she's back in her father's sight," I say with a lot less determination.

"We don't know that. After all, it's her choice."

That stops me on my tracks because that's something I can't deny. Janelle's life has been a series of choices made on her behalf. I've spent countless hours listening to her suffering of having no choices. And here I am like every other man in her life, thinking I know better and choosing for her. The thought of her seeing me right now cements my decision.

"It's her choice," I agree.

"Make sure you visit Amy Bee before going to Brandon," Roman says, getting to his feet. "Do you need me to help you there?"

I take a tentative step forward. I'm feeling better, but the tick in Roman's hands tells me he really wants to help.

"If I want to make it there today, I will require assistance," I say.

My brother breathes out in relief as he hooks his shoulder under mine and takes on some of my weight.

"Did you get lighter?" he asks.

"Fuck off," I say.

"Must be your depression diet. Soon enough, you will have the ladies asking for your secret."

"You know I can hear when you lie to me." I give him a side eye.

He chuckles. "I know. But what kind of brother would I be if I didn't tease you?"

"A good brother." I look to the heavens for help, but find none.

"A good brother lets you waste away only for a little while before making you see reason."

I say nothing in return because the words are far more truthful than I'm ready to face. I've been inside my head for so long that I failed to see how worried my family is for me. Thankfully, Roman is good at knowing when to drop a topic. He changes the conversation to his upcoming plans to move in with Isabel.

"During the tour we had a fall out that really reminded me to pull my head out of my ass and make a move already." He chuckles to himself. "Who would have thought that this entire time she returned my feelings?"

We all did and I told him as much. Didn't I?

"Who would have thought?" I remind him and grunt in pain as we keep walking back to the castle.

"I don't know what I would do if she weren't here after that night."

The serenity in his voice tells me he would be a shadow of a man if Isabel would have suffered the same fate as the others. Sofia. I think of her soft bright smile and innocent eyes. She was inside the library with a group of fellow students studying for their exams the next day. They were the last victims Ray took that night. Isabel would have faced the same fate if it wasn't for her gift. It kept her and Santiago alive. She was able to block the fire centipede before Bianca took him down.

That was also the last day Isabel was able to keep her gift a secret. Which has been for the best. Her gift is the reason we have a strong shield around the castle now.

"Ready to pass the barrier?" Roman asks as I feel the familiar pressure.

Isabel with the help of Lexi Blue was able to create a strong shield for the entire castle. It covers the structure on all sides until the forest edge. Every person attempting to cross the shield needs to be invited by the King himself. Only those who live in the castle are free to come and go.

"It's good that you have someone to lean on during these times," I say.

I take a deep breath in relief once we have crossed the shield. It's an odd sensation to walk past it. It feels as if you are entering the current of a river. The pressure against your skin is strong but momentary.

"How often does Isabel need to reinforce the spell?" I ask.

"About once a week," Roman says. He looks around as if checking the invisible shield. "Technically Lexi Blue is the one who does it by linking her magic to Isabel's."

I stop walking because this is news to me. "Lexi can do a spell?"

To our outer shock, Lexi Blue has not been able to successfully perform magic since she was born. My grandfather took a liking to the sisters from a young age since their mother and father worked with us for generations. He had professors who taught my brother and I try to work with her but to no avail, all had the same diagnosis. Her focus was simply not there. Not when she allowed her mind to wonder too much.

"You think they were wrong about her?" I ask.

Roman turns to face me. "I don't know but they have to be. It's possible she is a conduit. She is able to perform magic when linked to someone else's power."

I chuckle at the idea.

"What?" Roman asks.

"All that knowledge she has. If all she needed was a magic source to channel, Lexi Blue is going to be unstoppable."

"Well she better find another magic source because Isabel won't channel her all the time." He huffs as if any of this it's up to him. "Let's get you to the clinic."

Despite the events that followed that night, I am glad to see my brother in a solidified relationship. It's as stable and serious as we all knew it would be. It wouldn't surprise me if Isabel takes on my last name very soon.

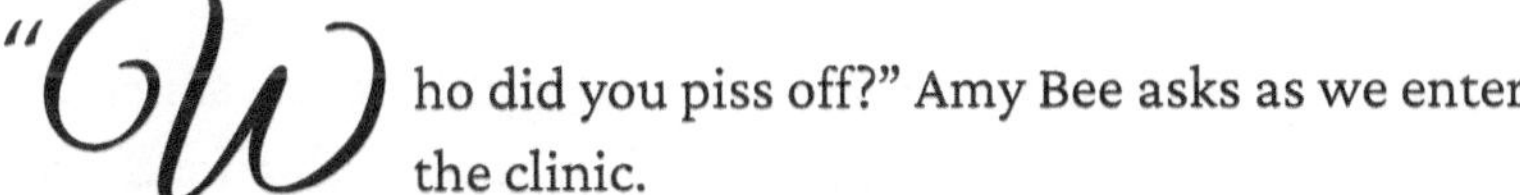

"**W**ho did you piss off?" Amy Bee asks as we enter the clinic.

She has been running this clinic for years now and despite having plenty of help around her she is always the first face I see when I set foot here. I often wonder if she ever takes days off. I rarely see her anywhere else outside of these walls.

"If we told you, you wouldn't believe his stupidity," Roman says as he helps me climb onto an open bed for treatment.

"I'll be right with you, Jesse." She takes a bag and begins administering her assessment of my injuries ignoring Roman.

I can see from the corner of my eye how Roman rolls his

eyes. He gives me a nod then departs silently. These two have never been able to get along or see eye to eye. It's a little funny to see how much it bothers him. Amy Bee is picky like that about who she fancies and who gets her cold shoulder.

She takes her time going over my injuries and pulling items from various cabinets.

"This will make you feel better." Amy Bee hands me a cup with boiling water and herbs she picked out. "Let me know if you need me," she says, then leaves me in the room alone.

I settle back onto the bed and absorb all the information that was shared with me. The cup on my hands cools down enough for me to drink the liquid. I know what is right and despite how hard it might be, cowering down has never been my style.

I find Brandon in his office later that day, with his office door slightly cracked open. This has always been a clear sign that one can simply walk in. As my feet cross the threshold, I wish I would have knocked. Bianca is hunched over by the windows, softly crying in Brandon's arms.

Her soft sobs gut-punch me, freezing me a few steps into the room. I don't have to ask what is wrong. Her childhood friend, Matias, has yet to return from his trip to the City of Sin. While we searched up and down for the traitors, she sailed on her own mission to find Matias. Just like our search efforts, she returned home empty-handed. Unlike our rage and determination that grows after every empty return, her journey brought her back sad and hopeless.

Brandon notices my arrival over her head. His eyes are tired and helpless. An emotion I can relate to all too well. If only I could ease his burdens. I look down at my hands. My clenched fist feels so useless. All of me does nowadays.

The Lord of Wisdom has no clue what to do. What a sick twist of fate.

"Jesse," Brandon calls my name. "Do you need something?"

Bianca pushes him away and turns to the window trying to compose herself before turning to me.

"I will go," I tell him and raise my chin.

"I will go with you." Bianca offers, stepping away from the window.

Her eyes are still red, and tear marks are fresh on her cheeks. The stress lines around her eyes look more pronounced today.

"You just returned." Brandon embraces her with so much care.

"Any news?" I ask.

"Matias made it to the clinic in Fierno and delivered the plants to LeeAnn. He got sidetracked on the way back," she says.

"What's next?" I look between them.

"I can't just sit here and wait." Bianca runs her fingers through her hair. The desperation slipping through clear as day. "I need to be productive."

"You can find something productive to do here." Brandon pulls her to his chest. "We don't know when Jesse will be back. I can't go without seeing you for an unknown length of time."

There is a knock at the door before a soldier enters the room. He passes by me and hands Brandon a box. My brother takes it and places it on his desk, then gestures for me to get closer. He opens the box and I see a cape. I look back at Brandon because I haven't seen this cape since we were children. At the sight of it, Bianca joins us.

Brandon nods, and the soldier hands me a piece of paper. The coordinates are of a location near the border between Fierno and the human lands. I don't have to ask to know it will lead me to the girl that I have worked so hard to put out of my mind.

"Look under the cape," Brandon directs me.

I lift the garment and find a golden envelope sitting at the bottom. I pick it up carefully.

"It's a letter from me to Janelle. If she signs the bottom, she accepts the conditions of the contract," Brandon says.

"A contract?" I look at the fancy lettering and the glitter hint that shimmers in the light. "A magic binding contract."

"She cannot be trusted," my brother says, like it's the easiest explanation. "Her life is not bound to it. Do not presume me to be so cruel. She was my friend too, you know." His voice lowers. "The contract will simply make me know of her disloyalty."

He refrains from mentioning that it is because of his lack of trust in my ability to inform him of any deceitfulness from her. The unspoken message is subtly implied. If I heard the tone of her dishonesty, would I say something? I'd like to think I would.

Brandon nods his head, and I take my leave. Bianca continues to argue her case about joining, but I can hear the reluctance in my brother's voice.

As I lay in bed at night, I look out the window and recall the nights I hoped to hear the familiar five knocks announcing my friend's arrival. Those nights feel a world away. The once eager anticipation has turned into a stressful reluctance.

23 years ago.

I look out the window and still see nothing. I tell myself to just focus on the picture book I have in my hands, but I can't help my eyes when they move to the clock on the wall. They move on their own accord. She should be here any minute.

Two rocks hit my window back to back. Then there is nothing but silence. After a beat, I hear the five knocks on the metal pipe running down the side of the house. I sit there waiting until a small silhouette climbs off the side of the window. Something inside my chest feels like it can finally breathe.

"Janelle," I say in greeting. I try to sound cool and not like I've been watching the clock tick by for her.

"Hi." Her sheepish smile makes me grin.

All my worries escape.

Our houses are now next to each other on the lake, and our rooms face one another on the side of the houses. We never talk about why she always ends up here. Every night at about the same time, Janelle throws a rock to my window, then knocks on the metal pipe, announcing her arrival. It has become something I look forward to. If my brothers have noticed how I lock myself in my room early, they have said nothing about it.

She comes into my room and climbs onto her side of my bed. A long sigh escapes her, as she finally relaxes after a long day. Despite being past dinner time, I've placed a snack for her on the side table. She wastes no time diving into it. I watch and take notice of how much she eats every night. Sometimes she is much hungrier than usual. She trains hard every day with tutors. Even in the summer, her studies are drilled down on her with so much urgency I feel bad for her. She deserves a break.

She is ten, and I am twelve. I can't imagine being friends with any other ten-year-old, but Janelle is different. Maybe it's the fact that she's already learning magic at my level. We only see each other in the summer when our families come to the lake for two months. Occasionally, we cross paths during the year at a royal family party. Still, we hardly get to exchange more than pleasantries.

"Alright, I'm done." She puts aside her leftover sandwich. "What do you have for me?"

I lift my leg and fold my pants to my knee.

"That's gnarly," she says, but her face shows amusement at the gruesome scratch.

I got hurt today with my brothers in the woods.

"We angered some giants in the forest." I wiggle my brows for effect.

Her eyes widen as I tell her an elaborate, partly fictional version of the events. As I talk about the day, she moves her hand over my injury and heals it with her gift. This has become our thing. Every night, she comes over, and we do this. She heals all the scratches I gained with my brothers during the day. I tell her about our adventures, then spend the rest of the night together. We listen to music and read books.

Once it gets late and we both yawn, we lie down side by side, facing each other. We close our eyes and let the noise of the open window put us to sleep. She is always gone by the time I wake up, but I know without a doubt that she will be back the very next day.

CHAPTER FOUR

JANELLE

I rub my hands together attempting to warm up my frozen limbs. There's a noticeable change in the mornings as the temperature drops. The hot summer months have quickly passed, leaving the chill of a fast-approaching winter.

I wrap my cover closer around me as I walk down town to the market. It's small with about twenty stands all lined up in one street. I despise getting up this early, but it's the only time I can get what I need. The market only comes once a week on Sundays. During the week, they are in Perla, the second biggest city in Paz.

Without my magic, I'm as good as a human. That prompted me to settle here. Close enough to the outskirts of Fierno and far enough from the capital of the human lands. At first I wasn't sure if my lack of magic would be enough to allow me inside Paz. I still don't know exactly how they know when a magical creature is inside their borders but if I had access to my magic they would have made notice of my presence within a day of my stay.

I've heard already of two magic wielders that overstayed in

town and were found by the King's soldiers soon after. My only guess is that there are two spells over the land. One that blocks spells from being performed and another that alerts the king's guards to the presence of magic wielders. Whatever the case, my current state is enough to help me blend.

A few of the sellers nod in greeting as I pass their stands. I've been here for weeks now, and I cannot say that my presence has gone unnoticed. Not as much as I had hoped. Young women living alone in a cabin in the woods are not common.

My hair has attracted more than one second glance. I've contemplated cutting it or dying it a dark color, but I never fully commit to the idea. So much of me feels stripped and ripped out. I yearn to keep something of myself untouched.

I get the items I'm looking for and quickly make my way back. Recently, the sight of the small cabin brings me peace and joy. A piece of this world that is mine and mine alone. Regardless of the quiet nights, I have found peace in the silence.

My cabin sits at the edge of a river a couple miles inside the forest. Even from inside, I can hear the water's current. When I bought it, it was nothing more than walls and a ceiling. Now, it's a home.

The colors that paint the sky this high in the mountains feel so much closer to paradise. I often wonder how long my eyes will see this picture before they grow accustomed to its beauty.

The first sign that someone is in my home comes from the smoke of the chimney. I spot the cloud from a mile out. I'm instantly alerted that whoever is inside wants me to know in advance they are there. Their reasoning for announcing themselves could be many things. As I walk that last mile to my front porch, I think of all the possibilities.

A pair of boots outside the door clues me in that my visitor is male. What gives me pause is the manners they displayed by ensuring no dirt is tracked in with their entrance. No man trained by my father would be so conscientious about their intrusion. If anything, they make it their job to be a nuisance to me.

"Do you plan on staring at my shoes all day?"

I jump back at hearing the voice. My heart is nearly beating out of my chest. I cannot believe I allowed someone to catch me off guard like that. I look up at the roof and find Jesse Oscuro sitting there. The open window to his left leading to my room tells me how he got there. He is also wearing shoes on his feet. The ones by the door were a distraction.

Our eyes meet, and I'm confronted with the oh-so-familiar hues of gold I know so well I could paint from memory. The sight that once brought me so much fulfillment now only reminds me of my shortcomings.

I didn't mean to, but I was never strong enough to stop it. That's something I need to live with. After all I've taken from him, I can't even meet his eyes.

"What do you want?" I ask. I don't allow the unease to reflect in my tone.

A flutter of hope spreads in my heart at the sight of him. I never thought I would see him again.

He looks off to the horizon like the sky will answer. After a beat, his eyes turn back to me. His expression hardens, like his determination has concluded on something.

"Let's talk inside," he says.

I try to get a hold of my breathing. He has already slipped inside the window before I can even gather my thoughts. He is in my room. *Here.* I hurry inside, forgetting about my own dirty shoes, and meet him as he comes down the ladder that heads to the second floor.

My cabin is technically two rooms: the bathroom and

everything else. The kitchen and living room are one small space. My bedroom is on top, connected by a small ladder. The entire space is open, and despite its size, I love it. I chose every single detail that makes this place what it is.

I wipe my hands on my pants, feeling more self-aware than I have been in so long. "Would you like something to drink?"

I move to the kitchen, mentally listing all I have to offer. It's not much. I put down the bag of things I purchased at the market this morning. I consider putting the groceries away. My hands ache with the need to do something.

"This is not a friendly visit."

His voice stops me in place. Of course it's not. What was I thinking? That he would come here looking for me because he missed me? After everything I've done?

The pain that strikes through my heart at the thought is almost paralyzing. A day hasn't gone by that Jesse doesn't cross my mind. A tiny piece of me held hope that in my new freedom, I would find my way back to him. But the coldness behind his eyes kills that tiny piece of me that dared hope.

I close my eyes and swallow down all my emotions. I raise a wall between us and tell myself it is for my survival. When I open my eyes, I'm more determined than ever. I raise my chin and look at him head-on.

"State your purpose." There's an edge to my tone.

"I came here with an offer from your King," Jesse says.

I don't live in Puerto Quinn, which means Brandon isn't my king, but I keep quiet. He has my interest.

His eyes are not on me while he speaks. Instead, his eyes scan the place like he is trying to piece together this new version of me. There are used blankets on the couch, watercolors on the table, and dirty dishes in the sink. Each thing scattered around is a puzzle piece of the person I am today. The version of me he's not part of.

"A trade, if you wish to call it. The Red Book was stolen the night of the attack. We need you to get it back."

His eyes finally find mine, and once again, I wish to be buried with the souls we lost that night. The hurt and brokenness I see is my fault, and I will never forgive myself for putting it there.

I swallow the guilt. "You want me to get the book?" I ask.

"The King has made the offer. Not me." His tone is sharp.

"What is the offer?" I cross my arms.

"Your magic back." He stares at me like I am a stranger to him. His eyes are cold and detached. "Accept this mission as a spy of the realm, and you'll get your magic back early in return. We know your father heads the rebel group. Find him, find the book and return it. Simple."

I want to laugh at the choice of words. There is nothing simple about what they're asking, and Jesse very well knows that.

"The King would like me to infiltrate my father's circle and betray them?"

His tone is bitter as he says, "You certainly have experience with the act. I'll accompany you on your mission to make sure it's carried out properly."

I can tell he expects a fight, but I think of the opportunities this mission will bring. I knew my time here was borrowed. The late night thoughts that followed my nightmares prepared me for this. I knew it was coming to an end.

I can finally do things right, not just for Jesse, but for myself. My inaction brought shame to my name in more than one way. By doing this, I will fulfill my duty as a member of a royal family serving the Crown once again. The Duelo name won't die in the flames that spread that night in the Black Castle.

The Fates might forgive my past if I make things right. I

asked them once to intervene and now I know I never should've. Perhaps there's a way to fix it.

Although, I will also make myself my father's number one enemy. Brandon might have punished me for my part and let me go, but my father is not as forgiving. I know the moment I sidestep him, he will come for my throat. He will never forgive me.

The question is not if I can or will do it, but if I'm ready. My time has come like I knew it would.

Movement to my left takes my attention away from the conversation at hand. I go over to the window and watch a man make his way down to my cabin. His silhouette tells me exactly who he is, but even if that wasn't obvious enough, his punctuality is impeccable. Almost as annoying as his insistence on befriending me.

"Who is that?" Jesse asks over my shoulder.

His movements are so quiet I don't hear him until he is right behind me. I don't care to explain to him who Ulysses is, and I don't care to explain to Ulysses who Jesse is. If they never meet, even better.

I turn and see the glint of a knife in Jesse's hands. "Put that away." I swat at his shoulder. "I accept. But we're leaving now."

Jesse eyes me curiously as I rush to pack. I shove all my clothing, which isn't much, in a backpack. The bag already has a few weapons on the bottom. I carry those with me everywhere. I grab a piece of paper and write a quick message, then drop it on the table. Ulysses might not make his way inside the cabin today, but he eventually will after not seeing me for a while.

"Gone for a while. Be back eventually," Jesse reads behind me. "Not very detailed. Is this for the man making his way to the porch?"

"Can you mind your business and start heading out from the back door?"

"Why not the front?" He takes a step to the front door. "I think we should head through the front door."

I take Jesse's hand in mine and nearly drag him out the back door. I hear a knock at my front door a second after the back door shuts close.

"That is just rude," Jesse says, far louder than necessary.

I ignore him and head out to the backwoods. One thing I have learned these past few months is these woods. I know them like the back of my hand. I also know exactly where in them my father is hiding with his men. It will take us a day to make it, but the day is young, and if we are lucky, we will be there tomorrow morning.

"Wait," Jesse calls after me. He pulls out an envelope from his back pocket and hands it to me. "Your contract," he says.

I look back at my cabin. We have walked far enough into the woods that we aren't easy to spot between the trees. I take the envelope and open it. Jesse stands there staring at me as I take out the paper and read it. The glint of gold letters alerts me to the type of contract this is. His eyes are trained on my expression like my decision would change because of the bond I'm expected to make. I expected nothing less from the King of Puerto Quinn. I once knew Brandon as a childhood friend, but even then, that would've been a stretch of the word. Now, even the only real friend I had back then looks at me with distrust. I swiftly dig out a knife from my bag and make a small cut on the tip of my index finger.

"What are you doing?" Jesse steps forward but stops when my finger lands on the dotted line at the bottom of the contract. "A signature could've been enough."

I shake my head at his naiveness. "Then you've no idea how magic contracts work. They are not only frowned upon because of the intrusiveness, but the gross act of signing with blood." I fold the paper, then shove it to his chest. "Not my first and I presume not my last contract signed in blood."

"Janelle," he says in a near whisper.

Before he can add anything else, I say, "We have a day and a half of walking to the first destination. Taking the roads will take longer and they are monitored by the human guards. Going through the mountains will be our best option so you won't trigger an overstay alarm."

The majority of the hike can be done on the Fierno side. I have no clue what kind of magic allows the human guards to know when a magic wielder is in their territory for longer than a day but I've seen it in action. I know it works. I might be going under the radar but Jesse wont.

My father's man said I knew where to find him and this would be the first place I would look.

"I can't be sure he will be there, but it's my first guess." I slid the backpack on and tightened the straps. "No time to waste."

"Can I carry that for you?" He asks, gesturing to my backpack.

"No," I say.

He nods like he expected the answer, then moves next to me as we start the path. "Since we have all this time to talk, maybe you can tell me who that was?"

I don't let the smile that fights its way to my lips win. Jesse is curious, but I can't allow myself to take it as anything more than that.

"The more breath we waste in talking, the less we have for walking." I don't care if that makes little sense.

I don't expect Jesse to be quiet for long, but I'm surprised at how long he actually makes it. We cover far more ground than I expected us to. The hike made in silence becomes a comfortable tread after a while. Using a compass and my knowledge of the river banks, I play guide.

We have been hiking for over seven hours now. This spot is just as good as any other for setting camp while we still have daylight.

"Do you know where you are going, Lady Janelle?" Jesse asks me.

The title sounds like a taunt. It has always sounded like that coming from his lips. It felt playful back when we were friends, but now it feels like a reminder of my place and debt.

"Yes, Prince Jesse Oscuro. Far more than you know."

His eyes narrow. "I have been searching these woods for your father for months. He is nowhere near here."

I sigh, in part because I'm tired and in part because he is about to feel so stupid for not seeing it. My father is a cunning person. Jesse shouldn't feel bad. No one would've been able to find him. Not if they didn't know where to look.

"You probably never found him because you looked on this side. Not that one." I gesture deeper into the woods on the other side of the river. "His hideout is in the human lands."

"Impossible. Magic cannot function in Paz." His eyes widened in realization.

"His secret hideout is in a small town called Divina." I let the words drop heavily between us.

I say nothing after so he can make his own conclusions about the implications. My father's idea of setting his hideout in that town was both bold and crazy smart. Divina is the only town in Paz that allows magic to function at its full potential.

I personally refuse to believe the entire realm is magic-free. There are rumors that the King of Paz himself descends from powerful magic. There is no way his bloodline has completely cleared of that. However, not being as powerful in the magic spectrum, living in magic-free territory is safer.

"Divina is where angels land in order to access the human lands," Jesse says, more to himself than to me.

He is working out the details in his head. I can see it in his eyes.

The small town isn't visited very often by angels, but at least a few cross through the downtown daily. It's the only access point to cross into and out of the Human Lands. Their angelic magic ceases to work the further they go into Paz.

"Exactly," I say.

My father knew the location would be perfect. Due to its access to magic, few ordinary humans actually choose to live there. The town is so small that bribing the few locals to turn an eye wasn't hard. However it remains complicated to make sure no angel would pick up on what was going on. My father acquired a mansion that appears more like a farm from the outside.

"It makes so much sense," he says at last.

We set camp on the Fierno side of the river and eat pre-packaged dry food Jesse brought. There's not a lot of talking before it's time to rest. Sleeping under the stars is not as romantic as people make it out to be in books. It's my least favorite way to sleep. When I left Puerto Quinn, I had to do it a lot before I found my cabin. I thought it was the fact that I was alone, and I felt so exposed to the elements. Tonight, even with Jesse a few feet away, a feeling of unease passes over me.

"How did you come to get the cabin?"

I don't turn to look at him, and I know he isn't looking at me. The sky has both our gazes captured amongst the view full of stars.

"I gambled my way to ownership," I say.

"You won that cabin gambling?" His disbelief is evident.

I shake my head. "Not in one game. You know I'm quite good at cards."

"I know," he says. The hint of a smile on his words.

"I won enough to buy the bare bones. I have slowly worked on fixing it."

"It looked complete," he sighs.

I don't say that the walls need paint or that the little items around were things I got secondhand from village vendors. That would be oversharing and opening up a lot more than I need to. Jesse doesn't care to know more than what would explain my whereabouts. That's the only reason he asked all these questions, after all.

"And the man that arrived just as we were about to leave?"

I sit up and finally meet his gaze. "A neighbor."

"That's all?" he asks.

"That is all. We aren't friends, if that is what you are asking. Not the way we are."

I reach for the words as they leave my lips, wishing I could take them back and never let them out, but it's too late. They are out there.

"We are not friends." Jesse turns away from me. "Can I truly do anything other than hate you?"

I shake my head. I want to say that he is right, but the words get stuck in my throat. I say nothing and allow the noise of the forest to fill the silence.

I lie there, unable to sleep for a couple of hours. It's uncertain whether I'll be walking into my ending. I'm going to seek the very people just a couple of months ago I couldn't get away from quick enough. Their reactions to my presence could be anything.

A scenario that finds me with little to no choice is the one that I am hoping will never happen. My father might attack at the sight of me. I need to be ready to react. The thought takes away my sleep because, despite it all, I love my father.

I've lost count of how many times his eyes have shown love

and appreciation for me. It was never free to take but priced at my worth. I wish I could turn off the switch that seeks that love, but it's not that easy.

I turn to my side and watch Jesse's profile as he sleeps. I am glad at least one of us won't be sleep-deprived. His chest rises and falls so peacefully. He is adorable like this. I want to take a mental picture to remember this. Nowadays, I only get glares from him. Well deserved ones.

I don't have a high moral code or delude myself into seeing me as a good person. It's not that the lives lost at the Black Castle didn't matter to me. I didn't want to hurt anyone. But I also didn't do enough to stop it. I knew how my father felt about the King and the Oscuros but never thought he would take it this far. I spoke up in meetings and disagreed with ideas. I thought that would be enough at first.

Pushing some common sense and practicality into those men's heads only caused me to be kicked out and left out of crucial information. If I had stayed quiet and listened more, I could've prevented the attack. I would've learned about his plans in time.

But would I? I'd like to think so. To believe myself that brave, but I never told Jesse, the one person in this world I love, about my father's disloyalty. And all because of fear.

I knew I loved Jesse as a child. I knew it as easily as I knew I possessed magic. A knowing deep in my bones. I wish I would've said something and spoken up, but wishes will only get me long, hopeless nights. I need to act, and my time to do so has come.

As much as I would like to say that I'm doing this for the realm, for my bloodline, and for the people I let down, the selfish part inside knows I'm not doing this just for me and my magic. I'm doing it for him. Because even though the possibility of not making it out alive looms over me, I am not turning back.

For the past two months, I have been on my own. I love the freedom I gained. In that short time, I thought of me and only me. The only time I have ever been able to do that. My time is up.

CHAPTER FIVE

JANELLE

The sun finally breaks through the mountain peaks an hour into the remainder of the trip. If the markers I memorized are correct, we're getting close. The forest in this area is more wild. I'm on high alert as the vegetation is dark and my footing is unclear.

I look at Jesse behind me. I'll know we are close when he feels the presence of magic return. Despite being alert to his surroundings, he doesn't look any different. I've been keeping an eye on him. Then Jesse stops walking and stares at his hands.

"You feel it?" I ask, referring to the magic tingling in his skin.

He nods.

I spot a large bush at a distance and rush to it. If I'm correct, there will be a clearing on the other side and the farm not too far after that. I peek through the gaps and see the white structure of an old farm.

"He's in there?" Jesse asks, looking through a gap above my head.

"I guess this is where we part ways," I say.

He chuckles. "I don't think so."

I look back at him. "What kind of spell do you have up your sleeve that will allow a long-term concealment?" I shake my head. "You need to stay here and I will try to sneak you in once I get the layout."

"You cannot be trusted."

I roll my eyes. That line is starting to sound cliche.

"So what, you will make yourself invisible?" I ask, half amused.

"Exactly," he says.

I'm not surprised to see Jesse pull out Brandon's invisibility cloak. He must have brought something to conceal himself if he so boldly demanded to accompany me to supervise this mission. What I wasn't ready for was the emotions that surfaced at the sight of it. Memories of us as children flow through my mind.

The image of a young Brandon and Jesse fighting over the cloak almost makes me smile. They would pull it from end to end until the material stretched thin. My hands would be on my cheeks, dreading the noise of ripping thread that never came. Roman was always the authority around. He would use the threat of taking it away as leverage to make them stop fighting. Those moments when the cloak would bring us midnight snacks and late-night adventures on long summer nights feel so fleeting now. In the blink of an eye, duty pulled Brandon away and Roman quickly followed. Jesse was the one who never left. He never became too mature for my friendship.

I wish I would've told myself to stay up longer during those summer nights. To be more patient and appreciate the way things were. I was in such a rush for things to change that I never imagined I was in the good part.

We never know how good we have it until we're looking back and the moments have become memories.

"You look at it like you've never seen it before." Jesse drapes it over his shoulders.

In the blink of an eye, he is no longer there. He is gone, and I don't bother correcting his assumption about my expression. Instead, I clear my throat and watch the front door of the farm. I've been thinking of how I plan for this to play out, but the simple route might be our best bet. My father needs to think I'm coming here seeking him to take me back. Therefore, we need to stop sneaking around and just come right out.

"Stay vigilant," I tell Jesse as I step out of the woods.

I walk out of the tree line. The second I step out, I expect one, if not more, of my father's men to have seen me. If they were doing their jobs, my father would've learned of my return by my seventh step.

I'm closing the distance between the treeline and the front porch of the farm when the door opens. A human man steps out. He is hunched over due to his old age. From the frown on his face, I conclude he is not thrilled to see me trespassing.

The old man raises one hand in the air. "Get out of here, girl. There are no jobs if you plan on asking for one."

"I'm here to see my father," I tell him in a calm voice.

"What?" he asks.

"I'm here to see my father." I try again.

"What?"

It is obvious he cannot hear me from where I'm standing, so I take another step forward. At my step, the man pulls a gun from the back of his pants and points it directly at my head. I stare at the weapon in shock. I've seen many since living on the outskirts of Paz. But I've never had one pointed at me. Jesse's body moves closer to me, close enough that I can feel his warmth.

Ordinary humans use guns for protection and crime. They're not used by magical creatures, as the magic we possess is far more deadly and easier to wield.

"That is enough, Jill," says a man who exits the front door of the farmhouse. The cocky smile on his face is familiar. "Forgive him, Princess Janelle, for he has never met your highness before." He turns back to the old man. "This is the lost daughter of King Duelo."

The title my father has given himself almost makes me laugh. Of course, he would start calling himself that. The King who's fighting for his rightful throne. His men have been calling me princess for so long that I've grown accustomed to the taunt. But that is all it ever was, a taunt. I never took it seriously. It was meant to point out my privilege and status amongst them. In front of family and in polite company, they always used my correct title as a lady.

I always found the secrecy to be cowardly. If my father truly felt he could take on Brandon Oscuro, he wouldn't need his little army of men. He wouldn't have sent me and my brothers to fight his battle.

"Take me to my father, dog. Is he already aware I'm here?" I say to my father's soldier and don't make eye contact like meeting his gaze is beneath me.

His smirk falls as the nickname falls from my lips. I refuse to learn his name because he is nothing more than a follower of my father. Jumping on his every whim without a single original thought to himself.

"Everyone is aware you are here." He looks around the land. "You cannot set foot on this property without me knowing. I'm the head of security."

"Yeah, yeah." I roll my eyes. He surely doesn't know of the man standing just a few steps away under a cloak. "Well, quit wasting my time and take me to my father."

The old man tries to raise his gun at me again. His dislike for my disrespect is evident. The dog pushes the gun down without moving his eyes from me.

"Follow me," he gestures to the front door.

I can feel more than see Jesse walking next to me. I make sure I pause in front of the door, allowing him to step before me. The dog and the old man follow me, shutting the door.

"You sure have a lot of attitude for someone who—"

"And you talk a lot for someone whose job is outside the walls of this house." I point to the main entrance before he can finish talking. "Shouldn't you be getting back to work?"

"Janelle," my mother calls.

Her frail body looks just as fragile as the last time I saw her. I leave everyone else behind as I rush towards her. I hug her tight to my chest, breathing her in. Her skin and hair always smells like sweet honey. It's the one thing that hasn't changed about her. The day that does change will be the day I worry she is no longer here.

My mother suffers from a sickness very few have ever guessed at. Her skin is nearly paper thin, and so are her bones. She doesn't just look fragile. She is.

My gift for healing first surfaced when I was three. My mother was bedridden after a fall. I rested my palm on her arm, wishing I could do something to keep her from getting hurt. Like a miracle came to life, I did it. I healed her. From that day on, I healed her weekly.

My healing gift has its limitations. I cannot heal myself and I can only heal small surface wounds and pain. The latter is more important than I ever thought possible.

Something I didn't understand was why she made me promise I wouldn't tell a soul about my gift. Most of all, my father. I later found that the reason for her sickness was him. She feared if he learned I could help her debilitated state, he would attempt to take even more of her power. She wasn't protecting me but herself.

See, my father and mother are soul bonds, and a little secret about soul bonds is how, once established, one can access the magic of the other one. That is how Ray was able to command my fire. He never tried to take my magic when we bonded, but that didn't mean he wouldn't in the future. He watched, like many others, how my father grew in power while my mother nearly faded away. Once taken, the power cannot be given back. However, I question if my father would've returned it if he could.

My mother has done little for me throughout my life, but unbeknown to her, by keeping my gift from my father, she shielded me. I thank her for that even if it wasn't her intention. She kept me safe from him before I knew how to do it myself. I'm certain he would have found a way to use and profit off my gift.

She pulls away and looks at me. I can see tears lining her eyes, but they don't fall. They never do. "Your father is waiting to see you. He is so happy that you're back."

I know those words are hollow. If they were true, it would be even worse. Because it would mean I was playing right into his hand. I take a deep breath and nod. There's no point in delaying any longer than necessary. I can't see Jesse, but I am certain he is still somewhere here. I follow my mother as she leads the way down the hall. We enter a long dining room where a formal wood table is at the center. He might be okay with hiding out on an old farm, but he would never allow his surroundings to be anything but the best.

My father's eyes look up to watch me as I cross the room. He scans me from head to toe. I don't think he is searching for injuries as much as assessing what he has in his hands.

"Janelle," he says.

His disdain for my attire is conveyed in the tilt of his lips. I'm a far cry from the tailored dresses he always insisted I wore.

"Father," I say, unclenching my tight jaw.

The silence that follows could be called uncomfortable for anyone who didn't grow up in a family like mine. I'm used to pregnant pauses and moments of tension. Mostly when my father is contemplating his next steps. He's a man who plans, after all.

He extends his hand to the chair in front of me. The invitation comes as a relief to my mother, who's still standing next to me. I can almost hear her sigh as I take a seat. This new concern for me and my father might come from the fact that she no longer has other children, or that she has not seen me in a while. The most likely scenario is that she is here all alone with *him*. She has his focus and rage.

My brothers and I were never close. They were both much older than me. Despite their best attempts, their magic abilities were never up to par with my father's ambitions. They spent most of their time avoiding my father's plans. They bailed whenever they could and just lazed around the rest of the time.

I look at my father and see so much of my brothers in him. They were walking portraits that depicted him, from the short curly red hair to the sprinkle of matching freckles over his nose and cheeks. His big nose and heavy brows always made him look upset at the world.

The more I grew in power and drew my father's attention, the more they got away with. I was the distraction they needed to live their lives. The brotherly love the Oscuro brothers displayed was something I never had.

For a while, I resented them for their lack of interest in me. As I got older and I realized who our father was, I couldn't hate them. They saw an out in me and I couldn't begrudge them the opportunity. Even now, I wish I had done more for them. I had the Oscuro brothers, even if it was in secret. My brothers were older than the boys and never found friendships that didn't want something from them.

I look over my shoulder to where I sense Jesse standing. I always had him and, in part, he was all I needed to stay sane. The summer months were always my favorite.

A servant is at my side, dropping a plate of food in front of me. I hold back a gasp as I look down at my plate. The amount of food is something I've not seen in a while. Did I really used to eat like this? And why does it feel like that was years ago and not simply months ago?

"None of your brothers made it out of that castle alive, but you did. Took you long enough to find your way back."

Not an ounce of remorse at the fact that his own ambition had two of his children dead.

His statement wasn't a question, but I know he wants me to say something to acknowledge I've been paying attention. The reminder of my brothers hurts. The fact that their lives were sacrificed for the ambitious man sitting across from me makes me nauseous.

"Ray never returned." My father leans back in his chair, done with his food. "For a while, I thought he had left with you, but the Oscuros would've never let him leave."

"Ray is dead," I say.

My words cut off whatever other rant he planned on delivering. He doesn't ask me how it happened, and I'm glad I don't have to make up a lie. Instead, he takes me in with new eyes. I can see the plans mapping out behind his eyes. The roads on which my future might take me are being paved this very second. I'm more open and freer for him to use than he expected. Or so he thinks.

"You have cost me much, Janelle, but I will overlook your shortcomings. Your time to make it up to your family will come. For now, you must earn your keep with labor. The maids would appreciate the extra set of hands." He wipes his mouth with his napkin, then tosses it on the table. "You're used to a life of comfort, you've done nothing to earn it. That life is over."

The irony of that statement is humorous.

"Sweetheart," my mother gasps appalled at the request.

My father and mother have been together for so long that many forget it's she who comes from royal blood, not him. He seems to have forgotten about it, too. My father was only an ambitious soldier with no name or title. Being my mother's soul bond was his only way in and has been her dismay ever since.

"Since you're a common human now, you'll have ordinary duties. Prove that you can be trusted with more, and you'll move up. I have faith in you, Janelle. You were never just a pretty face." My father narrows his eyes on me. A cloud that I recognize comes over his eyes. His voice lowers, and his tone darkens. "Don't embarrass me again."

Referring to me losing my powers as an embarrassment is disgusting when my brothers lost their lives. I swallow my pride and lean my head down. Playing the submissive daughter is the only acceptable role under his roof. I only have to do it long enough for me to find the Red Book. This is not forever, but as I tell myself that, sweat covers the palms of my hands.

There's a little part inside me that fears walking back in and getting trapped. I escaped him once. Could I truly do it again?

Jesse would never leave me here, would he?

I have to believe in myself. I'll get myself out. The girl from months ago isn't here. I've tasted freedom and therefore I'll never be the same again.

"Yes, sir." The words taste sour on my lips.

The nod and glint in his eyes tell me he is glad to hear it. He raises his wine glass. "To family being back."

My mother quickly follows his example and gestures for me to do the same. I raise my water cup reluctantly.

"The Duelo Reign will come. A setback is not the end." He pauses, then cheers, "To family!"

"Family," my mother says with a pitiful smile.

My father walks to the door and knocks the wood three times before calling, "Oliver!"

A guard quickly opens the door soon thereafter. At the sight of him, my heart nearly stops. I didn't expect to see him with my father in hiding. I make sure my eyes don't linger on him. The value of our friendship has always been a secret I treasured.

"Janelle has returned." My father gestures to me with a smirk. "I told you she would, didn't I?"

Oliver nods, "You did, sir."

"She will earn her keep by cleaning. Let her start on the cells. The maids keep complaining of the stench of the place."

Oliver looks between me and my father. "Sir, that is no place for a lady."

My father laughs with a sinister smile on his face. He looks back at me before departing with no other words. My mother promptly follows him, avoiding all eye contact as she passes by. Maids enter the room quickly after and pick up the dishes.

"I should take you there now," Oliver says.

I nod and follow him. Completely forgetting that Jesse is somewhere behind us. Oliver gives me a smile as soon as we are outside the dining room. When we round the corner, he stops walking and looks me up and down. In a swift move, he pulls me to his chest and hugs me tight. I fight the tears that gather in my eyes.

The warmth that envelops me is the only warmth I knew inside the Duelo home. As a young child, these were the only arms that ever comforted me from my father's treatment. There is no doubt in my mind that if Oliver could, he would have taken me away. Sadly, he couldn't, so instead he stood by me so I wouldn't be alone. Choosing to endure my father just to stay by my side is the biggest act of loyalty I've known. His kindness towards me was never conditional.

Oliver is a big man with a protruding stomach and thick black mustache. His black hair is cut short and his clothing is neat, always smelling of lavender. He has never been like my father and I have known him for just as long. Since my great grandfather's time, he has been a member of the Duelo soldiers. Time has changed a lot inside the Duelo home.

"You are good?" He asks with gentle concern. The wrinkles around his eyes have become much more noticeable since the last time I saw him.

"I'm good." I assure him, stepping out of his reach.

"Why did you come now?" The mood is suddenly serious.

I look down the hall. "After my failure, I felt the need for some time to myself."

"You were asked to do something ridiculous." He glances down the hallway. "It was suicide. Yet you're alive."

"I am hard to kill." I allow a smirk.

"You have always been a survivor, my girl." He leans over and kisses my forehead. "Do not trust a soul inside these walls."

"I can always trust you," I say confidently.

"If I knew it would come to this, I would have stolen you away. You would've known true freedom away from your name."

The truth is, whatever the Fates have chosen for me will come to be. There's no escaping what the stars have written for you.

A creak of a door opening has us both stepping back. The soldier I call dog steps into the hall and walks towards us with a slight smirk on his face. I want to slap it off. It's instinctive.

"Right this way." Oliver gestures to a door with a staircase leading down to a basement.

His tone is now stone cold and detached. The only tone he has ever used for me around guards. I don't even flinch at the abrupt change.

I walk ahead of him down the stairs, leaving enough room for Jesse to quickly move in front of me. The stench of body odor is the first thing to hit me as my eyes make up the shapes of the basement walls. Long metal bars stretch the length of one side. Dirty, disheveled men sit behind the metal bars.

A few of them look up as we walk inside. No one makes a move closer to the cell bars. As a matter of fact, each of them seems to move even closer to the opposite wall.

"Prisoners already?" I didn't think my father had been hiding long enough to take on hostages. As I take a closer look, I notice something else. "They aren't human."

"The majority are from the City of Sin. Your father's test subjects."

My eyes move to one man who looks slightly familiar. In his dirt-covered face and downcast expression he doesn't jump in my memories, but my heart rate picks up alerting me to this man's presence.

"You know the young boy?" Oliver asks behind me. "He was found wandering in the woods near the Black Castle right after the attack. He is the only one from Puerto Quinn."

I hold back my gasp because, at the very moment his eyes shift to mine, the gaze that holds mine is no longer filled with happiness and wonder. The warmth that once held a gentle smile is gone. The boy that taught me basic hunting skills and shared words of wisdom that saved my life more than once is looking not at me, but through me. He is now a mere shell of the boy I once briefly met in the woods.

I want to scream until my voice breaks. The fury that drives through my veins feels dangerous. It's seething through my body. His freedom has been seized by the very same individuals who took mine.

All the prisoners are worse to wear, but he is specifically beaten and dirty. There are holes in his clothes and parts of his skin are black and blue.

"What was his crime?" I ask between clenched teeth because I know the answer.

He never committed one. My father doesn't need a reason to do gruesome things to innocent people.

"His crime was being at the wrong place at the wrong time," Oliver says and shakes his head. "He is a survivor. The book hasn't killed him yet. I can't say the same for the ones before him."

"The book?" I turn to Oliver and away from the boy at the mention of the Red Book.

"Your father has the book. He used it on the boy. It didn't kill him like it did the others but he isn't cooperating so it's unclear what happened."

A stomp and knock on the door at the top of the stairs has us both turning towards the noise.

"I am needed." Oliver points at a door at the end of the room. "That is a closet with cleaning supplies. Do your best. I will come help you as soon as I can."

Before I can say anything, he is climbing up the stairs. A second later, Jesse unwraps the cloth from his body and steps closer to the cell bars. His eyes are looking at the man inside in disbelief.

"Matias." Jesse gasps then tries to wave in an attempt to catch the boy's attention, but he is lost in space.

"Where do you know him from?" I take a step closer to Jesse.

His eyes pour into mine, trying to read my interest. "He is family to Bianca. Meaning he is family to me." His eyes move back to the boy.

"The boy with the soul lost to the curse book." I recall the story Jesse told me in secrecy.

It feels like a lifetime away since he would confide in me that way.

"You recognized him." Jesse's tone is accusatory. But I don't bother getting offended.

"I met him the day of my exile in the woods. He saved my life."

The truth of these words resonates when spoken aloud. I'm here getting a second chance, thanks to the boy behind bars. My mind and heart decide on a course of action as I gaze at him. I turn to Jesse and look him in the eyes. I need him to understand how serious I am about what I'm about to say.

"We will not leave this place without him." I turn to face Matias. "At least I am not," I vow.

CHAPTER SIX

JESSE

I pace back and forth along the length of the basement. The prisoners are no longer looking our way and have instead resorted to staring at the walls or converse with one another. All except for him.

Matias.

The one variable I was not prepared for. Janelle's connection to him still makes no sense to me, but it doesn't matter. The fact of the matter is that I can't leave without him. Bianca will never forgive me.

Bianca is the future queen of Puerto Quinn, if my brother has his way. I've known him his whole life and never would I've imagined his ruling partner to be a woman like Bianca. She's such a wild card and unpredictable. The total opposite of all the women that came before her. I've spent days watching my brother worry himself sick over her whereabouts while she was looking for Matias, and here he was all along.

Matias stares at the wall with no expression. His body might be here, but his mind is gone. I fear Bianca will hate me if I don't bring her Matias back, but I also fear what seeing

Matias in this condition will do to her. He is a shadow of a person. I never got to meet him, but from what Roman and Santiago told me, the man before me is not him. What remains here is the shell of who he used to be.

"If you help me, this would go a lot faster." Janelle is holding two mops and a bucket.

She has filled the bucket to the brim and from the bubbles at the top, I'm inclined to believe she has already added some type of soap she probably found in the supply closet. Uncertain if she really thinks I'm going to let her do the manual task, I approach her.

"You don't need to do that." I place my hand over the cleaning supplies and spell the inanimate items to do the task themselves.

They move clumsily but quietly. Beginning at one edge of the basement, they scrub and wipe the floor.

"Thank you," she says.

I clear my throat and move to look at Matias again. He remains unmoving.

"What is your business with him?" I ask.

She steps to my side, her eyes train on the boy. "Like I said, I met him once. He was kind."

"Outside of the Black Castle?"

"Yes," she says and inclines her head. "After my exile. As I made my way out of the forest."

If she saw him after she was kicked out, then he must have been on his way back. He was going to make it back in the time frame he gave Bianca. He was so close. I can't help but pity the guy.

"What do you think they did to him?" I ask her.

He is in terrible shape. No wonder he has this gone look in his eyes. He has escaped to a place in his head to survive.

"My father is ruthless. But I can only imagine. We have no

real clue how the Red Book works, but I know what my father wants from it." Her eyes are pained.

"And that is?" I ask.

"To uncap his magic and be as powerful as he can be. He plans on taking down your brother and his reign that way."

My brothers and I had guessed as much in the meetings after the attack. There are only so many reasons the traitor would choose to take the Red Book. I look back at Matias' beaten form and broken spirit. The Red Book sealed something in us to cap our magic and whatever Lord Duelo is doing to uncap it, it's simultaneously breaking the person.

"Your father must first figure out how to do it on others before doing it on himself."

Janelle gives me a look that says I'm stating the obvious. "My father might be brave enough to declare war on the Black Castle, but he sent us, his children, to do the battle."

"I saw him, you know." I recall clearly the moment my eyes landed on him that night.

At the sound of distress, Brandon and I had agreed we needed to get to my grandfather. He had departed to his office to relocate the Red Book. Brandon took the route inside the castle passages and I, with a group of soldiers, took the castle halls. The smell of burning wood, the loud screams of people scared and in pain echo in my head.

I made it to my grandfather's office first. Lord Duelo was already inside with his hand on the Red Book as my grandfather laid unmoving on the floor. The moment his eyes met mine, a smirk painted his lips. Ethan, his son, stood over my grandfather's body.

"I killed him," I say. A part of me is glad but another dreading the response."Your brother."

Would she hold it against me? A pause echoes in the space between us.

"I'm sure you had to," she says.

I did. There was no choice. But she had choices.

Her eyes aren't on me but on her own hands. The dread that must exist on her conscience must make it hard for her to sleep. Everyone back at Puerto Quinn thinks of the Duelos as soulless evil people who attacked us completely unprovoked. The latter is true, but I know the soul that lives inside that chest. At least I did, and it wasn't evil.

At what point does the responsibility weigh on her, considering how much of what she did can be blamed on others?

"Do you feel guilty?" I ask her, not knowing if I will like the answer.

Her eyes finally meet mine once again. "There are no words to explain all I wish I could do over. But I cannot dwell on the past. I can do something about today, and that's what I will focus on."

A yes was all I wanted to hear to know the girl I once knew was still there.

"What about Oliver?" I ask her.

I've known Oliver far longer than Janelle knows. I knew he lived and worked at the Duelo home but I didn't know his connection with Janelle was deeper than the one between a soldier and the lady of the house. The hug and appreciation in both their eyes as they embrace one another tells me I am missing important information. It also fills me with fury because he should have taken her away at the whispers of Lord Duelo's plans.

If I had known, I would have never left her there.

"Oliver isn't like my father. He is good."

I point at Matias over my shoulder. "He helped your father do that. He's obviously not that good."

Anyone that can look at Matias and not want to get him away from here is a monster.

"You don't know what you're talking about." She frowns as if I'm the one who doesn't understand.

"Sure, Janelle, what I know is that you will make excuses."

I once believed I knew Oliver, but after the night at the Black Castle, I cannot trust anyone. Including the girl in front of me. Regardless of how much I wish I could. Oliver obviously has affection for Janelle and the feeling is mutual. I've never seen her hug anyone before, let alone one of her father's soldiers. Having Oliver on our side inside these walls could be instrumental for the mission, but after laying eyes on Matias, I'm afraid that is not an avenue I'm willing to take.

She says nothing and instead turns away from me and the conversation. I let her have her space and peace. For the sake of having something to do, I move around the room and try to talk to the other prisoners, but none of them do anything but twitch or murmur to themselves. These people aren't far from the brokenness Matias is in.

***

A loud buzzing from above blurts through the walls, making the prisoners instantly move away from the cell bars towards the back of the prison walls. This urge to get away at the sound of the buzzing is the most reaction I've seen out of them in the past couple of hours.

I wave my hand toward the cleaning supplies still scrubbing the floors. They instantly drop. I pick the cloak up and wrap it around me just before a figure reaches the stairs landing.

The man who recognized Janelle outside looks around with suspicion. "Did someone come out here to help you?" he asks.

He probably didn't expect Janelle to get this much done in just a few hours. We should have been more conscious about this. I turn to look at Janelle to see if she also gets the feeling we might have messed up. She doesn't look concerned. If anything, she wears a bored expression on her face.

"No," she says. Then picks up the cleaning supplies and places them off to the side by the wall. "Is that why you're here?"

"Dinner should be ready soon. Your father wants you to be cleaned up and presentable to sit at the table."

I look out to the only small window on the back door and see that the sun has begun to set. The small amount of light coming from there is nearly all gone.

"I'd rather have it in my room."

"You have a room because of him, so I would show more respect if I were you. When the King asks you to be present for dinner, you do it with a smile."

"Has being his dog given you the satisfaction you want out of life?"

"My name is Ernesto, not dog," he says, and waits for Janelle to react, but she doesn't. "Iris is upstairs. She will show you to your room."

Janelle doesn't address anything else as she makes her way up the stairs. I follow her and hurry past her once at the top.

An older woman waits for Janelle at the end of the hall. There is no pleasant expression on her face, but a familiarity passes her eyes as they land on Janelle. Regardless, she says nothing to her. Janelle knows to follow the woman to the second floor of the house. I'm always a step behind.

On the second floor, the floor plan spreads into two sides. Each side looks to be hallways with doors to either side. We take the left one.

"The soldiers are to the right," the woman says without looking back. "Female staff and your parents are to the left. It will be best if you stay to the left at all times."

We pass several doors before we reach one at the end of the hall. The hall turns left again and another hall of doors. At the end of that hall, there is a set of double doors.

"The end leads to your parents. Don't go there. If you need to speak to them, do it when they are up."

There are still ten doors that need to be crossed to reach Janelle's parents' door from her own. She walks into her bedroom, and I'm glad she remembers I'm right behind her. Leaving the door wide open, she waits for me to come after her. She looks so natural you would think there was nothing amiss. The maid doesn't wait for Janelle to inspect her room. It's not like Janelle would make any requests. It's clear that the staff is currently providing a "You get what you get" service.

The room is a sad white and beige space with just a bed and a nightstand. The mattress looks lumpy and old, but at least the space smells clean.

I remove my cloak and move about the room, inspecting it. Janelle stays seated at the foot of the bed while I conduct my inspection. There is a bathroom adjacent to the room. That in itself is going to prove very useful.

When I exit the bathroom into the bedroom, Janelle passes me, then locks the door behind her. After a few minutes, the sound of running water begins. A shower sounds amazing after sleeping outside and then spending hours on the cells downstairs.

Janelle is speedy with her clean up. When she walks out of the bathroom, she's changed to a dress I recognize as hers. Her hair is down her shoulders, wet and curling at the tips.

"Where did you get that?" I ask.

I think I would remember this dress being packed in her bag. Perhaps not since her bag can very well be spelled to have more room than appears.

"The dresser in the room is full of my clothes," she says as she laces up her boots.

I look at the dresser in question. Starting from the bottom, I open each drawer one by one, finding Janelle's clothes, neatly folded and smelling fresh and clean.

"They expected you to come here," I say.

"Of course they did," she says with a smirk. "Well, I'm off to dinner. I will try to get you something, but it might be easier if we get it when everyone is asleep."

I tell my heart not to confuse her concern with whether I eat for anything other than assurance that I won't hinder her mission. But my stupid heart still argues with me because when it comes to Janelle Duelo, it has never cared for logic.

CHAPTER SEVEN

JESSE

Janelle leaves for dinner with her parents, and I start the job of getting myself clean. The water feels like heaven as it hits my skin. I don't even want to look down and see what goes down the drain. I keep the time of my shower short to decrease the possibility of a maid passing by and hearing the water running.

Unlike Janelle's freshly laundered clothes, mine have been packed into my bag for days now and they don't smell anywhere near as fresh. I need to find the laundry room and throw in my clothes with the maids. When they come across them, they will probably think it's one of the soldiers and put it aside. Hopefully, if not, I can always steal from one of the men here. One of them is sure to be my size.

When I'm changed and ready to go, I press my ear against the door and listen in for anyone going or coming. When I hear nothing, I open the door and shut it quickly behind me. The cloak is already over my shoulders, but I make sure no part of me is showing. The halls are far more empty right now than before. As I make my way down to the first floor, a flow of voices come from different directions.

I turn left and the kitchen comes into view. The doorway is open and from my place I can see the maids and other staff eating while leaning against different countertops. Jokes and laughter ring out of the room.

I must return here when everyone is gone to bed and pick up some food. I ignore the growl coming from my stomach at the smell of roasted potatoes and meats in the air. Whatever they made smells amazing and I'm hoping there are some left at the end of the night.

I keep walking deeper to a louder gathering down the hall. There is no light in between rooms, making the hallways fall into darkness. But a small light at the end brightens as I get closer. The noise coming from the room also increases. This is where the soldiers have dinner, if the loud laughter and hooting are anything to go by.

Before I can reach the dinner hall, I notice a small dark hallway to the left. A solo soldier stands guard outside a set of doors. There can only be one thing behind that set of doors if a soldier must stand guard at all times. I take a closer look and realize I know the man standing there. This might be the best opportunity to hash out this conversation.

"Oliver," I say.

The speed with which his hand snaps forward to take my neck is impressive, coming from the old man. The cloak falls off my head to my shoulders, revealing my face.

"What do you think you are doing?" Oliver asks me. His eyes widened in surprise and a hint of fear. "Even you are not immortal, boy."

His face is so similar to the ones I saw growing up inside the Black Castle walls. His eyes are a copy of his mothers. The main chef of the Black Castle, Rosa. She was a loyal tough woman with a spine of steel. I witnessed her run a kitchen full of people with command and precision.

Three generations of his family have served the castle and the King. That's how I know Oliver. He lived in the Black Castle with his family growing up. I personally didn't know him as by the time I was a child he had married and moved to the Duelo home. But my grandfather always made time to greet him when he visited the Duelo estate.

"Let's talk somewhere where we won't be spotted," I say.

We go into the room Oliver was guarding and as I predicted, I'm inside Lord Duelo's office. The red oak wood desk in the middle of the room looks just like the one he has in his home back in Ignis. His bookshelves are a burnt orange color that reminds me of the city of fire. Janelle had similar colors in her childhood bedroom.

"Are you here for her?" he asks, obviously referring to Janelle. Before I can answer him, he continues. "You need to convince her to leave. It's not safe for her here. It never truly was, but her father is doubling down on his plan."

"Doubling down?" I take a step closer to him.

"Thank you for not giving up on her." He looks outside to make sure no one is coming. "She needs you now more than ever."

"What do you mean, doubling down?" I ask again.

"He is seeking allies, and he is finding them. Maybe it's an urge for change or maybe some find boredom in the status quo, but more than one type of creature wants to see your brother fall."

I grab Oliver by his shirt collar and forcefully push him against a bookshelf. "What are you talking about?" He doesn't say anything right away, stunned by my sudden outburst. "What is Duelo planning?" I seethe.

"It will be best for you to see it. In two nights, there will be a gathering just outside the woods' clearing."

I let him go and move to the window as I don't hear a ringing in my ears.

"I'm here with her, not for her." Silence follows my words. "We're here for the Red Book."

"Brandon will have her back?" he asks. "That must be why she returned."

"She must return the Red Book first." I look around the room. "Where is it?" I wonder if I can locate it somewhere among these bookshelves.

"It's not here. He's not forthcoming with its location." His eyes look up.

"This is not the time for you to have conflicting loyalties," I say with irritation.

I push regardless of the fact that I know he's not withholding information. I want him to give me something.

"You think I'm loyal to that monster?" Oliver looks appalled at the thought.

"Why else would you fail to warn us, Oliver?" My words are closed to a breathless whisper.

The betrayal that cost so many lives weighs so heavily on my heart.

"I didn't know." His head hangs low. "Did they make it?"

He is asking me about the remaining family he has in the Black Castle. His first thought at seeing me wasn't about them but how I could help Janelle.

He had one cousin left inside the castle before the attack and he survived. Everyone else departed out of their own accord as they built families of their own.

"Your cousin is fine. Your niece left the year prior when she married."

The relief on his face doesn't match his actions. If he cares about those two people in the castle, why allow the threat at all? He could have stopped it. My grandfather might not have believed Oliver over a royal family but my brothers and I would have taken precautions. We would have been on alert. Lives would have been spared. A lot of would haves are only sorrows now.

"Why did you say nothing?" I ask him.

The words come out choked. If one person should have told us, it's Oliver. The people who found themselves running from the flames were people he knew.

"If I would've known what his plans were, I would have done something, Jesse. Her being there should tell you how I didn't know."

"What is she to you?" I cross my arms.

How is her existence any more proof than the ones in the castle?

"The child I've always protected." His words are a near whisper.

"Does that child know you were born in the Black Castle?"

Oliver shakes his head. "I got hired by her grandfather. Then her father came to power. His opinion of your family was evident so I kept my history to myself."

"He never asked?" I raise a brow.

"He assumed and I allowed him to keep the false assumption."

I wait for the ringing in my ears to sound but the space is dead quiet. Nothing of what he shared was a lie. But I know that for my gift to work I need to ask the right questions.

"Plotting for the crown should have started long before. How about before?" I ask, trying to hold back my rage. "Why did you say nothing, then?"

There is no way he simply decided one day to march into The Black Castle with no plan. They coordinated the attack with only a few soldiers but the planning of the attack must have taken weeks. None of them would know the halls of the castle more than the man before me. He took his first steps in them.

"I was never part of those meetings. If he had any sights on your brother's title, I hoped the whispers were wrong or he would come to his senses."

I shake my head because I can hear the clear ringing in my ear that tells me he is not being fully truthful. There is a little of the truth in there but not enough.

Duelo might not have walked the halls of his house announcing his plans to take my brother down. But I also find it hard to believe that Oliver didn't know a single thing about it. He stayed in the Duelo home despite rumors for a reason. Whatever his reason, I can see he won't freely share.

"You are both here for the Red Book?" He looks concerned.

I nod, not sure if I'm going to regret telling him anything.

"I will do all in my power to help you both."

His words don't ring in my ears but that's left to see. He looks back out the door.

"We cannot be here long. The book isn't here, anyway." He closes the door after me and walks ahead to the main hall. "The kitchen staff must be cleaning up."

Making his way to the kitchen, he discovers only a handful of staff members are still there. After a terse conversation, the remaining staff vacates the kitchen.

"They are going to assist the dining room. Lord Duelo is not done eating until fifteen past seven." He looks over at a clock on the wall. "He will send the staff back. We don't have a lot of time."

With a bag in hand, he tosses different food items inside. Snacks go in first. Two containers with tonight's dinner go into the following bag, making my stomach growl again. The food is no longer hot, having sat on the countertop this whole time, but I don't care for that. He stops and goes into the pantry. He climbs a shelf to get a box at the very top. After a huff and puff, he hops down with something in his hands.

"These are Janelle's favorites," he says.

He hands me a box of cookies I used to stock back in my summer house. I hate these cream and chocolate concoctions, but if you asked my mother, she would have said I lived for them since we would go through boxes of these in a month. The fact was that Janelle and Roman would consume about a sleeve of cookies each night. Disgusting.

"I need to get back to my post. Duelo makes a stop at his office every night after dinner."

"Sounds good." I wrap my cloak around my shoulders, covering the food in my arms.

I'm out of Oliver's sight when he speaks again. "For what it's worth, I'm sorry. If I had known, I would have done things differently."

"That's a sentiment I can relate to."

There are countless things I would've done differently if I knew what lay ahead. Nevertheless, those will only ever be boundless wishes.

I leave Oliver and decide to explore the other side of the lower floor before going upstairs. As I make my way back, I take extra care to be quiet while passing the formal dining room. The door to the room is open and I can't help but look inside. Lord Duelo is at the head of the table. As always, the sour scowl on his face is ever present. His wife is at his side and across from her is Janelle. All three of them have plates and silverware in front of them, but Janelle's plate is empty. The sight is odd, as it's also spotless.

Looks like I need to go back to the kitchens before heading

back. We are going to need more sustenance to complete this mission.

The rest of the floor plan seems to include a small library and a couple of sitting rooms. The small library looks deserted, but I plan on stopping there the next day to check out the catalog. It might be too obvious, but I have to double check he didn't decide to hide the book in plain sight.

I make my way back to Janelle's room without having to cross paths with anyone else. I throw the cloak off my body and waste no time finishing one of the meals Oliver gave me.

Twenty minutes later, Janelle opens the door. Her eyes look droopy with tiredness and the bags under her eyes look darker than they did earlier today. She instantly finds the food I left for her on the bedside table.

"You need your sleep, so hurry to eat and we can get to bed," I say.

"How did you know?" she asks as she sits on the edge of the bed with the container of food on her lap.

I shrug my shoulders. "I went exploring today."

"What did you find?" She asks between bites.

"Oliver knows I'm here. I tried to get answers from him."

Her eyes snap to me. "He spoke to you?"

"I figured since you seem to trust him so much I would give him a chance. He might prove useful."

I am ready for her to ask more questions and dig but she doesn't. The narrow eye glare she shoots my way does tell me she knows I am not totally forthcoming with information.

I watch Janelle's face for any intentions, but she's too focused on her meal again. Her parents really sat her down at the dining table and denied her food. Looks like some things never change with them. Their forms of punishment have stayed the same over the years.

"He said he doesn't know where the Red Book is, but in two days a meeting will take place. He thinks I should witness it."

"I would like to keep him out of this as much as possible," she says with a full mouth.

"You sure are protective of him. How come you never mentioned him before?" I ask.

"Oliver is nothing like my father. If their beliefs aligned, he wouldn't have snuck in books to me growing up." Her voice lowers, as if what she's about to share is too embarrassing. "I don't know how I could have survived without him."

I sit up in realization. "He is the man that used to give you the books."

"The same one," she says.

The only clear memory of him being mentioned is when Janelle would tell me she got a new book from the man. She never said his name, elaborated on who he was or what relationship they had.

She loved those books. They were about adventure and action. In every book, the lead was a young girl that saved the world from destruction with her bravery. Janelle was obsessed with those books for a couple of summers. She lent me one once but I was too ashamed to admit I never read it. I never brought it up the following summer.

Janelle being vague with details regarding her life inside the Duelo home wasn't odd. She never said much. She said little about herself, but we all knew in one way or another that the silence was louder. At least that's how I see it now as an adult. As a child, Janelle was simply a mystery. The parts of herself she chose to share were enough to hook me deep into her gravity. I can't help but hate myself for not asking more. If I knew, would I have been able to do anything?

"You were so obsessed with reading for a while." A chuckle escapes my lips. I shift my attention to Janelle, and her eyes meet mine with a perplexed look, as if the sound is unfamiliar to her. "What happened to that?" I ask.

"I outgrew the stories. After all, they were just stories."

"Stories that gave you hope," I say.

She never belonged to me. Her soul being bound to someone else is enough proof of that.

"One day my father found the books Oliver was giving me. He was furious because this was physical proof of someone giving me something he did not approve of at all."

"What happened?" I ask in a whisper.

Her eyes take a far away look. "My father went on a witch hunt. He never flat out blamed anyone but a sweet maid was fired soon after and tossed out." Her eyes water but tears don't fall. "I never truly felt guilt until that day. My father took the books, and I begged Oliver to never bring me more."

I picture a little girl with fiery red hair crying over her books. I picture her having misguided blame for her maid's situation. Her little heart felt the guilt, thinking she brought it on by reading a book. Not understanding that the monster she has as a father is the root cause of all her misfortune.

"How did your friendship with Oliver come to be?" I ask, with ideas already circulating in my head.

"Oli's mother's name is Rosa. He says I remind him of her. Something about my eyes."

I turn to look at Janelle's eyes. I have seen them a hundred times, but as I lay eyes on her again, it finally dawned on me. Her eyes do, in fact, resemble Rosa's.

"He never had children, but he always wanted one. His wife had been a loyal maid to my mother since childhood. He took a job as a soldier for my grandfather after marrying her. Sadly, she died a few years later from an illness."

"Where did he come from?" I ask, already knowing the

answer but fishing for pieces of this puzzle I don't fully understand.

"He never told me," she says, putting away her plate.

The ring of lies never sounds.

I cannot fathom why anyone would stay under the Duelo command unless absolutely needing to. But as I watch Janelle get ready for bed, I know exactly why Oliver never left the Duelo estate, despite not agreeing with Lord Duelo. I understand why he didn't alert us to any conspiring whispers. Oliver's duty to do what is right will forever be second to the loyalty he has to her.

Would I have done any better in his place?

"We should go to sleep," I say, and settle in for the night.

As we lay there side by side, I take a deep breath. The sweet spring smell of Janelle fills my lungs. Her soft breathing quiets down, reassuring me that she has drifted off to sleep. It's a relief that she didn't complain about sharing a bed, but it's not the first occurrence. It's unsettling how comfortable and correct this feels. I wish I could despise her and eliminate these uncontrollable emotions I have towards her.

I am starting to believe that is impossible.

20 years ago

The sun is high in the sky. Brandon was recently announced as the next in line. Mother has spent the day crying about it. I'm not sure if it's from happiness or sadness. She looks at him like she pities him. Being the chosen one is a huge honor. At least that is what Grandpa says. But that is not what it feels like when Mom congratulates Brandon with tears in her eyes. She doesn't really sound like she means it.

Brandon has said little about it. I doubt he has thought much about it. I never imagined myself being the chosen one because it's too much responsibility. I might not know exactly what Grandpa does, but I know it's a lot, and he always has to be busy. Brandon's fate isn't something I wish for.

"Is he excited about it?" Janelle asks me.

"Not exactly."

She doesn't ask me much about my family other than the antics my brothers and I get into. We are pushing a small old canoe we found on the lake a few years ago. We usually paddle to the middle of the lake and just sit back. Alternating between eating, reading, and talking. It's always a peaceful day when we do this. I spot the figure of Roman at the edge of the lake, waving his arms like crazy, but I ignore him, hoping he will go away.

"Isn't that your brother?" Janelle asks me, but I don't look. "He is swimming towards us."

That makes me snap my head up. Sure enough, the monster is swimming laps toward us. Roman is a year older than me, but he had a growth spurt recently, leaving me a foot shorter than him.

I shake my head in disbelief. One day. That is what I wanted for myself. And Janelle, but she doesn't count.

His head pokes to the side of the canoe as his fingers grab the edge.

"Careful before you tip us over." I gesture for him to let go, but he doesn't.

"Neither of you could hear me?" Roman looks between Janelle and me.

"We didn't." Her tone is sarcastic.

"Janelle Duelo," my brother says her name with a knowing glint. "It's nice to see you in daylight. I was beginning to think you were part vampire since you only sneak into my brother's window when the sun has set and then leave before it rises again."

"Are you some creepy peeker?" She crosses her arms.

"What?" his head shakes back and forth. "No!"

Janelle gives him her best chastising look. The edges of my mouth tilt up.

"I was just wondering why you two don't invite anyone else." He doesn't wait for us to answer. "What do you guys do here?" He looks inside the canoe and scrunches his nose at the books.

"Today I am water painting," Janelle tells us as she picks up her bag. She opens it and shows us all the supplies inside.

"It's summer. Shouldn't we be having fun?" Roman whines.

"This is fun." She mocks, offended.

"Jesse?" His question comes with an over-enthusiastic head shake. "Let's go jump from the swing dad tied to the tree branch."

The idea sounds enticing, but it would take much more than that to persuade me to leave.

"I am right where I want to be." At his outraced expression, I add, "We will paddle closer to the swing. We will score your jumps."

With a smile only Roman Oscuro can muster, he turns toward the swing. "Let's race there. If I win, you two have to join me eventually."

He won that race and we eventually joined him in the lake. We swam until our skin wrinkled and the sun set. The laughter mixed with the sounds of the night.

Everything shifted that day. A new normal was created for us. Every day that summer, Brandon found us after a long day of doing whatever his training intended. We never talked about it per his request, but we helped him let loose and forget, even if it was just for a few hours every night. When Janelle visited my room after that, Roman and Brandon would find themselves there, too.

The four of us spent countless hours together. However, even with them in the room, it never felt like she blended with them as she did with me.

CHAPTER EIGHT

JANELLE

The dream is always the same. It starts with the smell of smoke, and then the heat of the fire skims across my skin. It's followed by the screams of people. I never see their faces, but I see their shadows running away. I don't realize they are running away from me until it's too late. It's not until the flames my body is composed of have devoured everything in my path that I stop and look behind me. It's chaos and agony as far as my eyes can see. I think I'm rushing after them to help them until I realize what I am. I'm the snake made of fire that my magic creates.

"Janelle," a voice calls.

I snap my eyes open and look up at Jesse's confused gaze. His hands are holding my face in a tender touch.

"You are okay." He lets me go and stands up.

"I am," I say and look around. "I'm awake."

I'm not the one being chased by the fire. I am the one wielding it. The dreams come every night while my eyes search for sleep. If I would have slept the night before, they'd have come in the woods under the sky.

I wipe sweat from my face and realize my skin is hot to the touch. Jesse doesn't say anything else as we both get ready for the day. I can see the questions in his eyes, but he holds them back. Regardless of the reason, I am thankful for it.

I start my duties with the rest of the staff. Jesse goes on his own to search for the Red Book. In contrast, I have tasks on my to-do list of places that need my attention before the end of the day. I survey the paper and calculate the number of things I need to do. It's clear my father doesn't expect me to finish by the number of items, which only fires me up higher. But there's one place I plan on visiting first.

"Matias?" I try to get his attention, but not even a flinch registers on his face.

He is lying on the hard floor with nothing underneath to cushion him. The other prisoners move around him with ease, as if they know he is harmless and will continue to be. I might as well be invisible to them. They act and move about as if I'm not even here.

"He will not answer," one man says from the other side of the cell.

I'm uncertain which one. They say nothing else, so I can't attribute the voice to someone in particular.

I look into Matias' eyes and see a glimmer of something familiar. "I hid in there too, you know," I say, tapping my temple.

His eyes are still focused on something beside me. I stop trying to catch his attention and think of that night. How I got there and what brought me back.

"The night of the attack, my father had called for a household meeting."

When I entered the door of his war room, I stopped to see that only his soldiers were present. It had been months that I wasn't allowed to attend meetings with his soldiers.

"Seeing all his soldiers there should have been the first sign of trouble. But I didn't leave. I walked in and sat down." I recall the way their eyes followed me as I crossed the room. He extended his hand in my direction and asked me to join him. "My soul bond Ray was already sitting at the table with my brothers."

I look down at my hands and see the same tremor that took over them. My body knew what was about to happen before my mind could catch up. At least that's what I want myself to believe. That I didn't know the tea pushed into my hand was odd at the first sip. That despite the sour taste overtaking the normally minty flavor, I had no clue. I was tricked.

Coward.

The truth is that I was very much a coward. Now, looking back, it's a shameful memory. I should've spat it out and fought my way out of there. I might not have known what my father was planning, but the second I figured it out, I should have acted. Staying quiet and compliant didn't make me a victim, but a silent ally.

By the time I stood up for what I knew was right, it was too late. The damage was too great to make up. There's nothing I can do to make amends.

"I was given a tea that allows my soul bond to take full control of my magic. I became a passenger of my own mind. He accessed my power without my conscious decision to allow it." A tear runs down my cheek as the image comes back to the front of my mind. "My mind became fuzzy and the events that transpired played out before me as a dream. They didn't feel real until I came to my senses. But then I hid." I hiccup and push down a sob. "In a hallway, my dragon rushed a group of people. My eyes focused enough to watch them be consumed to ashes."

The smell of burned flesh and wood fills my lungs. The

taste in the back of my throat is vile. I made the first choice I regret from that night. My first choice was the wrong choice.

"I chose to hide inside my head. I didn't try to stop him. It wasn't fear of him, it was fear of facing what I had allowed."

The thought of how I ever let it go this far echo in my head. I hear them sometimes even while awake. Their running footsteps as they try to outrun the fire. They never get too far before the footsteps cease all together.

"Then I saw Bianca," I say.

I look at him to see if her name would get a reaction out of him. I might be seeing things, but I think his eyes twitch.

"She was facing off with Ray. The determination and bravery in her eyes caught my attention. She wasn't ready to die defending the castle. Her eyes told me she was sure she could win."

The thoughts that follow flash through my mind at lightning speed while Bianca and Ray move in slow motion.

"I was jealous of her bravery and confidence. Then I realized the only difference between us was her determination to come out on top. I just need to take action. So I did. I killed him."

My second choice that night is not one I regret.

"You killed your soul bond?" a man across the cell asks with a mixture of shock and disgust.

I am completely unfazed by his expression. Some people are attracted to the idea of a soul bond and idolize it. Ignis is the only city that continues the tradition, and many visit the city hoping to find their soul bond. I abruptly ended the precious connection with a blade. According to traditions and legends, what I did shouldn't be possible. Being able to harm your soul bond goes against our biology, but while holding the blade in my hand, all I could think of was how free I would be.

I had not noticed that the men in the cells had stopped

whatever they were doing to listen to my story. They are all staring at me from various places on the cell.

"I freed my soul," I say.

I get a few shakes of the head and some strange looks.

"Take your time Matias," I say, reaching inside the cells. I place my hand on his, laying under his head. "But come back. You can't hide forever. We always have to face the events the Fates have planned for us one day or another."

I scrub the last of the toilet bowl with soap and flush the bubbles left behind. I've been given the responsibility of cleaning all the bathrooms in the common areas today. That is a total of five bathrooms, all on the first floor of the house. Jesse said I should be thankful I'm not tasked with cleaning all the bathrooms inside the bedrooms. I find it hard to be thankful for anything while I'm still stuck here. Since he went off on his own to investigate the whereabouts of the Red Book, I'm left to do the manual labor alone.

I close the bathroom door behind me and head to the next one. A grunt that can only belong to a big man with a thick mustache makes me redirect my steps. I find Oli in the kitchen, under the sink, with a flashlight. He peeks out from under the sink as I enter the room but quickly turns back to his task at seeing me.

Since scrubbing bathroom bowls doesn't take much mental work, I had plenty of time to think. Especially about the Red Book, and the cursed book.

"I have to ask you a question." I move closer, but make sure no one is outside first.

The last thing I need is for my father to get word that I'm curious about anything.

"This is not the best time, Jan." Oli's words come out with a grunt as he tries to tighten a pipe under the cabinet. He sits up and rubs his wrist.

"Here," I say, taking his wrist and pushing healing energy into it. "Did it work?"

"How? You don't have magic, do you?" he asks.

"Sadly I don't. But I once read that gifts cannot be taken away. I haven't tried it yet."

I am unsure if Brandon knows of this loophole or if he even cares about it. Not many people know of my gift all together.

Oli gives me a soft smile. "Let's see if it worked." He gets up in two tries and a couple of huffs. The uninterrupted flow of running water makes Oli's smile widen. "Okay, what do you want?" he asks, shutting the water.

I get right to it. "My father attempted to steal the cursed book written by Klause from the Oscuro library, correct?"

When Jesse first mentioned the cursed book it hadn't occurred to me that my father was the man behind it. I figured that I would have heard of it first before he made a move. Now I know it couldn't have been anyone else.

The attempt to steal the cursed book is what alerted the Oscuros that something was coming. Bianca was hired to acquire it by one of my father's men, and it trapped Matias's soul in it. Then she struck a deal with Brandon Oscuro to help them in exchange for Matias's soul. Little did my father know that by bringing Bianca to Brandon, he would position a key player against his rebellion.

Oli rubs his eyes, the tiredness evident on the lines of his face. "The idea came from one of his men, I think." He looks at the clock on the wall. "Must we talk about this right now?"

I follow his eyes. "Why?"

"The kitchen staff will begin preparing lunch soon."

"It won't take long. I'm just wondering if he is in possession of more than one book written by Klause?"

The lengths my father went for the cursed book has me thinking he knew something else. There must be more than one journal by this infamous Klause person.

"Not exactly." He looks to the doorway as voices alert us to people coming. They are still far enough, but Oli hurries to whisper, "Klause is not the only one of his kind. He is not like us. I'm sure you know as much. There are cousins of his who knew of his movements. Your father had one journal by a cousin but he destroyed it."

"What was their name?" I ask, but it's too late.

A cluster of people enter the kitchen. Without sparing us a glance, they get to work.

"You must return to your duties, Lady Janelle," Oli says with a strong authoritative voice.

I don't bother arguing with him because when he starts his role as a soldier in front of others, it's impossible for him to snap out of it. I know he thinks it keeps everyone guessing about our friendship, but he has to know it doesn't fool everyone. All I care about is that it fools my father.

I salute Oliver and march my way out of the kitchens to find the next bathroom I need to clean. I'm dragging my steps, but the sooner I finish my tasks, the sooner I can go searching for the names of the people who knew Klause. What they wrote could be crucial to deciphering what my father is doing to Matias.

With that in mind, I make my way to my father's office. It's close to lunchtime, so he will not be here for the next few hours. With a hint of excitement, I slowly turn the doorknob to his bathroom. If someone happens to inquire why I am here, I plan to use this as my excuse.

I look over the bookshelves first. I pay close attention to the spines. If this journal was made around the time the Red Book was created, it's very old. I go spine by spine but it's not long before I've gone through all the books.

It's very possible it's not here. There's a small library on the other side of the house. But that hide-out would be too obvious. That's if my father even thought of hiding it. Would it cross his mind that someone will look for it?

Only the Fates know what crosses that man's mind. After all, he declared war not just on the Oscuro King, but on a young, powerful one. Only a desperate man would resort to that. I should have seen the signs of my father going off the deep end, but I was too busy trying to survive his controlling grip and rigorous schedule.

My father never trusted the other royal families. I grew suspicious of them by the way he spoke of them, but the truth was that he envied them. He was an outsider, and despite marrying into the family, he never truly belonged.

The oldest sibling carries on the title and duties according to tradition. I was the youngest, meaning my oldest brother would be the one to take on the title and duties. But due to my birth name, I never saw myself as free of responsibilities. I try not to let my thoughts linger on my brothers. They were strangers to me. Two fallen soldiers of my father's schemes. I shake my head and stop myself there.

I always watched the Oscuro brothers, not with jealousy, but with wonder. Knowing those close bonds weren't meant for me, I was glad they were out there. I was happy simply to know that they existed somewhere out in the world.

As a child, I felt that if those kinds of connections existed, one would eventually find me. Well, one did and I destroyed it.

Before restarting the search and pulling each book out, I decided to check my father's desk. Despite his organizational style, it's worth checking if the books are here. My father never locks his desk drawers. He is far too impatient to unlock them every time he needs to get something.

On the right side, I see all the accounting documents. My father is the type of person who might not do the work, but he sure will double-check it. I have no clue who is doing all his accounting work here, but it looks like he's still running a tight ship. I look over a few lines and see all types of food items being documented and accounted for. The sight of various fish makes me roll my eyes. There's no doubt they belong to his favorite dishes.

A hushed tiptoe of rubber soles carefully paddling on the floor alerts me to the presence of someone trying to sneak up on me. I first imagine it's Jesse trying to be playful, but I dismiss that as soon as it crosses my mind.

I close the drawer and move towards the bathroom. I'm a few steps away when the intruder stops trying to conceal themselves.

"What are you doing here?" Ernesto asks. There's a smirk on his face, like he caught me with my hands on the cookie jar.

The bathroom is only one foot away from me. I hold back from explaining that I was cleaning it because that would be odd. I don't explain myself to this dog. Starting today would only raise suspicion.

"Is it any of your concern?" I ask.

I don't wait for him to answer as I open the door. I realize I left my cleaning supplies in the office, but I make use of the few wipes under the sink. In addition, I pick up the toilet brush and toss it into the toilet.

"You have some high and mighty air for someone scrubbing toilets."

I can't deny he has me there. Thankfully, he hasn't noticed the lack of cleaning supplies.

"Shouldn't you be doing something for my father?" I ask. "Like bark."

Ernesto lets out a booming laugh that fills the room. I move out of the bathroom and pass him. He keeps taking steps closer, and it is only a matter of time before he blocks my way out. His laughter keeps me from hearing the horde of footsteps until my father and his man are at the doorway.

I must've been looking for far longer than I thought.

"What is happening here?" my father asks entering the room.

The rest of his men, who are a total of five, stand by the door, carefully watching the scene unravel. I might be mistaken, but I believe I see a flicker of something in mid-air. It could very well be Jesse. It makes sense that he would resort to following my father around if searching the house was unfruitful.

"Your dog won't leave me alone," I say to my father as I gather my cleaning supplies.

Crying to my father with complaints has never been my way. I haven't made an attempt since childhood, when I was punished for it. But I need a reason to leave before he notices I shouldn't be here.

Ernesto joins us by the door. He crosses his arms and sends a cocky grin my way. "I was simply supervising the quality of the work, King Oscuro."

The mistake is done, and as soon as the words leave his lips, he knows it too. His eyes widen and his mouth gapes. The poor dog just called my father by his enemy's name.

My father is not a forgiving or understanding person. He will not simply acknowledge that there has always been one King Oscuro longer than any of us have been alive, regardless of first name. The title has stayed in that one family since the beginning of the Red Book. It's normal for a person to make a mistake and have that well-known name attached to the title roll off the tongue.

Hoping my father would be thoughtful is naïve. My father doesn't want to be king for the people but for his selfish needs. There is something broken in him. I first thought his faults came from not having a father himself.

How can a boy not raised by a man learn to become one?

There is something further wrong and hollow inside my father. His darkness is not just the absence of love and care. I have come to learn his darkness is sinister. He is not unique. He isn't the first and he will not be the last. Hunger for power takes many shapes and faces but persists through the years.

My father's eyes do not leave Ernesto as I scurry away. The soldiers outside the door move apart to let me pass, then walk inside the room, shutting the door. I make my way to the stairs, then up to my room. I don't stop moving until I reach my bed and kneel at the foot of it.

The door opens after me and clicks shut.

"It's not your fault."

I look at Jesse, who stands before me with furrowed brows.

"What?" I ask and my voice comes out like a gasp.

"Regardless of how much of an ass that man is, you feel guilty that he is about to be punished." He kneels next to me. "Breathe, Janelle."

His words break through my haze, and I realize I'm hyperventilating. I need to get a grip. What is wrong with me? I don't care about Ernesto or his fate at my father's hand. It's his choice to be here.

I look down at my hands and see they are shaking. I fist them tightly and take a deep breath. *One, two, three, four, five.* I breathe out, then repeat. The five count is something I haven't had to do in a while. As a child, it's what I used to do to keep myself sane. Whatever my father threw at me between training sessions and social expectations, the counting always centered me and helped me gather my bearings. After all, screaming until my lungs were empty was never an option, despite being far more relieving.

"You still do the five count," Jesse says while staring at me.

We are eye to eye on the floor.

"I counted out loud?"

"No," he whispers. His hand traces my lips. "But I can see them make the sound of the numbers."

He snaps his hand back like my skin burned him.

I lick my lips, and I rise to my feet. "I will go find us food."

"Actually, I will," Jesse says.

Before I can object, his cape is over his head, and the door is shutting after him. I look back at the bed and decide this is where I'll be spending the rest of my day.

CHAPTER NINE

JANELLE

The following morning, I woke up earlier than usual. My nightmare was just starting when a hand shook me awake. Jesse didn't say anything and even pretended to sleep as he lay down looking away from me.

Once I am up and ready, I waste no time in looking for Oli. With renewed energy, I navigate through the house. Our ancestral home is significantly different from this house. The Duelo home has been passed down from generation to generation. Over the years, the structure has seen additions and renovations, but it has always been an impressive building. I can only imagine my father's dismay at this home lacking the luxury he has grown accustomed to, regardless of the amount of magic he has put into expanding it.

I find Oli on a ladder changing a light bulb in the middle of my father's office.

I hate how my father pushes Oli to do things like this. He could easily ask a younger soldier. Ernesto could do it, but he asks Oliver, who is thirty years older. There's a trail of sweat coming down his forehead, dripping to his chin.

"Isn't there someone else that can do this?" I ask.

Oli looks down at me and shakes his head. His focus is on tightening up that light bulb. Once he's satisfied with the number of turns, he brings his hands down to the top of the ladder. He pulls a rag from his back pocket and wipes his face. A heavy breath huffs out of his chest before he climbs down slowly.

"Oli," I say, as he reaches the landing. "One day, I will make things right. I will get my magic back and I'll take you home."

The smile on his face is sad. "You don't need to do anything for me."

"Of course I need to take care of you. I didn't forget about our deal."

"What deal?" he asks.

I cannot believe he forgot our deal. Even when I ran away and grabbed onto my freedom, I remembered Oli and our deal every day. My plan was always to return for him and my mother. I wanted freedom. I wanted to taste it and know what it felt like, but there was no doubt that running away from who I am was a momentary thing. There's no avoiding fate. The Fates have made it known to me.

"I'll take care of you when you are old like you took care of me when I was little. It was our deal," I remind him.

He sighs and takes a step closer to me. "Janelle, I only told you that because your little girl's mind couldn't understand why I was nice to you without reason. Being raised by your father always made you suspicious of people. From a young age, you never believed that anything would come without a cost. The deal was my impromptu solution."

I don't let his words choke me up. My heart warms at the explanation. I met Oli very young, and even if I don't recall feeling suspicious of him, I do remember promising one day that I would care for him like he has done for me.

"I'm keeping my promise, Oli," I say.

He doesn't argue with me, instead the smile that spreads on his lips is gentle. "That is something to look forward to," he says.

We hear a group of steps approaching from down the hallway. Oli looks up to the ladder.

"I left my rag on the top." He points at it. "Can you get it quickly?"

I'm not sure why we're rushing, but I don't question him. I climb up the ladder for the rag. As I reach the top, the footsteps stop at the doorway. My father and a couple of his new favorite soldiers enter the room. I look down for Oli, but he is gone. The handle on the bathroom door rotates slowly, alerting me to where he went. I cleaned that bathroom before, and there was another door that connects it to the hallway.

"There you are," my father says as he circles the ladder.

I follow him with my eyes while clutching tightly to the wood.

"I wondered how you manage to get so much done in a day." He watches me closely as I climb down. "I suppose you cannot blame me for wondering. You have never done real work before. Who would've thought you have work ethic?"

The irony.

"And you have?" I ask.

The question comes out before I can help it. I don't flinch away as my father raises his hand on me. He has never hit me before, but the mental torture he has subjected me to is far worse. He stops when someone calls for him.

"Sir," Oliver calls from the doorway. "Your men are waiting in the dining room for further instructions about tonight."

"That's great." My father turns in his direction. "Would you look at that?" My father points at the changed light bulb.

"Janelle has completed most of her tasks without help once again and it's not even lunch time."

My father moves quickly to my side and takes my hand in his. "Yet these hands remain unblemished. One would think manual labor leaves its mark."

It's only been a few days, but he is already suspicious of me. Then his words dawn on me with the accusation. Everytime I found Oli these past couple of days he had been working hard but also in a rush.

I meet my father's eyes. "A true Duelo is tougher than that," I say between clenched teeth.

I might be suicidal. I cannot help but remind my father the royal blood of the family name does not run in his veins. Before he can answer, we hear a loud fight down the hall. A few of the soldiers with him rush out of the room.

"You can't expect them to stand in one place for too long before fighting like toddlers," Oli says, shaking his head in disgust.

My father straightens his collar. "This is all we have to work with, I'm afraid." He moves out of the room quickly after his men.

"You have been completing part of my daily tasks, haven't you?"

The list I was given is already extensive. I can only imagine how many things were in the actual list.

Oli does not deny or confirm my statement. He gives me a gentle smile that is tight at the edges.

"Whatever you are planning, make sure it happens soon. He's getting dangerously paranoid," Oli says, then leaves after my father.

I don't say out loud, but my father is paranoid for a good reason. I'm planning his dismay. He's right to feel danger coming.

There's a light knock on the door, but no one is standing there. A light touch on my shoulder raises goosebumps up my arm.

"Are you okay?" Jesse asks.

I had no clue he was around, but I'm not surprised. I expected him to find me later in the day or meet me in my room.

"Of course." I gulp.

I can't see his face, so I don't know if he believes me, but after a pause he says, "I will go see what your father tells his men in the meeting. I will meet you later in the room to debrief."

"That's fine," I say and move to fold the ladder. "I want to visit Matias."

I haven't seen him today, and a part of me wants to confirm with my own eyes that he is still there. Whatever remains of *him*.

The hallways are quiet with only a handful of guards on duty. The remainder of my father's men are meeting with him, allowing me to make my way down stairs without intrusive eyes.

I notice something is different the moment I reach the bottom of the stairs. The heaviness in the air is suffocating. The space isn't filled with the soft murmurs of the prisoners. Their complete silence scratches at my skin with awareness. I look around and watch how their gazes are fixed to the opposite side of the cell.

Matias is on the floor. It's not until I take a step closer that I finally see it. His skin is covered in blisters. The burns are running down his arms with a mixture of red and blue marks. There are more wounds on him than unblemished skin. Despite the agony he must be in, he remains unmoving.

This is why he retreats into his own head. It's clear as day.

If my father's attempts to uncap his magic don't kill him, the pain should. But he is alive. He is a fighter.

The rage inside my veins rises. I can feel the impotence and frustration underneath my skin vibrating with the urge to do something.

I look at my shaky hands. "If I do it they will know someone helped him," I say to myself in a near whisper. "But not doing it will allow his suffering to continue."

The stakes are much higher now. If I do this it will only be a matter of time before a soldier finds out and my father is notified. *Knowledge is power, and no one keeps secrets for free.*

I risk jeopardizing the mission, but at what cost? Being a silent ally stops with me taking action.

I cross to Matias with determination. I place my hand over a section of his skin that has the least amount of open wounds. I close my eyes and push all the healing energy I have in me. Even as I feel my reserves empty I know it's not enough.

The damage is too much.

I open my eyes and feel tears track down my cheeks. Even as a child with miniature reserves I always managed to help.

I lay down and mirror Matias on the other side of the cell bars. The majority of his open wounds have healed but I know there is far worse damage deeper in. His eyes are still gone but I speak to him softly anyway. He might not hear me but in case he does I need him to know.

"It's okay to hide Matias." I wipe down my face with my sleeve. "Hide deep enough that you don't have to feel any of this. Vengeance is coming. You will have it."

I don't know how long I lay there watching his chest rise and fall. I take that sign as a victory for the night. By the time I reach my bedroom door, Jesse is already inside with the cape off.

His eyes meet mine and without saying a word his arms

open for me. I cross the distance between us in a rush. I feel once again like the little girl who found peace in these arms. Oliver gave me comfort and support inside the walls of my home. But even he couldn't give me safety. Jesse gave me something different. He gave me hope for a future. It might not have belonged to me from the beginning but hope is sometimes enough.

I bury my face in his chest and breathe in. I fill my lungs and count to five looking for my sanity. As always I find it in Jesse.

When I feel my voice is stable again I say, "they did it to him again."

Jesse's arms pull me in tighter. "Is he alive?" His voice is full of worry.

I nod. "I don't think he will survive whatever my father did again."

"Then we need to hurry," he says into my hair. "We will."

Knowing we are both on the same page fills me with something. We are running out of time, and now more than ever, we need to find the Red Book and take Matias far away from my father's clutches.

We will.

CHAPTER TEN

JESSE

I close the door behind me and take a deep breath. My focus needs to be on what I'm doing. I cannot afford to get distracted. I've failed my people and my family once for the girl behind that door, and I can't allow that to happen again.

From the meeting earlier today, I know Duelo plans to have his men meet him on the first floor at nightfall. I follow the low glow of lanterns illuminating the hall down to the other edge of the house. Janelle's room is at the end of the hall, apart from everyone else. She might see it as yet another way for her father to alienate her, but I'm glad for it. I see the way those men look at her. The princess, falling from grace, looks almost attainable to their hands.

Over my dead body.

These past couple of days have taught me the feelings I bury are closer to the surface than I expected. The longer I spend by her side the harder it gets to fight them. I've just hoped for them to fade but they never left. I have no clue how anything between us can work after the attack but there is no sense in thinking about that right now. We have to free Matias and return the Red Book.

I swiftly make my way down to the next floor, seeking any noise or movement, but the place looks and feels deserted until I touch the threshold of the first floor.

Lord Duelo stands before the front door above his men with his nose high in the air. I can't hear the end of his speech, but his men nod in unison, and a choir of affirmation echoes through the room. He leads the way out of the house into the backyard. Some of his men carry torches lighting up the path. I fall into step at the edges of the group.

I stay vigilant to listen with my gift. Any and all information is essential. I wouldn't put it past Lord Duelo to tell his men one thing but truly mean something else. He isn't a trusting man. Neither am I, after all.

I stay close to the edges and follow them with my cloak over my head. Just before I'm about to cross the door to the backyard, I look up the stairs and watch Janelle's mother leaning over the edge. A handkerchief is balled up in her hand, covering her mouth, while shaking her head lightly.

"Hurry boy!" Duelo Senior snaps.

I watch a young boy rush to pull a small wagon. His feet slide on the dirt as he pulls with all his body weight. A dark blanket covers the top, keeping the item inside hidden. Whatever is inside cannot be too big, considering the way the blanket drapes over the wagon. But the boy huffs and puffs loudly with every pull. None of the men offer to help the boy, but Oliver watches over him, staying behind and waiting for him to catch up.

I look at the trail of mud the wagon is dragging leading to a shed in the back. The structure is old and a breeze away from falling apart.

The men are quiet as we walk into the forest clearing near

the back of the house. The torches are the only light illuminating our path in this cloudy night sky. They stop walking at the edge of the circle, and a path opens for the boy with the wagon. He keeps walking to the middle of the circle where Lord Duelo and his two top soldiers stand.

There's creaking coming from the other side of the circle before we watch the trees and bushes move. Two tall creatures break through the greenery first. Their tall figures are masked by the night, their skin helping them blend in the dark, but I have seen giants once or twice. Their bodies are about ten feet tall and their skin is covered with bumps that resemble horns.

None of the surrounding men look alarmed or worried, so I stay frozen in place. Not a single murmur is heard amongst them, telling me they have seen these giants before. It's not a common sight that would be easy to breeze over.

The creatures do not venture close enough to magic wielders and, as far as I know, they definitely shouldn't be anywhere near the human lands.

A second and third rustle of leaves announce the entrance of two more groups. On the right walks a trio of orcs. They are tall, but not as tall as the giants. Their height is usually around eight feet, and they are built like tree trunks. These three are no exception. Their faces are also not unfamiliar to me. I've seen them before at social events. They are the three sons of Kro, the current commander of their kind. They are to their people what Brandon, Roman, and I are to ours.

On the left are four duendes. The small creatures are human-like but also have a tree-like texture on their skin. They are usually kind and quiet creatures that care more to keep to themselves in the depths of the forest. The four here tonight are not any I have seen before.

"You are late," Lord Duelo says to the duendes. "Did you bring what you promised?"

"We did," they say in unison, then move out of the way to allow someone else into the circle.

Murmurs finally break out amongst the men around me as the creature walks forward. This must be their first time laying eyes on this creature. Mine too. I've read about it and heard stories here and there, but nothing concrete.

"She's beautiful and scary," a soldier says to my side.

"That is not a woman. Death has no gender," another man whispers.

Their kind are not like the others in the group. They don't organize powers and negotiate treaties. They do not claim lands or establish villages. Their homes are rumored to be in deep caves and only seen by the light of the moon.

"Calaca," Lord Duelo greets.

His eyes take in the tall figure with glee. Long white sheets drape over its body, covering everything but the face. Calaca's face remains unemotional and doesn't return the greeting. Instead, it looks around. For a second, I fear its eyes might see under the cloth because its eyes stay on me for a beat, but after a blink, it turns back to the men in the circle.

"I have come here to hear your offer. Not to offer my services," it says.

Their voice is like a strong wind. It carries through the circle and beyond without being loud. The sound is soft yet powerful.

Lord Duelo nods his head and turns back to his men. "For hundreds of years, we have been limited to what we can amount. Our level of magic has been restricted to keep some above others. The balances are about to change."

He moves to the wagon and pulls off the cloth covering the top. The murmurs that follow are not from the surrounding men, but the creatures across the circle.

"Impossible," the duendes say to each other.

"You have spoken true, dragon." One giant inclines his head to Lord Duelo.

The Calaca takes a step forward, making the men around Lord Duelo raise hidden weapons. They point them at it, making it raise both its white bony hands in return. I do not think simple swords and daggers can do much, but I also don't know if its magic works the way ours does in the human lands.

"I simply wish to take a closer look. It's not everyday we see the infamous Red Book," Calaca says with a glint in its eye.

Lord Duelo shakes his head. "You've seen enough. The book is not up for negotiation. It's going to be a tool used to dismantle the restriction on all our magic."

"How certain are you that it has any restrictions on our magic?" One orc asks. "We have found nothing in our ancestors' books about our magic being limited by any law."

"That is how long and forgotten it is," Lord Duelo insists.

The tone that rings in my ears at his words tells me he isn't all that sure about the statement. It's not a lie, but it's not fully the truth. The partial truths have their own tone, and the noise is definitely coming from Duelo's words.

"Will you keep the book?" the oldest looking duende asks, taking a small step forward. His eyes don't leave the wagon.

"I don't plan to get rid of the book. I plan to uncap the magic only of those who stand by me." Lord Duelo doesn't pick the book up, but his hand strokes the spine.

"By fighting the king of Puerto Quinn?" A giant asks. He turns to his companions. "What do we care if the magic king lives?"

"As long as the Oscuro reign continues, our freedom will be threatened. Many of you today live under constricting reigns of your own kind. The power of this book will bring us all an edge above our enemies. By fighting with me, you will choose your side and show your loyalty. You will earn your turn then and only then."

The missing ringing in my ears punctuates how much he believes this to be true. Brandon, Roman, and I, by association of blood, stand in the way for Duelo. He probably believes that without Brandon, another Oscuro will be chosen to the crown next.

"We cannot guarantee all our people will follow us," another duende says, while looking at his companions for reassurance. "We can try, but peace has been kept for centuries with the magic king. The new king is well liked."

"I do not need them all. I need a few," Lord Duelo says.

"Have you done it yet?" Calaca asks, nodding at the book. "Have you uncapped anyone's magic?"

"Not yet, but very soon we will." Lord Duelo looks at everyone that has gathered. "We will meet in due time to take over the Black Castle and destroy King Oscuro."

Out of the corner of my eye, I watch as a man moves to the edge of the circle, then back into the forest. His slight steps are going unnoticed by everyone in the gathering. I look around the faces of the men in the circle. One face is evidently missing in the crowd.

The dog.

I rush after him quietly. He's quick to make it back to the house. He is diligent about watching the halls for servants. Something tells me to hurry after him. He passes the side of the hall where the soldiers stay and I know I was right to think so.

A maid steps out of her room down the hall but at spotting him walking rushes back into her bedroom. The lock clicks into place quickly after.

"I'm not here to see you today, Leah," Ernesto says with a chuckle. "Someone needs to learn some respect."

He passes her door and walks to the last hall of the floor, the one I know only hosts one person.

I'm about to cross the maid's door too when it flies open again. She looks in his direction, then rushes towards the opposite side of the hall. I'm so preoccupied watching him I don't move before she slams into me. I take a step back, and she lands before me on her knees. Her wide eyes search all around us to explain what had just happened. After a second, she quickly rises, then turns on her heels and runs out.

I stand there frozen in place as I watch him reach the door across the hall. My feet hit the ground with loud stumps as I close the distance. The cape drapes over and behind my body as I carelessly let it fly. My focus is only on making it across the hall as soon as possible.

His body disappears behind her door and my heart beat skyrockets.

My breaths are coming short and shallow. I throw my shoulder to the door and thrust all my weight on it. The door flies open and bangs against the wall with enough force that a lamp across the room rocks from side to side.

Ernesto is holding Janelle by the neck against the wall across the room. His eyes instantly travel to me, and shock paints his expression. Janelle takes this opportunity and knocks him to the ground. Her knee strikes his stomach and her elbow hits his throat.

The man falls to the floor coughing until she deals him a kick to the side of his head. We both stare to see if he's getting up again, but he stays on the floor completely out. Janelle stands before him. Her breathing is heavy, and a hand is holding her waist with a pained edge on her face.

"Are you okay?" I take a step inside, dropping the cape by the door.

"I expected him to be you at first. I was not ready." Her eyes reach mine and then the room, like she is making an account of everything around us.

She hurries to the door and closes it. The man on the floor grunts and turns to his back, holding his throat and stomach. His eyes open and they narrow on me.

"Jesse Oscuro. You will never stay away from her, will you?"

I think it's funny that even the dog knows the answer to that question.

"Jesse," Janelle says in a stern tone.

Her eyes tell me there is no other way. He has seen me and knows who I am. After telling Lord Duelo this piece of news, it will not take long for him to conclude I am aware of his plan involving the forest creatures. He wants me and my brothers dead. He will not stop until we are no longer an obstacle to his plans.

Lord Duelo thinks he will bring war to us. He doesn't know what is coming to him. War begins today. I focus on the man on the floor, then gaze at the woman standing in front of me.

I hold her gaze as I extend my hand out and allow a dark cloud of smoke to flow down from my hand into the floor. Before he can think to scream, it surrounds him and his senses. There is no disgust or judgement in her eyes. There has never been. This is not the first time Janelle has seen what I can do, and I am sure it won't be the last.

"We are leaving tonight," I say when it's done. "I know where the Red Book is."

CHAPTER ELEVEN

JANELLE

We wait for the guards to return from the meeting. Only those on duty are left patrolling the grounds by the time we step out. Thankfully none of the night patrols take place inside the house. We silently make our way down the hall. From the sounds coming from behind the doors, the men have just turned in for the night.

I know whatever Jesse saw and heard in tonight's meeting is the reason we're acting on the spot. I've never been one to ask too many questions but given the circumstances, I would like to know. However, Matias doesn't have time. He is going to be subjected to that torture again if we leave him here. I need to take this opportunity to get him out.

"We need to make one stop before we go," I say and gesture for Jesse to follow me.

I walk past the stairs and head towards the soldiers' bedrooms. Jesse doesn't argue with me, which means he knows whose room we are going to visit.

I place my hand on the door handle and slowly twist it, trying to make no noise. Once open, I move inside in quiet feet.

"Oli," I say into the darkness.

There is a rustle of sheets, then the bedside table light turns on. Oli's sleepy form comes into view. His eyes are squinted and hair turning in all directions. A glint of guilt stabs at my chest at the idea I will leave him behind once again. But there is no way I can take him with us now. We will risk our lives getting out of here.

I'll return for Oli when it's safer to do so.

"You are leaving?" He asks, already looking more awake than he was just a second before.

"I am."

Oli looks over my shoulder. Jesse has removed the cloak from his head. He's currently a floating head, but with a look of determination in his eyes.

"Be safe," he says to both of us.

I lean closer and kiss his cheek. Oli pulls me into a hug and I soak in as much of the goodness as possible. It's hard, but I pull away from his embrace.

"This is not goodbye, but see you later," I say.

"You can only keep your promise to me if you keep yourself safe enough to fulfill it," he says, referring to my promise of one day being able to take him home.

"That's right." I nod, trying to look away before the tears threatening to spill win.

Jesse's hand on my shoulder is a reminder that we need to get moving. With one last look at Oli, we step out of the room and into the dark hallway. Everyone seems to be in their rooms, but we are still careful to not make noise as we pass the soldiers' rooms. As we reach the stairs to go down, I see a silhouette standing in front of my bedroom door. I don't realize who it is until they walk closer to the stairs.

"What are you doing, Janelle?" she asks.

One of her hands is on her chest and the other is brushing

her bottom lip. Her wide eyes move from Jesse's to me. He never placed the cloak back over his head.

"You're not supposed to be friends with him. I already told you. How many times did I tell you?"

"Mother." I take a step closer to her and gesture with my hands to lower her voice. "Please stop." I look behind us to the hall where all of my father's men are sleeping.

"His friendship was never a good idea. Why wouldn't you listen and stay away?" She shakes her head with disapproval.

Her voice sounds lucid and very much the woman she once was, but the back-and-forth questions remind me that my mother will never be fully back. Not to the normal person she was before my father took it all from her. Losing her magic took part of her sanity.

"He is going to be very upset." She looks off to the stairs railing. "Whatever you are planning, stop and go to bed."

She crosses her arms as if her request isn't ridiculous and I will simply obey. She knows exactly what I'm going to do. At least part of it.

"You know I can't do that. You know why. He can't get away with this. The book belongs to the King." I try to reason with her, to no avail.

"He might not be a good man, Janelle, but he is your father and you need to obey him."

"At what cost?" I ask.

I always wanted to know. Where would she stop? What truly would be the point my mother would no longer fall victim to him.

"He took your magic and your title. What else will you give him?"

"This is wrong." She stumps her foot. "You will ruin everything!"

"I would?" I take a step back and bite down the bitter laugh in my throat. "You are the blood relation of the Duelo family. He took your last name. You were a lady brought up as a royal now living in a hideout scared of your King. How much further will you fall for that man?"

"You wouldn't understand. He is my soul bond, Janelle. The Oscuros took away yours, so you never had a chance to find out."

The bitter sound that escapes my lips is unavoidable. "The blade that took his life was wielded by my hand alone."

"You killed your soul bond?" Her shock is so honest and innocent. Her eyes are wide and scared. My mother's expression shifts as she is finally seeing me for the first time.

I know what she plans to do.

"If you call for my father, he will kill me."

"He will not kill you." Her expression is appalled at the mere idea I would suggest something like that. "After losing your brothers, do you think he would do anything to hurt you?"

"He has done it my entire life, mother. Are you willing to bet my life on it?"

"He only hurt you to toughen you up. You are so strong and he always saw potential in you. I told you to dial down your power and pretend certain things were beyond you, but your magic was too great to mask. He did what he needed to do to prepare you."

Listening to her reasoning is mad. I always imagined my mother was ignorant of the truth about my father's actions. It crossed my mind many times to go to her for help, but even as a child, I saw her as too weak to do anything. After all, if she couldn't help herself, how could she help me? I would love to think that there is a piece left in her willing to protect her children. Surely my mother would never give me up.

"Mom, let me go," I say, but it's too late.

The resolve is written all over the harsh lines in her face. She takes a step back and yells, "Help! Someone come and help. They are escaping!"

No anger flows through my body as I stare at her. I feel only sorrow. I don't tell her to stop, try to reason or beg her. With one last look at the woman who brought me into this world I say goodbye. This might very well be the last time I see her.

Her voice echoes once in the space before her gaping mouth makes words, but only silence comes out of her lips. Perhaps once she would've been a challenge for Jesse, but my mother is close to as powerless as I am. One spell takes her voice, and another puts her to sleep.

"She will be okay when she wakes." Jesse catches her before she hits the ground and gently places her on the side of the stair railing. "Let's go."

In the dark hall, no one will see her.

Jesse leads the way down the main stairs and into the back of the house. I follow him outside and into the night sky. The backyard is cold and other than the noises of the farm animals, the night seems to be dead silent.

Jesse stops in front of what looks to be an old shed. Keeping the doors locked is a new shiny golden lock. His hand hovers over the lock as his eyes close. The lock shakes a bit, but it does not open. Jesse's head turns to the side before he repeats his attempt.

"Is the Red Book in there?" I ask.

"It's not working." Jesse takes a step back to take a better look at the structure of the shaggy building.

Its appearance was intentionally designed to be inconspicuous. My father has always loved to hide things in the most unassuming of places. He has always wished for me to do the opposite. Perhaps he believed if people were too busy looking at me, they wouldn't see what he was scheming all along. Or he couldn't help himself from creating a puppet all would see and admire.

I know my father better than anyone else in the world. I know him better than my brothers ever did, and perhaps more than my mother. She definitely has suffered the most by tying herself to him, but a long time ago she checked out and stopped wanting to know what he was up to. I wasn't offered that opportunity. The only time I was allowed to be excused from his attention was when my soul bond was announced. He found a compliant ally with access to my magic. My presence became solely for show. He needed nothing else from me and was relieved to find access to my power without my consent.

He must have seen the rebelliousness building in my eyes. Over the years, his eyes grew weary of me.

"Let me see." I take the lock in my hand and do a closer inspection.

"You don't have magic, or did you forget?"

I give Jesse a glare over my shoulder, then turn back to the lock. The metal vibrates with magic, but not the spell kind. Spells are light and fleeting. They can fade and be modified so easily. Like the frosting on a birthday cake. The magic on this item is deeper and heavier than that. The weight it possesses is inside, like the middle filling of the cake.

I don't need magic to know what it needs to open.

From the crevices of my mind, a vivid memory surfaces, a younger version of myself standing in my day school uniform. The same item in my hand secured a small chest, keeping secrets hidden. I don't recall what the small chest contained or why my father asked me in his office while this took place, but I remember what he did next. I remember it strikingly, like the feel of the blade and the sting of pain across my palm, the shortness of breath that came from my small chest and the absolute fear that any of the tears gathering in the rim of my eyes would descend and mark me as weak.

I grab a dagger that's attached to my thigh and bring it down the side of my palm. The burn of this cut does not fill me with emotion like it once did. I watch as the line I draw fills with crimson.

"Janelle," Jesse says. His eyes look at my cut, then my eyes searching for answers.

"It's an ancestral lock. Created with Duelo blood and sealed with it. There is only one way to open it."

I don't even want to think about how my father opens and closes it.

Jesse steps back as I position myself to the side so he can see. I carefully push my hand to the lock mechanism. We both watch as the artifact lights up in a low glow before clicking open.

My hands slightly shake as I remove it, and the door creaks open. The room has no light, but Jesse is quick to remedy that by creating a flame before us.

"There." He points at a wagon in the middle of the room. Before I can ask anything, he is across the room removing a cloth covering the top surface of the wagon. "Why does he have it just on this wagon?"

Jesse extends his hand towards the book but nothing happens. "It cannot be picked up with magic," Jesse says and leans forward to pick up the book. A grunt of exertion comes out of Jesse before he turns over his shoulder. "Did you ever hear anything about the book being heavy?"

I shake my head and step closer. The red velvety cover of the familiar book comes into view. The light of the flame illuminates the space above and around the wagon. It's a big book, but nothing out of the ordinary.

"How heavy?" I ask.

Jesse attempts to pick the book up with magic but is unsuccessful. "It must only be able to be moved by touch."

His posture becomes stiff as he leans down and grasps the book with both hands. He takes a deep breath and pulls it up. The book lifts this time. Jesse's hands are extended in front of him, with the book hanging low. He takes a few steps towards the door with much difficulty.

"We have to leave," he huffs.

I freeze in place. While I don't wish to go back, I'm unable to leave without Matias. Not after what he did for me. The only act of kindness a mere stranger has shown me. He didn't want a single thing in return but for me to show that kindness to someone else. Little did he know he would be the one needing that aid in the future.

"Janelle Duelo pays her debts." I turn to Jesse. "Go to the tree line. I'll meet you there, but if you hear commotion in the house, you run."

"Where do you think you are going?" He reaches for me but stumbles with the weight of the book.

"I'm going for Matias. I cannot leave him."

Jesse puts the book on the ground, then turns to fully face me. "I more than anyone wishes to put a stop to his suffering and take him home, but we have to go now. The book takes precedence."

"Not for me," I say, shaking my head as I step closer to the house.

I mean every word with my full chest, knowing very well that my freedom and my magic depend on the delivery of that book.

"Do you understand what you are risking right now?"

"I found my father and helped you get the book. I did my part, Jesse, but now I need to make sure I keep my word to Matias, too."

"Janelle, do not take another step."

I have to make amends, and it starts today. Rain starts to fall quickly, drenching me from head to toe. With one last look at Jesse, I run towards the house and head for the side door that leads to the basement. The steps are slippery, but I do my best to keep quiet as I make my way to the wooden door. I press my ear and hear nothing but the soft noises of the prisoners.

"Move aside," Jesse says behind me.

He is holding the Red Book in his hands, but he sets it down on the ground to place his palm on the lock. Unlike the one in the shed, this lock clicks open instantly. His frown is firmly in place, but he is here. Part of me wants to tell him to go back to the forest and wait for me, but his magic will be useful for this rescue mission.

"Quickly, in and out," he says.

I nod and focus on the now open door.

We slide inside and allow our eyes to focus on the dark space. Due to the rain outside, the amount of light has decreased to nearly pitch-black darkness. A series of lightning and thunder lights up the room enough for us to see that the prisoners are not the only people in here.

"Hey!" a guard yells from the other side of the room.

He is leaning against the opposite wall in a chair. His disheveled hair and sleepy face gave away the fact that he had been dozing against the wall. The thunder or the door opening must have caused him to wake up.

Before Jesse can react, the man pulls on the bell against the wall. The loud ring seems to echo in the room, then follows outside the basement wall. The thunder that follows doesn't come from the storm raging outside, but from the dozen feet landing on the old wood floors.

They are coming.

Jesse takes care of the soldier as I open the cell doors. Everyone is up at this point. I run inside the cell as the captives rush out, staying out of my way. They hold on to one another as they stumble out. Instead of running towards the open back door, they coward deeper into the room by the cleaning closet.

We're about to be outnumbered any minute now, judging by the thundering footsteps in the hallway.

"Janelle!" Jesse calls, probably after having the same revelation.

I flinch at the urge behind my name, but I cannot leave Matias behind. He's leaning against the wall and his eyes are as gone and spaced out as any other day. The chaos doesn't faze him at all. I pull him to a sitting position and try to get him to look at me, but my efforts are in vain.

"Listen to me. I need you to get up and walk."

No response.

"Matias!"

There is no time. I lift him by the armpits from behind and try to drag him down to the door, but from the sorry expression on Jesse's face, I know it will not work. I will not be able to get him up the stairs. Jesse is already breathing hard from carrying the Red Book. Why did that damn thing have to be so heavy?

I kneel next to Matias, already half defeated. "Please," I beg as tears gather in my eyes. He doesn't respond and I'm not surprised. I look up at Jesse. He is already shaking his head before I can open my mouth to tell him to leave me behind and take the book.

"Absolutely not."

The sound of footsteps draws near. He drops the book on the floor and rushes to my side as the door on the top of the stairs is thrown open. Twenty men march down. Some of them have wet hair sticking to their foreheads. They must have been outside in the rain. Someone might have noticed the open shed. It's not like we bothered closing it after we took the book.

Jesse stands before me, shielding me, but between his legs I can see how the men move aside to let my father through.

"I shouldn't be surprised to have a traitorous child. After all, you are your mother's daughter. She was always too weak for her own good."

"You made her weak," I say between clenched teeth.

He steps on the landing and only spares Jesse a disinterested look before focusing on me once again. "You will not leave tonight, Janelle, and neither will that book. Hand it over quickly or forfeit your life, girl."

"Bowing down to you is as good as killing the remainder of my soul," I say.

"You have always been one for dramatics." He shakes his head. "There you are." He walks to the other side of the basement, near the back door.

My father picks up the book where Jesse left it. He too struggles to lift it, but once in his arms, he gestures for his men to move forward. Without another word, his men surround us. Despite how good Jesse is and my training, there are too many for us to take on. I don't even make eye contact with them. The humanity I would search for departed the day they followed my father into this mission. My father climbs up the stairs and departs back to the house, leaving his men to do his dirty work.

We take a few steps back deeper into the cell. The men take their time closing in on us instead of attacking. Like a predator, too damn sure that the prey has no chance of coming out on top. The absence of my magic has never felt as heavy as it is at this moment. If only Brandon Oscuro could see the future. Would he take away my magic, knowing I might as well be the only chance his brother had of survival? Did the fates not warn him of that? This feels like a set up.

"You shouldn't be here," I say to Jesse.

Jesse spares me a glance before turning back to the crowd.

"This should have never been your ending. Not here, not with me, and not because I couldn't let a debt pass. You wanted to leave him, but my pride would not let me. He helped me and dying trying to free him is my choice, not yours."

"I would never leave you. Do you not see it?" His eyes don't meet mine, but his voice alone conveys all the truth behind his words.

"I see how you continue to suffer due to your association with me."

He finally turns in my direction. His gaze moves from my eyes to my lips as if searching for something. I am about to ask him what he is doing when he steps closer and kisses me.

The touch of his lips is fleeing but scorching.

"Willingly," he says as he steps back.

Someone throws the first blow. Jesse deflects it easily, casting a shield above the three of us. The hit radiates off us and bounces back. The men expect this counter attack and deflect sideways. We can only watch as the blow is sent to the back side of the room. Screams from the remaining captives ring in the room, but it dies as their voices do.

"Harder!" a man from the back barks at the front line.

Like good obedient dogs, they collectively push forward, tossing blow after blow our way. Jesse's shield holds on, but from how sweat trickles down his temple, it won't be for long. I'm useless outside of hand to hand combat. Even the shittiest soldier would have me dead in a minute if he used magic against me. I have no way of helping Jesse.

"Tell me you have daggers on you," Jesse says between clenched teeth.

I pat my pants down. In the commotion I forgot I don't have to be next to someone to be deadly. I nod and gesture at the two men ahead. Having some background info on my father's men is finally coming in handy. I narrow my eyes to my targets. Jesse promptly lowers and then raises the shields. There's just enough time for me to throw and bury my two daggers in the front of two men's skulls.

Their bodies drop to the ground in what feels like slow motion. Their knees touch the ground before their heads flop forward. The men behind them take a second to process what happened before a blooming red puddle grows beneath them. Anger erupts in growls and renewed energy. Their attempts to break Jesse's shield triple. We keep getting pushed back until our backs touch the wall behind us.

We hold on for a while longer. My father's men might be trained, but they are not as powerful as an Oscuro. When I think one of them is tiring out and the amount of attacks thrown our way is going to decrease, another man steps forward and takes over. Waiting out seems to be the only way out of here, but how long will it possibly take?

"I won't be able to hold forever," Jesse says.

Sweat is dripping down his chin, and his skin is taking a pale tint. The shield he has formed splinters with each blow. We both stare at it, knowing that any minute now it's going to fall.

Jesse opens his mouth, but before he can say anything, grumbles from the other side of the shield snap our attention. We watch in horror as the two men with the blades in their heads raise to their feet. If it wasn't for the look of horror and disgust from the men around them, I would have thought they did this. No, the men instead shout to one another and scurry away from their dead friends.

We all watch as one of the dead men yanks out the blade from his head and turns on his friends. One corpse jumps on a soldier and bashes their skull in two moves. The other one uses magic to fend off attempts by the others to stop them.

"They can use magic," I say.

"How?" Jesse asks.

"Me."

The voice is small and shakily like it hasn't been used in a while. Jesse and I don't move from our spot against the wall, but we turn to the sound of the voice.

Matias.

"It's nice to see you again," Matias says to me as he raises to his feet. "Sorry it took me so long. I was far away from here." He taps his temple like it's a place he departed for.

"You did that?" Jesse asks him while pointing at the now three dead men fighting my father's soldiers.

"I guess I did." He looks down at his hands like he is also having trouble believing what just happened.

"How?" Jesse looks between Matias and the walking corpses.

"Every time they tried to uncap my magic, and I didn't die, they thought nothing happened. They were wrong."

"Wrong?" I ask.

"The book," he says. "It wants revenge."

Matias takes his head between his hands and bends down. His face is scrunched up in pain.

"What is wrong now?" Jesse asks.

I look back at the now six dead men finishing the soldiers. They were first hesitant to fight their own fallen men, but they no longer are. Now it is too late, and they are outnumbered.

"It has to stop," Matias says between clenching teeth.

"I got it from here, buddy," Jesse tells him, kneeling next to him. "Let go."

Matias does and the walking bodies drop instantly. The

remaining men take a minute to look around and absorb what had just happened. Jesse doesn't hesitate to finish them. Black smoke drips down his fingertips and surrounds the few men. They do not notice the smoke enveloping them until they lose their senses.

The Oscuro brothers have always been known for having dark, dangerous magic despite only a very few ever witnessing it. I, myself, have only watched it happen a handful of times over a lifetime. It never ceases to impress me. Magic like theirs is not common.

The smoke cuts their senses one by one until they see, hear, and feel only darkness. Then they become it.

"Oscuro dirt," a man on the floor says before the smoke completely covers him. His hand waves in the air and from the drills of smoke, a glint of silver shines in the light.

It moves almost faster than possible. Perhaps we did not see it coming. Jesse grunts in pain as the dagger thrown from the smoke hits him in the shoulder.

"Jesse," I call as his body hits the ground. I lean down over him and see the wound is a slight cut. "Oh, good."

I place my hand above it and push healing magic into his skin.

Jesse looks at his shoulder, where now only a pink fading mark remains. "Looks like not even the King can take away a gift."

I once read that gifts are not like regular magic because they weren't given to us by the Fates. The gifts given by angels only last a lifetime. Gifts like mine are passed down from generation to generation.

The sound of footsteps above snaps our attention away from our musing.

"They will soon come to check what is taking them so long to apprehend us."

"Them?" Matias asks. "Is there more?"

"Many," Jesse says, getting up. "But we will not be here to greet them."

We exit out of the back door. With no time for second-guessing, I lead Matias across the backyard and we hastily enter the forest. I think of my mother and Oliver, the only two individuals inside those walls that I care about. I send a little prayer to the Fates. May they keep them safe and burn the rest of the house down.

The first fifteen minutes of walking into the forest are easy as the path is mostly tame, but as we get deeper inside, the flooring becomes a lot harder to cross. I'm lending Matias my shoulder as a crutch while he tries to walk on his own. That is when I sense we are not alone. The creatures in the forest are damned to be curious about us going so deep inside, but this specific energy is darker than anything I've encountered. Before I can warn Jesse, who is walking in front of us, he stops and signals for me to freeze and be silent.

The wind picks up beside us and from the high vegetation around us, it's not natural wind that rustles our clothes. From the darkness in the trees, a figure takes form. A long, tall figure is draped in a cloth that flies around its form. The Calaca steps in our path. A menacing scowl on its face quickly turns into a scary grin.

I have never seen one in person before. They are creatures created from darkness. Servants of death, yet not connected to the underworld or the demons that rule its premises.

The Calaca steps closer to Jesse and tints its head lower to see him. I have only ever seen a few who have towered over Jesse, but never with this magnitude. I move before Matias, but I don't let go of him as I shield him with my body.

"I saw you amongst the men and knew you were unseen by the rest," Calaca tells Jesse. "I knew you were going to take the book back to your brother."

Its cloth moves effortlessly with the wind, showing glimpses of the bony structure underneath.

"As you are aware, we do not have the book," Jesse says.

"Yes, I see you have failed." Calaca looks between Jesse and me, then looks past me. Its eyes land on Matias for a second before it gasps and steps back. "You." Calaca points at Matias like it has seen a ghost.

"Me?" Matias asks with furrowed brows.

Calaca doesn't answer him. Instead, it inclines its head and bows low. "Sire."

"Me?" Matia looks between Jesse and me before looking down at its hands. "Did I make you?"

"Your magic created me a long time ago." Calaca moves closer to Matias with its head down.

"Back off," I say, moving between them.

"I would never harm my sire." The creature actually looks appalled at the idea.

I've no idea what the Red Book did to Matias, but it cannot be a good thing. Whatever can create a creature like Calaca isn't good or pure. The darkness that creates a server of death is dangerous.

"Calaca, can you explain yourself?" Jesse says.

Calaca halts and raises their eyes to the sky. After a bit, it turns back to us. "You are being hunted. You must go." It turns to Jesse with conviction. "Will your King keep my sire safe?"

"Yes." Jesse nods.

No hesitation that the Black Castle will welcome Matias with open arms.

"Then my loyalty lies with your successful journey," It says.

"My name is Matias, by the way. Sire makes me uncomfortable." He looks between Calaca and Jesse.

"Matias," Calaca says as it bows low. "I will do everything

in my power to protect you, sire. You all go on. I will distract the hunters from your trail."

I look at Jesse and our eyes meet. The concerned edge in his eyes is mirrored in mine. We don't have to say a word to communicate how bad this is. Matias is no longer the same boy who crossed my path in the forest months ago. He isn't the boy whose soul was stolen by a cursed book. Whatever the Red Book did to him changed him forever. The darkness that answers to him is unnatural and dangerous.

CHAPTER TWELVE

JANELLE

While Matias walks, I observe him, attempting to piece together the events. Leaving in the middle of the night sounded like a good idea. We counted on the soldiers being sleepy and tired. With no preparation, we also fell under that description. The tiredness hits harder when the adrenaline drains from our bodies. I can see it in Matias' slow steps and Jesse's heavy breaths.

My brain is having a hard time making sense of all I witness. Matias brought people back from death. As if that isn't crazy enough, he controlled them enough to have them fight for us. He can essentially create an army of immortal soldiers. My father's biggest dream weapon was right under his nose, and he just watched it leave.

But how does any of it even work? The logical rules of magic don't allow for something like that to exist. Matias possesses something odd to the magic world. His expression when he realized it left no doubt in my mind that he had no idea he could do that. It has to be because of the Red Book.

"So that is what you can do, huh?" Jesse asks. The casual tone rings comical at the intensity of the situation.

Jesse brushes away more vegetation as we walk. Matias doesn't answer, but looks between us. We walk past Jesse. He waits for us to make it a distance in front of him before turning and mending the vegetation behind us. He does this every few minutes to conceal our path.

"I've never met someone who could do even close to what you did," Jesse continues.

Matias keeps walking. Seems he's not in a chatty mood. I turn to look at Jesse working. He is growing tired and I'm not sure how much of a difference hiding our route might do. There are only a handful of routes that can take you to Puerto Quinn from the hideout.

"They know where we are going." I point out.

There is no other place for us to go, but I guess my father doesn't know that. He is unaware of Matias' connection to the crown. But he knows Jesse and if he puts two brain cells together, he will conclude we are running back to King Oscuro. Who else would have put us up to this?

"If we can beat them there, it will be enough. Your family might've been able to enter the castle freely once, but that is not the case today," Jesse says with a sharp tone.

His tone reminds me he hasn't forgotten who we are to each other. Despite that less than an hour ago he had chosen to die by my side fighting.

Jesse walks past us and begins chopping away on a path we can walk through.

There are only small patches of sunlight and blue sky peeking from the tall branches of the trees. Jesse makes it a few meters down before turning back to us. We walk the distance in a minute while he goes to the back and covers the path step by step.

"What did I miss while I was mentally checked out?" Matias asks.

"My father has the Red Book. The plan was to steal it back."

"That didn't go well." Matias gives me an apologetic look.

"Nope," I say.

"Regrets?"

I look over at Jesse. "None. And I am sure he doesn't regret it either."

"Are you sure?" Matias looks over at Jesse with distrust.

"Yes. He is the King's brother. A friend of Bianca's. Loyalty cannot get stronger than the bonds Jesse creates with those he cares about."

"Roman's brother?" Matias' eyes brighten slightly.

"You met the oldest Oscuro?" I ask.

"Briefly." He pauses. "You sound protective of him. Is he the reason you're here and not with your father?" Matias gestures behind us. "The last time I saw you, you were cutting off a dress and running off into the human lands."

For someone who had been inside his own head for the last few weeks he surely is observant.

"Things didn't go as planned." I clear my throat. "I thought so. At first, at least. But I don't think he is what is keeping me going now."

The honesty feels freeing.

Matias' eyes show something like contentment. He likes what he's hearing. "Who does?"

I ponder that, and the longer I think about it, the more clearly the answer becomes.

"Me." The word drops from my lips, and I feel like I can breathe easier. "It may sound crazy, but I need to do it. I need to stand up to them for the young girl I used to be."

"I haven't heard anything more sane." His words make me smile.

We aren't too different at the end of the day. Two souls tortured by the whims of the same man.

A genuine smile, the one you can only share with a friend. That's what Matias feels like he could be. A real friend. I never had one of those, not outside of Jesse, and even then, our friendship has always been different.

"Care to clue me in on the joke?" Jesse asks us with a grunt. He is standing there with his arms on his hips.

Matias gets to his feet. "No," he says easily and leaves.

I don't have to look in Jesse's direction to see the scowl on his face, mostly after he utters "asshole" under his breath.

Using Matias' directions and my experience in the forest, we cross from the human lands to the edge of Fierno by nightfall. We are hours away from the Black Castle, but continuing is impossible. We have been walking for hours. If it wasn't for my gift to heal, everyone in this traveling party would be limping. Unfortunately, I can't heal myself.

Jesse starts a fire in the middle of a small clearing. Matias finds a spot under a tree and settles back. We settle in and share the small number of belongings we have among us. The flavor of dry food packets becomes incredibly satisfying after hours of hunger and non-stop walking.

It doesn't take long before soft snores come from Matia's side. The boy can sleep quickly and just about anywhere. The position his body is in doesn't look comfortable, but I'm sure he has experienced worse. I find a spot to sleep too and just lay there for a bit.

As Matias sleeps the night away, I toss and turn.

"Hey," Jesse whispers.

I roll to my side so I can face him.

"When Matias said the book wants revenge. He was lying. I'm not sure why, but I heard it in his voice. It did not ring true."

The Lord of Wisdom is what people call Jesse. The gift of truth was given to him a long time ago by an angel of the land of the bless. I have personally witnessed him hear lies from people and if he says Matias did, I've no doubt he is right. Even if it doesn't make sense. Matias looks genuine and trustworthy. He has gone through enough already and being called a liar is not what he deserves after what he endured.

"Why would he lie?" My question is not meant to question Jesse's accuracy but the intention behind.

"I can't say." His words are soft. Jesse rises to his elbows and moves closer to me. "Stay vigilant. Whatever his motive might be doesn't change the fact that he is keeping secrets."

"I will," I agree without hesitation.

His breath is so close to me and it might be the chill of the night, but goosebumps spread all over my arms.

"Jesse," I say but stop when a bush begins to rustle.

He is up in a blink of an eye, and I'm right behind him. A second after, Calaca steps out of the bushes with an unreadable expression. It looks over at Matias' sleeping form before turning back to us.

"You will make it to the King. They have taken a different route to search." It moves to Matias and plumps down next to him. Not close enough to touch him, but close enough to guard him.

Jesse and I share a look.

"Well," I say to Calaca. "If that was your doing, we appreciate it." I gesture in the direction of the Black Castle. "We have a six hour walk that way and we will be at our destination."

It doesn't move.

"You don't have to accompany us." Jesse crosses his arms with unease.

"I'm not leaving my sire," Calaca grunts.

Matias stirs. He doesn't seem surprised to see Calaca next to him.

"What's going on?" Matias asks.

"Your pet doesn't want to leave," Jesse says.

"I'm not leaving my sire," Calaca says again.

Matias rubs his face, the tiredness evident on the bags under his eyes. "It's not hurting or bothering anyone. Why does it have to leave?"

His question surprises Jesse and me.

The Calaca makes a noise in the back of its throat and I could swear it's a version of a laugh. A sinister noise.

"You want to keep it?" I ask Matias.

"Why bother trying to get rid of it?" His question is obviously an excuse to avoid my question.

"Do you think it's attached to him because of whatever your father did to him with the Red Book?" Jesse asks me.

A glint of something passes through Matia's eyes, but he looks down to hide it.

I clear my throat. "His soul was taken, then returned to his body. Maybe that is why?"

I know my reasoning makes less sense. However, I can tell Matias appreciates the commentary because the tension on his shoulders lessens. Whatever happened to him under my father's care isn't something he is ready to speak of. Whatever the reason might be, he needs to come to terms with it first.

"Any ideas?" Jesse asks Matias, but he chooses not to answer.

Jesse sits back down and crosses his legs in front of him. It's still dark out, but after the recent addition to the team, I know neither of us will sleep anymore. I sit next to Jesse, careful not to touch him, and wait for the day to come.

It's not long before Jesse says, "I can't sleep with it staring at me."

I can't help but agree. It could at least turn its vacant gaze to the trees instead of boldly staring at us.

"Matias," I begin to say, but he stops me by raising to his feet.

"If we won't sleep, we can start walking."

I want to object and tell him that the sun hasn't risen yet, but a few rays are peeking from the tops of the mountains. There is something beautiful and peaceful about them. That moment of the day before the rest of the world wakes, where you feel ahead of the rest just for that second.

The six-hour journey I had expected turned out to be a fifteen hour walk. Turns out we were all far more sore than we predicted and with me being so tired, I couldn't keep taking away aches for anyone. Neither of the boys let me try at all.

The edge of the forest finally comes into view and it almost feels like it has come too soon. I'm not ready to face the walls of the castle I terrorized. I step into the clearing behind Matias and Calaca. The creature has made no allowances for being near Matias. Jesse was right to call it a pet. Even if it is, the creature acts more like a protective knight. Ready to risk it all for its master.

The day has gone by in a blink of an eye. The night lanterns are on, illuminating the outside walls of the Black Castle. We are crossing the clearing when I hear voices. My eyes shut because I know the screams are only in my head. The smell of burning itches my nose and the stinging in my eyes is not from heat. It's all attached to the walls inside this castle. The images haunted my dreams for weeks before I was able to rest. In the depths of my nightmares, I realized that the trauma haunting me was nothing compared to the one experienced by the people here. My own personal hell was a walk in the park. I have no right stressing over the events when they were part of my own doing.

I shake my head to clear it. It must work because, almost immediately, I realize something isn't right. I look around and the quiet empty backyard becomes a warning sign. There has never been a time I have seen this yard empty. The gardens can be seen from here and the lack of walking bodies feels alarming.

"It's empty," I say.

They must know we are here.

Matias stops walking and turns to me. Jesse doesn't notice that we have stopped. Calaca doesn't turn but raises its head and looks from side to side. Its eyes narrow at the castle like it's waiting for something, but nothing happens.

"Alright, we are about to come to the protective shield." Jesse stops and turns to us. "Brandon has to grant you entrance for it to allow you in."

The castle's security was strengthened in response to the attack with this shield. There must be people inside the shield that can see us, but we cannot see them. It's a tricky show of power. Things this advanced are not common to see.

A group of soldiers riding horses steps out of the shield, inspecting us at a distance. A crowd of onlookers follows them closely. Their faces carry mix emotions, but most of their eyes freeze at the sight of Calaca.

"You idiot," Roman shouts at the forefront of the crowd. He dismounts a horse dressed in metal gear and runs to his brother. In one swift movement, he takes Jesse into his chest and holds on to him tight. "We were wondering where you were."

The crowd parts slightly and through the middle Brandon carefully walks forwards, eyeing the rest of us with apprehension. His eyes land on me and search my body for the missing item.

"You have failed." His lips mouth the words, and I can hear them despite the distance between us.

"Matias." Bianca breaks from the crowd. Her steps are slow and careful. The apprehension in her face fears hope. From her new angle she asks again, "Is that you, Matias?"

He doesn't look like the boy who found me in the forest all those weeks ago. The most recent events have not helped his appearance, either. Sleeping under the stars never does.

Before he can answer, her feet hurry until her arms are flapping and her legs cannot run fast enough to meet her strands. Brandon tries to stop her, but she side steps him expertly. Her arms are around Matias before Calaca can even react. The tears in her eyes are testimony of a sibling's love. She only allows him to step an arm's length away to search his face.

"Where have you been?" She asks him between tears. He doesn't get the chance to answer before she continues. "I have been looking for you for months. Do you know that?"

"We found him as a prisoner of the rebel group." Jesse steps away from Roman and hugs Brandon next. "I don't think they knew his connection to Bianca."

"You made it to their keep, but don't have the book with you, which means things did not go well." Roman crosses his arms and scowls at me. "Care to explain what happened?"

"We fled for our lives when we attempted to steal the book," I say to them.

I don't mention my choice to take Matias over the book. I expect Jesse will fill them in on that instead. There's no remorse for my decision, but its weight is becoming apparent.

"You did not complete your part of the deal," Brandon says in his King voice.

"Not yet." I clear my throat. "I still plan to do it if you allow it."

Now that we have fled, my father is sure to move locations, but there are a few other places he might be. Best of all, I don't have to be the one seeking these locations. Calaca should be able to travel through the night and scout the locations at a fraction of the time it would take by foot.

His eyes narrow. "You think you can find them again?"

"I just need time," I say.

My voice comes off far more confident than I feel. It might also be the exhaustion. Thinking of doing anything other than sleeping right now sounds horrendous.

The King nods his head, digesting all the information.

"You gotta be joking. She can't stay here," Alejandra says from the back.

I recognize her instantly as the castle's head guard. She also happens to be a close friend to the Oscuro brothers. I remember her following Brandon around during the tour. The blank stare she once directed my way has now been exchanged for hatred.

An echo of boos travels through the crowd. Their opinion of me is evident.

"Are we to just welcome her as a royal again?" Someone shouts from the crowd.

"If she goes, so do I."

The words make everyone turn to the side. Matias is standing tall with the dark shadow of the Calaca at his back. The duo is scary from this angle. His sharp cheekbones and eye bags make him look dangerous and deranged.

"The Red Book was used on me multiple times. I can show you what it did, but I can only do it if I stay. I'm not doing that without her." His arm is limp as he tries to point at me. Matias is on the verge of collapsing any moment now.

"Matias, you don't understand." Bianca gives him a sympathetic expression. "While I appreciate Janelle's help in bringing you home, it's not as easy as it seems to allow her to stay."

"It's you who doesn't understand," he snaps. "None of you understand what I had to endure these past couple of months. None of you understand what the rebel group is even doing. What they did to me changed me and they are only getting started. I was their test subject and only I have answers to your questions."

"Is that your final stance?" Brandon asks.

"Wait a damn minute." Bianca rounds on Brandon. This time her back is to Matias standing between him and the King. "He's not going to be thrown out."

"He is not," Brandon says simply and calmly. "Janelle and he may stay as long as both of them cooperate with our plans. The Calaca must remain outside. Too many magical shields have to be lifted to allow their kind inside."

"Are you welcoming back the daughter of the traitor family?" Alejandra doesn't back down. "She herself has taken the lives of loved ones. You might not feel the loss like we do."

"Is our late king not loss enough?" Brandon pushes closer to her space. "You are not the only one who has lost someone. We all did. I'm not allowing the grief to cripple me from fighting to get my people peace. That peace comes when the Red Book is back safely, and the threat is exterminated."

At the look of utter hatred in Alejandra's eyes, everyone can tell she is about to object yet again.

"This is not a democracy, soldier. We are all wounded from that night." He turns to the crowd. "We must do everything in our power to find a solution to our current threat and I can assure you that is not Janelle. She is not even in possession of her magic."

The majority of the people who are looking at the King nod

their head with determination in their eyes. Some in the group avert their eyes, staring at the ground instead. There are only a few who hold my gaze, and their eyes show utter hatred for my existence.

Brandon turns to me, but his words are directed at his people. "Lady Janelle Duelo will not stay in the Black Castle as a royal family member. She will be allowed accommodations with the condition that she earns her keep and continues to work to fulfill her arrangement for the Crown."

I can feel Jesse's eyes burning the side of my face. I fear what I will see if I turn and meet his gaze. Does he feel sorry for me like he did back at my father's house? I cannot take his pity again. Despite his hate for me, he cannot help himself. Or does he fear I will decline the low bargain?

I swallow my pride.

"I accept."

It's not like I haven't cleaned toilets these past couple of days. My words make the King nod and perhaps a sliver of relief leaves his shoulders too.

People dispense soon after at the order of Roman. I could be mistaken, but I think it's he who calls for Isabel. The small young woman I've seen him around with on multiple occasions stands next to him. Brandon approaches them and they all speak in hush voices.

"That was dramatic," Matias tells me. He turns to Calaca. "I'll be fine here. Will you be fine there?"

Is he serious?

"If you ever need me, just call for me." Calaca walks to the forest edge and, as if a shadow in the wind, it fades into the darkness.

"Calaca is a creature of death," I say to Matias. "Not much can hurt dead creatures."

Before Matias can say anything, Bianca and Isabel reach us.

"Matias," Bianca says in a soft voice. "Let's go inside and get you looked at by Amy Bee."

Her demeanor is as if she's approaching a wounded animal. I don't blame her, mostly after how he snapped at her, but the tone is annoying.

He looks at me with a pained expression, like I can save him from his fate, but I agree he should visit the clinic. They might not heal what my father did to his magic or the trauma he caused, but they can at least aid exterior injuries.

"I'll be taking you to your room for the duration of your stay," Isabel says, distracting me.

Listening to Bianca and Matias feels wrong, so I nod at Isabel and gesture for her to lead the way. We are met with many stares as we cross the yard into the castle. We walk into a long hall, and I recognize my surroundings right away.

I have been here many times throughout the years. The visits I managed to sneak out of my father's sight always ended here. It always started with late night quiet, yet hurried steps trailed by laughter.

"You will take Roman's old room," Isabel says as she opens the door to a suite.

I have been here before. The space has a central shared room with two adjacent doors that lead to bedrooms. The other room belongs to Jesse. I let that detail go and instead try to pay attention to what Isabel is saying.

"This will be your room." She opens a door and looks at the space inside from the doorway. "Your job at the castle will be with me at the plant nursery. After the attack," her eyes downcast as she has to be ashamed of anything that happened that day, "Many job duties in the castle have been vacant. Having an extra pair of hands in there would be a lot of help for me."

I turn sharply at her words. The job vacancy comment

rings in my ears. Her eyes meet mine and my expression must convey my shock at the information.

Isabel takes a step forward. "Oh, no. Not because they died. I mean, many people did. But the man who ran the plant nursery left for his hometown after the attack. Many people don't feel safe here anymore. Not when whispers of war linger in the wind."

My father has hurt the castle far more than he even knows. The lingering effects of his attack have caused long-lasting consequences for the King.

"Settle in and rest. We will begin tomorrow in the morning. If you need anything else, you can ask me or Jesse. He is just next door."

Next door.

I try not to linger on that thought. We will both be here every night. Just a wall away. After years of sneaking into his bedroom at late hours it is ironic that now that we are a door away he wants nothing to do with me.

"You don't have to be so kind to me, Isabel. I have done horrible things and I don't deserve your kindness."

She needs to understand that I mean those words. I don't need nor want her pity. Her kindness is best saved for someone more deserving of it.

Her bold stare and stone-like expression convey more emotion than I've ever seen in her. "I don't think you're an evil person. You were forced to do grave things. Now you've been given an opportunity to do the right thing. Your next actions define you."

The punch I feel in my gut is not real. But it feels like it is. Before she closes the door behind her, she stops and looks at me over her shoulder.

"You are safe now, Janelle."

I stare at the now closed door. The silence in the room feels like a warm blanket on a frosty night. Despite more than one person inside these castle walls probably wanting me dead, I will never be subjected to my father's cruelty again.

"I believe I am," I say to the empty room as I take it in.

I'm safe, at least for now.

CHAPTER THIRTEEN

JESSE

Brandon paces the length of his office wall. He stops to look outside the window, then turns to face me. From my angle by the door, I can see the back garden through the window. Bianca and Matias are sitting on a bench a few feet from each other, speaking. They might not be aware of it, but there are a few guards monitoring them from a distance. It's evident from the glances my brother throws at the window that he is who instructed the guards to be present.

My brother is not a trusting guy, but I am certain he thinks of Bianca as a capable woman. She has taken care of herself for a while all on her own, but Matias is a blind spot. A blind spot that my brother has less influence on than he likes. Bianca has a love and kinship to him that resembles the one my brothers and I have for one another.

Brandon doesn't trust Matias right now and neither do I. Not after I heard the lies in his words. I'm not sure what secrets he is keeping, but I plan on finding out.

The light of the setting sun illuminates the burgundy tone of the room. I take a break from looking out of the window and look at my surroundings. I used to come to this office and sit around with Grandfather as he worked in silence. This used to be his office, and I loved the way silence never felt lonely here.

I'm glad to see Brandon more settled. After all, the last time I saw him here, he still acted like the office was borrowed.

How different my life feels in just a matter of days since I was last here.

"What did they do to him?" Brandon finally asks me. He stops pacing and sits behind his desk. "I want to know every-thing. From the second you found her to the second you both abandoned your mission."

The harsh tone of his words strikes me with accusation. His problem is with the scene happening out in the gardens, not with me. My brother fears what he cannot control. That happens to be Matias at this moment. He has not just an unex-plainable power but a Calaca at his beck and call. Most impor-tantly, he has influence over Bianca. My brother must be out of his mind worrying she might not stay behind if he leaves.

I try to keep my attitude from slipping into my words. "That was never a conscious decision until we were surrounded and staying alive became the priority."

He fixes his gaze on me, as if he has finally recognized me. "Jesse, I am sorry."

The words ring true.

A knock at the door stops his next sentence. Roman doesn't wait for permission before opening and closing the door. I'm glad certain things have not changed between us as titles and responsibilities have shifted with Brandon's crown.

"What have I missed?" He asks.

"Nothing yet," Brandon says and gestures for me to go on.

I look at both my brothers. What I am about to say will forever change our lives. The people they were as they entered this room will not be the same when they leave. I wish I could keep them here a while longer but there is no stopping time. Regardless, nothing has been simple or peaceful since the tour started. At least for me. The excitement I once felt at the prospect of visiting Janelle in her hometown during the tour feels so far away now. Nothing could have prepared me for the events that would unfold.

"War is coming," I say. "Not just from the rebel group. I personally witnessed Lord Duelo meet with forest creatures."

"Did you recognize any of them?" Brandon crosses his arms.

"None of them were leaders that have peace treaties with grandpa." I look up to the ceiling.

I recall the moment in the forest. They looked desperate for the opportunity to finally decide something for themselves.

"If anything, they seem to be outcasts and power-hungry individuals."

"What exactly did Duelo promise them?" Brandon states his question with care.

I can see the wheels turning in his head. He is already laying out the field and working through the possibilities. The situation is playing as a game of chess in his mind. Although pieces are not always predictable, he can map out the next moves, ready for anything.

"To uncap their magic," I say and pause before adding, "I am not sure if he truly thinks he can do it or if he is trying to use them to his benefit. He wants them to fight us as his personal army."

How and if that is even a possibility is something I don't think anyone in his room knows. I heard the uncertainty in Lord Duelo's own voice. When he spoke I didn't hear a clear ringing in my ears but I heard something. There was definitely doubt. He wishes to believe what he says, that is for certain.

"Is that true?" Roman looks between Brandon and I. "Does the book cap their magic as well as ours?"

"I don't know if it even does it for us. They have been trying with Matias," I say.

"They attempted to uncap his magic?" Brandon freezes in place and looks at me for confirmation. At a nod of my head, his eyes move back to the garden. "Is he?"

I first shake my head but since Brandon isn't looking in my directions, I follow it with, "No. I don't think his magic was uncapped, but the book did something to him."

"What did it do?" Roman asks.

"Matias can awaken the dead, and control them. They don't lose their magic. He essentially has access to a dead army," I tell them recalling our exit from the hideout.

"I need to sit down," Roman says and takes the first chair he finds.

"You watched him do this?" Brandon asks. He is leaning against his desk, and I wonder if he also needs something to lean on. "With your own eyes?"

"He is the reason we are here. Janelle and I were completely outnumbered. Almost without meaning to, he raised dead soldiers and had them fight their own friends for us."

"He is new to this magic?" My oldest brother asks.

"That's what it looked like," I confirm.

"I am not sure if this is good news or bad," Brandon says.

Brandon's eyes move to the window and, not finding Bianca on the garden bench, searches for her. A knock at the front door has us all turning towards the sound. After a second, the door opens and Bianca walks inside. The utter relief clear in my brother doesn't go unnoticed by Roman and me.

Bianca makes a beeline for me. Her arms wrap around me tightly. I have never noticed how thin her arms have gotten. This only makes me realize she has lost a lot of weight in the past few months. While I was inside my head dealing with my demons, my friend was struggling with her own worries.

"Thank you for bringing him back to me." Her words are tired yet eternally grateful.

The tears in the rim of her eyes carry the appreciation I truly don't deserve. After all, I was more than ready to leave him behind.

"Did he tell you what the book did for him?" Brandon asks, breaking the moment between us.

"No, we spoke of other stuff." She wipes her face and tries to collect herself.

"What else could have possibly been more important than knowing what they actually accomplish?"

"Brandon!" Bianca barks with a lot more energy than she seemed to have a second ago. "He didn't want to talk about it. It's too soon. He needs a day. Can you give him at least that much?"

"Do we have it?" he asks her. "Because Jesse witnessed Lord Duelo gain allies in the forest to come and fight the castle again. So far, all we know is that he can rise and control the dead. That is no simple power to control and manipulate. If the book gave him that much, it must have told him how and where to use it."

"He can do what?" her eyes widened trying to compute what Brandon just said.

"He didn't tell you anything." Brandon shakes his head.

"I haven't seen him in forever. He asked for space to talk about what happened later on. I agreed. We mostly caught up on what he had missed and the attack on the castle."

"Interesting." Roman stands up. "I'm going to make sure Isabel is back to our quarters."

I look at my older brother with surprise. "You two moved in together?" I ask.

Have I been gone for that long? The last time I was here, he was still convincing her to take baby steps. Her attention has been divided on taking on new tasks around the castle. It didn't seem like he would get his way anytime soon.

I am happy for my brother. I am glad his love is returned at last. All the pining he did for years was not in vain. I once hoped the Fates would bless me in the same way, but I think they have done me a favor by not fulfilling my wishes. Perhaps it's time to move on.

CHAPTER FOURTEEN

JANELLE

The knock on my bedroom door comes promptly after seven in the morning. I've been up for hours, staring out of the window and into the walls. The nightmares have only intensified inside the walls as if determined to make me remember. As if I could ever forget. I don't want to leave this room and I can't sleep. So here I am in this in-between.

I open the door expecting to find a guard instructed to supervise me during my stay or one of the Oscuro brothers to give me a warning and instructions. I could even see little Isabel being here to guide me to the plant nursery. But none of them are here.

"Matias?" I ask because I'm puzzled by his presence.

I peek out of the room into the shared space. There is no one else walking around. All the doors in the room are firmly shut.

"Do you want to get food together?" Matias asks.

I shake my head. "I don't think so."

"Aren't you hungry?"

I am starving, but I also have an idea of what I will face if I venture into the dining hall of the castle. It's the busiest room at any given time of the day.

"Matias," I say in a stern tone. "Be serious for a moment and tell me you think it's a good idea for me to walk around the castle."

His stomach chooses this specific moment to growl.

"I don't want to go alone." His eyes drop and uncertainty enters his expression. "You're right. I will just go in and out. I'll be fine."

He walks away but before he makes it to the door handle I hear myself say, "wait."

His hopeful eyes turn in my direction. "Yes?"

"Fine."

I need to eat if I plan on finding my father on top of my new duties at the nursery. I hold up a finger indicating for him to wait and go into my bag retrieving a few items. I pull my hair into a low bun then tie atop a black bandana. The color will shield my hair color from being noticeable at a distance. There isn't anything noticeable about my clothing but just in case I stick to dark colors.

"What are you doing?" Matias asks me eyeing my attire.

"Trying to blend in." I shrug.

His expression tells me that I am not fooling anyone.

"Can you use your magic to disguise me better?" I ask, only half hopeful.

"I don't think so." He looks at his hands and then back at me. "I don't have much training. I'm sorry."

This might be for the best. After all, I already saw what Matias can do with his magic. Being touched by dark magic in any kind of way cannot be good. I am better off this way.

"Lead the way," I gesture forward.

"I don't know where to go," he says and I nod.

"I will lead the way then."

The first thing that catches my attention in the hall is how many guards are posted around the castle. The security has always been impeccable to the point my father found the trespassing of the castle defenses impossible. His one and only opening is already sealed, and I doubt he will be able to find one now. This might be more for the staff to feel safe than actual readiness for a future threat.

The second thing I notice is the amount of eyes that follow me as I make my way across the castle. Quiet sneers and hush whispers trail behind me. Matias goes unnoticed by my side. Clusters of people stop and stare with a mixture of expressions. Some of them don't hold my gaze, but others don't dare look away. So much for tucking my hair away.

Despite how much I wish to blend into the wall right about now, my appearance will not allow it. My hair is a flag announcing to every passing eye that yes, in fact, I am the traitor that caused the pain and destruction everyone inside these walls is recuperating from.

The hustle and bustle from the food hall is a welcome sight that allows me to be swallowed by the sea of people picking up breakfast.

Matias saddles up next to me as we make a line for food. His hair is messy and his clothes are wrinkled as if he rolled out of bed only a couple of minutes prior. I didn't notice it back in my suite.

He gives me a head nod but adds nothing else as we silently pick up our plates. The food is set up in a line that extends from one side of the room to the other. There are usually a variety of options and today is no different.

I put a bit of eggs and toast on my plate before scooping mix fruit and yogurt to the side. Matias watches me carefully and mimics every move until our plates look identical. At the last stop, I place my plate in front of the beverage stand and take a cup of coffee.

"There you are," Matias says to the beverage before yawning. "I'm not really a morning person," he says to me.

I look at the clock on the wall and see that it's eight. "How did you sleep?"

"Sleeping on an actual bed beats the cells or the outdoor camping." His smile is easy and honest.

He takes a sip of his coffee cup and looks at the crowd of people sitting in different sections of the food hall.

I stop next to him and ponder where I can go and blend into the wall. My eyes find Jesse, who is sitting at a table towards the end of the hall by the open windows that lead to the gardens. I didn't hear anyone else moving around the suite when I woke up. I wonder at what time he got up.

A table by the garden windows empties, leaving a spot at the corner of the room. It would be great if it wasn't because it's the table next to Jesse's.

"What are you waiting for?" Matias asks.

"A black hole to swallow me." I grunt.

"You are dramatic." He gestures with his chin.

I stop before taking a single step and think of something that should have occurred to me before. I look over at Matias and say, "being associated with me might damage your reputation."

"My personality will have to make up for that downfall." He laughs and puts an arm around my shoulders. "Plus, outsiders need to stick together."

I want to tell him he might not know the people here, but soon enough, he will find his place. Being around me can only hinder his chances, but I can't help but wish to keep him around. He has offered me kindness from the second he found me in the woods, when he had nothing to gain. I don't understand the warmth he offers me and a selfish part of me wishes to keep it despite the consequences.

As we cross the food hall, many glances follow. As we pass Jesse's table, I realize he's sitting with soldiers that must be part of Romans' guard if their matching badges identify them as head of the Royal Force. Each and every one of them raises their head as we pass by. The point is clear. Not one of them is happy about me being here and their disapproving gazes fixed on me say it.

Jesse, unlike them, doesn't raise his head in our direction. He doesn't even look up once. If anything, he makes a point of not looking my way.

I sit across from Matias with my back to the room. Despite how much many people might want me dead they will never act against their King. Brandon Oscuro might have many doubters in his kingdom, but they don't live in this castle. The people here idolize the Oscuro boys as if they themselves hanged the sun and the stars in the sky.

"Why is your boyfriend looking like he wants to kill us?" Matias looks over my shoulder, then back at me.

I don't respond. I eat my food and refuse to look up again.

"Matias," Bianca calls as she approaches the table.

Brandon is close behind her, but doesn't make it to our table. Instead, he hangs back with the Royal Force soldiers on the table next to ours. I have known Brandon for many years, and although his eyes are not trained on us, it doesn't mean he isn't aware of every single move we make.

"You were gone before breakfast." Bianca takes a seat beside me.

He points down at his plate. "I came to get breakfast."

Bianca looks from his plate to me, then back. "We usually get breakfast in our suite, Matias. You did not have to fetch your own food."

"Fetch," he laughs at the word. "I'd rather come out here and fetch my own food."

"Matias," Bianca tries again. The sigh she lets out is full of borrowed patience. "I understand what you went through was hard, but I can't help you unless you let me."

She lays her hand gently atop of his.

"Understand?" His tone is harsh. A few people turn in our directions, but Matias doesn't notice. "You understand nothing because you weren't there." He shakes Bianca's hand off his. "I am glad you weren't. But because you don't know what I went through, you cannot tell me how to fix it."

Brandon finally steps behind Bianca and settles a hand on her shoulder. The silent show of support is loud. However, Matias doesn't look phased by the King of Puerto Quinn.

"I'm going to meet Santiago at the library." Matias gives her hand a squeeze before getting up and leaving his untouched breakfast behind.

Brandon takes the open seat. His hand rubs soothing circles on Bianca's back.

"Why does he come to you?" Bianca asks me while watching Matias retreat. Her tone carries a note of resentment.

"My soothing and ever-loving personality?" I guess.

"Trauma bonding?" Brandon suggests.

"Perhaps it's because you saved him from that cell," Bianca says.

"We both saved him from the cell, but he doesn't seem inclined to entertain conversation with me," Jesse says from behind me.

I can't see him, but I can feel the heat of his body so close to mine. He must have been listening to everything that was exchanged in the past couple of minutes. Not missing a detail has always been his thing. I feel stuck between a family feud.

From the concerned faces on the Oscuro brothers, they consider Matias their problem too.

Bianca is staring out into space with a heartbroken expression. I've never had a true brother sister relationship with any of my siblings, so I have no clue how she feels, but from the looks of it, the guilt of his torture is something she is taking on.

I eat my food as the rest continue to rationalize why Matias seems to want to speak to me more than any of them. I wouldn't have given the issue a second thought, but now that speculation is being thrown all around me, my guess would be that it has something to do with what he endured during his time with my father.

My father being the key word.

"Janelle," Brandon calls for me. I look up at him and realize this is not the first time he called my name. "I said Isabel is waiting for you at the nursery."

I put my fork down on my now empty plate. Without another word, I walk my plate to the trash and head to my new day job.

The halls are busy with people coming in and out. I have to wait and slowly make my way out of the dining hall with a cluster of people. Once in the open hall I make my way to the nursery. I find Isabel already inside, standing in front of a set of pods. There are bags of dirt on the floor. Despite the smell of fertilizer and dirt, the plants and flowers perfume this space. It reminds me of peace. I have no clue what I'm associating it with, but it's relaxing.

"We are repotting these plants that are growing too big for their current home." She gestures for me to step beside her. "I've never taught before, so tell me if I need to explain something more. This is how I do it."

I watch her do it once, then follow along with my own. I am careful to follow her steps and I fall into a flow of sorts.

There is a long row of plants waiting for us and I'm looking forward to getting through it all instead of dreading the work.

"Magic can't aid this process?" I ask, wondering if she is doing it all manually for my sake.

"Magic can't be as careful and gentle with the roots as we can." She pulls a plant by the stem, roots up and over her head. The strands hanging off the base proving her statement.

"Alright," I say with a smile.

I'm ready to get my hands dirty.

CHAPTER FIFTEEN

JANELLE

The front door of the nursery makes a loud creaking noise as the wooden door swings open. Isabel and I stop our process of repotting plants and look behind us. The visitors are easy to spot as they tower over the majority of the greenery around us. Roman's steps echo as he crosses the room. The loud sound makes me wince. I cannot believe the old man that ran the nursery never thought of doing something about that. The slightest noise echoes in the space. It has been driving me crazy.

Roman and a soldier approach us with easy smiles. As always, the Royal Force general only has eyes for the woman standing beside me. His companion just gives us polite nods. His face looks familiar, but I can't quite recall from where until he crosses his arms. I remember him from my last day in this castle after the attack. He is the one who walked me out and into the forest.

"Hey there, gorgeous," Roman says to Isabel, pulling her into a hug.

The two talk to each other in hush tones. I resume my task

of repotting the plants, trying to ignore the company in the room.

"I will be right back," Isabel tells me, then moves to the small office at the back of the nursery.

Roman looks around, but not even a minute later, he clears his throat. "You weren't at lunch today," he says.

I don't stop what I'm doing. "I wasn't hungry," I lie.

The thought of going there alone and crossing paths with people who wish me gone isn't something I wish to do twice in one day. I'm not afraid of the stares, but I'm not mentally ready to face them. Isabel has lunch with Brandon in his suite and joining her was out of the question. It's not like I was offered an invitation.

"You could use some food."

I shoot him an unamused look.

"Sorry, well, while we are stuck here, we might as well talk." He shrugs.

I grunt.

"How was the trip back?" he asks.

"Are you seriously making small talk?" I give him a side eye.

He scratches his head and shoots his friend a look to help him, but the soldier remains out of it. "Yeah, you're right. Thank you for bringing Matias home. Some might not be happy that you chose him over the Red Book, but some of us wouldn't have done it any differently."

Does Matias know how much these people want him to be a part of them?

"I'm sure that is not the real reason everyone here hates me." Choosing Matias is the only right thing I've done in a while.

"Not all of us hate you, Janelle."

I meet his eyes. "It doesn't make a difference. I am here now and I have work to do."

"I can acknowledge the role you played was forced on you." He clears his throat completely ignoring my attempts to end the conversation.

I think back on every time I tried to speak up to my father. How I lower my head and move out of his sight. I could've done so much more if I had tried harder. If I wasn't such a coward. Shame washes over me.

Coward.

I sigh, already growing tired of this conversation. "I am living with the consequences of my actions, Roman. That includes all the rightful hate directed my way."

There is much more I wish I could say but the words get stuck in my throat.

Roman's eyes look at me as if he finally sees something he was looking for. His eyes don't see me, but through me. The slow smile on his lips hints at getting something I don't, a secret of some sort.

"Well, that explains why my brother is so in love with you. You two are just as critical of yourselves."

At the mention of Jesse, I straighten. Roman crosses his arms and looks at me expectantly.

"Is he still on that?" I try to sound casual. "He needs to get over that silly crush."

Roman laughs lightly. "I almost believed you." I give him my back to pick up another plant to repot. "If it wasn't because I've been watching you like a hawk. I would've missed the longing looks you give him when you think no one is watching."

"That is all very creepy. If you are crushing on me too, I will have to break your heart."

He pretends I didn't speak. "That was just recently. I

watched it before too. Every time you had the opportunity, the two of you would share giggles and small remarks. I never bought the best friend title." Roman's grin drops. "That was a placeholder for you two to grow up first. Then your father became a very obvious road block."

"I need to get back to work," I say.

"You two are adults and your father isn't around to tell you what to do." His words land in the space between us like heavy stones.

He clears his throat as Isabel returns with a small basket of herbs. He kisses her cheek, then shares goodbyes before departing with his friend.

I continue to work in silence. My mind can't help but think about the memories of a past full of hope for a future. As I sit here in the future I once imagined, there is no trace of hope left within me.

I close my eyes and remember the smiles. The stolen moments. The childlike crush I had on Jesse and how that grew as we did. Stolen smiles became stolen kisses. He was my first everything, including my first secret. The first time I dared disobey my father's orders. Then from there on, only more and more questions rose out of me. Even when I was told to stay away from Jesse, like magnets, we always gravitated toward each other.

I appreciate the silent nature of Isabel today more than ever. I never got to interact with her before, but, as a fly on the wall, she was always around in one capacity or another. Her younger sister is someone else I always watched around the Oscuro boys. When Isabel became Brandon's assistant, I wasn't surprised. She knows far more than she says and there is something amazing about that.

Hours pass us as we go from task to task. I'm tempted to ask her if some background music is out of the question, but interrupting this flow feels wrong. This is the first time being with my thoughts feels peaceful. The labor feels near therapeutic.

"We're almost done for today," Isabel says as we complete a row of plants. "I will be right back." She gestures with her index finger to give her a minute.

Isabel returns and hands me a basket filled with bags. Each bag has a bundle of leaves we cut down earlier today. Isabel mixed and arranged them into small portions, sealing them in baggies.

"I need to tend to Brandon. Can you please deliver half of the bags to the kitchen and the other bags to the clinic?" She puts on a cardigan.

I look tired and dirty. Isabel, on the other hand, just puts on a cardigan and brushes out her straight hair and she is fresh as a daisy.

I clean my hands on my apron and grab the basket as I leave the nursery. The halls are much quieter in the middle of the day. Lunch was a couple of hours ago. I begin to regret not venturing out to the dining hall when my stomach growled. Luckily, I have to make a stop in the kitchen. I might as well take some food to go.

Although the kitchens are on the same floor as the food hall, I have to navigate through the outside corridors in order to reach the entrance.

I spot Matias outside in the gardens from a hallway window. He isn't sitting alone, which catches my attention when I realize the girl next to him isn't Bianca. I step up to the window to take a closer look. Alejandra sits on the same bench a few feet apart. They are both looking forward as if to appear like they aren't together.

I see Matia's lips move and after a beat Alejandra's do. I'm leaning against the wall trying not to be caught blatantly staring at them. The conversation continues, but they never make eye contact. Their eyes remain forward the whole time.

"Nosy dragon," an older lady says under her breath as she passes by.

I straighten at the jab. Alright, I think that's enough curiosity.

I attempt to deliver the bags twice to different staff but each time I am redirected to a man named Pad. The name is said to me as if I should know exactly who they're talking about. I make my way to the back of the building and find a set of doors that I have never seen before.

"There you are." A big man with an apron approaches me and takes the basket from my hands. "I heard you were looking for me," he says.

There's something familiar about him.

"Is your name Pad?" I ask.

"The one and only." He pauses his perusal of the basket to look at me. "You should use the back hall to get to this part of the kitchen. You will rarely find me at the front."

"I will keep that in mind," I say.

I take a turn about the room. The kitchen is bigger than I expected, but I guess it takes a lot of space to make enough food to feed the entire castle. The only two people in the kitchen are me and the man across the prep table, picking bags from the basket.

"Isabel is an angel." He grins down at me. "She knows exactly what to send every time."

"She is taken, I'm afraid," I say.

His laughter rings in the empty room. I stop my observation of all the items on the tables before turning my attention back to the space.

"Are you looking for something?" He asks.

I'm about to tell him no when my stomach makes an angry noise.

"Hungry, huh?" he asks.

"I skipped lunch."

"Why would you ever do that?" He looks appalled at my decision.

"It's not that easy," I say without thinking.

I regret the words as soon as they come out. I have no business telling this man my problems. But I don't have to explain myself. A look of understanding passes through his face. He knows.

He moves to the side of the kitchen and pulls out a packet of bread. From under the table, he pulls a container of butter and jelly. As if materializing out of thin air, an apple and some water make it before me.

"I don't have much more here other than ingredients and from the number of bags in that basket, I assume you have places to be."

"This is perfect," I say, thankful for the act of kindness.

"Well, go ahead and eat while I put these things away."

I stand there eating while I watch Pad walk from side to side. He first puts away all the herbs sent by Isabel. Then he sets up items at different tables. When he doesn't take out ingredients, I realize he is prepping the kitchen for tomorrow morning. Listening to him move about the room while I eat creates the most peaceful dinner experience I had in the past few weeks.

"Thank you," I say when I'm done. I pick up after myself and drop the dirty dishes in the sink. "It was nice to meet you."

"You are always welcome back here," Pad says. "The best snacks are made after hours. Just not today. One day a week, everyone is done early."

"Might be better this way. I don't make many people comfortable."

"You might not feel you have many friends. That might or might not be true. But you have far less enemies than you would think," Pad says.

"I doubt that."

I get many who avert their eyes as I walk by, but for every single one of those I have four who narrow their gaze at me like staring me down is their way of making their discontent with my presence known.

"People dislike what they can't understand, but they also seek solace. They pity you more than they hate you. Then they hate you for making them pity you. We all heard whispers from those who actually saw you that night. The walls remember."

"Remember what?" I ask.

"Remember the ghost of you that walked the halls."

A fuzzy image of that night comes to mind, the way the shape of the walls would go in and out of my sight. The realization of what was happening as my senses came back to me and the horror at seeing what my fire snake was doing. The heartbeat in my chest feels loud in my ears. My lungs fill with smoke, but unlike anyone else, I don't lose my breath and cough. Due to my bloodline, the smoke filters out like fresh air. That is when I finally made my first choice. I regret how I dissociated. I don't fight back, nor do I ask my dragon to listen to me instead of Ray. I hide deep in the premises of my mind.

Coward.

I let Pad's words sink in. "They pity me because they think I'm now stuck living with the reality of what I did."

"Is it a lie?" Pad searches my eyes.

No, it's not. Every day when I close my eyes, I can hear them. I can hear each voice above the cracking of the fire. Their feet hitting the ground trying to outrun me. Their screams are the lullaby that accompanies me every night as I lie on my pillow. I don't want to describe it as a haunting sound because I have accepted it. It reminds me of my purpose and all the work I have left to undo what was done. I cannot bring those people back, but I can keep many from following after them if I stop my father and the movement he has created.

I snap myself from my thoughts and thank Pad for the food.

"Like you said I got places to be," I say and grab the basket.

He gives me a small wave before returning to his task.

The halls are empty and the reason for that is obvious as I walk past multiple windows. Clusters of people are walking about the grounds. The warmth of the sun and chilly air from the mountains are mixing to perfection. I allow myself one glance before returning to my task.

There are a few people moving around the clinic, but make themselves scarce as I cross the threshold inside.

"Hello there." A young woman greets me from across the room. She is sitting behind a desk looking over papers.

I recognize her instantly as the castle's head of the clinic. Amy Bee is hard to miss with her mismatched eye color and loud personality. She would always accompany the late King on visits to other regions once his health started to decay. At least that was the observation my father had made countless times. It was almost as if it served as a beam of hope to the rebellion. Her presence symbolized a weaker King and with that came the opportunity for attack.

"I came to deliver these," I say, lifting the basket higher.

She gestures for me to come forward. I drop the basket on her desk and she quickly empties it out, looking at the different bags Isabel sent over.

"She clearly sends what she wants," Amy Bee says under her breath, more to herself than me. "She obviously doesn't know what she is doing there. I'm guessing the shortage in staff means this is what we have to get used to, regardless of inconvenience."

So there's a person who doesn't think Isabel walks on water. Now, I'm intrigued.

"Would you like me to tell her to stop by so you can explain what she missed?" I ask.

She shakes her head instantly. "Absolutely not." At my pause, she looks up at me and softens her harsh expression. "That is absurd. You are already here." She takes a notepad from her desk and then writes down a list.

As I take the paper from her hand, I realize the harsh difference between her hands and mine. Dirt marks the edges of my nails and crevices of my fingers. I scrubbed my hands, but some dirt is truly impossible to get rid of. Amy Bee's hands are soft and clear of any stains or marks. If anything, they look like what my hands had once looked like.

"I'm not sure where her new room is since pairing up with Roman, but I will see her tomorrow morning," I say, folding and pocketing the piece of paper.

Amy Bee's eyes don't leave mine like the news is something she was not expecting to hear. It makes me wonder if the information has somehow not been included in the daily castle gossip. Isabel spoke of it so freely and casually that no hint of secrecy was implied on the subject. I'm also not included in any inner circle, so sharing information seems out of the question.

"There you are."

At the phrase, both Amy Bee and I turn to see the newcomer standing at the front door of the clinic. The sun has bathed the room in low orange light coming from the open windows.

Her smile widens and, looking thankful for the distraction,

Amy Bee turns her attention to the newcomer. "Hey Matias, have those pesky nightmares finally subsided with the herbs?"

His steps falter a bit as his eyes move from me to Amy Bee. Her cheeks instantly darken to a shade of crimson. The tension in the room takes a nosedive.

I wonder if he took those herbs before or after I saw him in the food hall in the morning. Matias looked tired when I saw him at breakfast, but I figured it was from everything else. After what he went through, I can only imagine how much rest is needed to finally feel healthy again. Lack of sleep due to nightmares sounds more like something everyone should expect after the ordeal.

"I am so sorry." Amy Bee touches her lips like she cannot believe those words came out. "I have lost my mind and all sense." She points in my direction as if to follow up her sentence with something else, but even I'm at a loss about what she could refer to. "Please forgive me," she finally says.

"They helped." Matias crosses the distance to us. "I would like it to stay between us three now." He looks from me to Amy Bee. "I don't want to worry Bianca. Not until I figure out what they mean."

"Of course. I will not utter another word about it." Amy Bee inclines her head.

"What kind of nightmares?" I ask. "Are you frequented by memories?"

I figure I might as well know exactly what kind of secret I'm keeping from the King and his beloved. I can already see their faces when they learn I know something about Matias they didn't.

"In my dreams I'm not reliving..." his words trail off as his eyes turn to Amy Bee, "my time in the cell. I am being spoken to."

"Trauma has a way of manifesting in the brain. It's how it

keeps us in survival mode. Did the voices quiet down?" Amy Bee asks. The concern clearly written on her face.

Matia's nod is reassuring and filled with thankfulness, but I can see the stress marked on the edges of his eyes. I witnessed a portion of what he endured the past few weeks, and I know what my father and his men are capable of.

While I lack the gift of wisdom, a person who frequently told lies raised me. Jesse was right. I can see Matias is hiding something. The question is what and for what reason.

CHAPTER SIXTEEN

JANELLE

I close the clinic doors behind me and head to my room. Today's gardening is weighing on my muscles. Especially my back, which feels heavy and tense. I roll my shoulders and feel the sting of pain. I know it will turn into a full ache by tomorrow morning. It's like whatever I did today affected the muscles I don't use often.

"Hey," Matias calls from the clinic doors. He closes them behind him and rushes in my direction. "We need to talk."

"I won't tell a soul of your secret," I assure him.

Not like I have anyone to tell, but if saying it makes him feel better, why not?

"Not that, but thank you. I appreciate it. I need your help."

"My help with what?" I tilt my head.

"Answers," he says, then begins walking the opposite direction without looking back.

Despite my exhaustion, I find myself following Matias. There are a lot of questions regarding him, but I don't have any answers as far as I know. That alone intrigues me enough, and I think he knows it.

He is walking beside me, but his eyes don't turn in my direction even once as we cross the halls of the castle to our destination.

I pause when a set of double doors comes into view. This is my first time back here after the attack. My heart rate picks up with every step I take. Despite smelling smoke, I disregard it as a figment of my imagination because Matias seems entirely unfazed. I watch a light glow under the doors. My mind tells me that when I open that door, flames will greet me on the other side. It's unreasonable for me to believe so, but not impossible, and that sliver of possibility is where I am.

Someone then exits the library, leaving the doors open behind them. The person casually pushes past us without sparing us a second glance.

"Are you okay?" Matias asks me. He looks between the library and me. His too-well-knowing eyes seem to understand the situation. "We are both going to be haunted by what happened to us for a while. The time to face the music is here."

"I'm haunted by what I did, not what happened to me." Not all the demons that haunt us are alike. We are not the same. Not even close. "You might not have learned the entire story of the attack, but I, with the help of the fire snake my magic conjures, killed a group of students assembled inside those walls." I point inside the library.

The news of their fate was shared with me by the old man guarding the prison cells the night of the attack. Back then, I felt so dissociated that I only recall the news being delivered. Not an ounce of emotion followed after. I watched people share their fate before choosing to hide in my mind, but they were just people in my head. Giving this group of people a label such as 'students' made them all even more real.

"I know." His eyes show a compassion I don't deserve.

"Sofia was a friend studying inside that very room when you and your snake came along."

"She was your friend?" I ask, taking a step back.

"A new one." He looks back to the room, then to me. "But I also know that you were not in charge of the snake. Your soul bond was. I also know you killed him and saved Bianca."

"I didn't do it fast enough."

Coward.

"That might be true, but it's also true that it's easy to toss out blame and pretend we will always make the right decision in that situation."

"You are far too kind and compassionate for your own good," I say.

"Or maybe I also know what it is like to be under your father's control." His voice lowers and to my ears only he adds, "I listened when you spoke to me that day in the cells. I, too, felt like a coward for not fighting back and checking out instead."

I look at Matias. The clouds of his eyes are no longer hidden behind the fake smile. His shields are down and I can finally see why he has been seeking me out. He doesn't feel thankful for my aid in his freedom. He seeks me out because I'm a fellow survivor of the evil that made him wish to disappear. I'm a flame akin to his fire.

"What are we doing here?" I ask, nodding to the open doors.

He clears his throat and after making sure no one is nearby, he says, "I want to figure out what exactly was done to me. That might give me an idea of how to make the voice stop."

"What voice, Matias?" I take a step closer to him and whisper, "Is it my father's?"

Is he somehow able to still communicate with Matias? My father is a powerful man, but his capabilities have limits. His hold over me always made me think he viewed me as his most powerful child, even more powerful than himself. I would come lacking to this extent of power, but I'm not sure what the Red Book might do for a person.

"No, I don't think so. I don't think the voice is of someone living."

The words give me pause. I finally realize why he has told no one about the voice. He allowed Amy Bee to have a slight misunderstanding of what he is dealing with because of this. Even in the magic world, no one can communicate with the dead. Well, no one possesses the magic to raise the dead either, and Matias has done that. His level of connection with those who have passed on is stronger than thought possible.

A few people sit at various desks throughout the expansion of the library entrance. With every step I take deeper inside, I'm in awe at how intact it looks. The smell of fresh pine wood hangs in the air as it has always been there and no disaster ever stained the walls.

"Can I help you?" A voice asks behind us.

I turn and look up at Santiago's impatient frown. His arms are folded before him and the tapping of his foot conveys he has places to be and we are in the way. I've known Santiago for a long time. It's hard to miss his existence when he is so close to the Oscuro brothers. However, the few times I found myself in the castle when I wasn't monitored by my father, I always spent time alone with Jesse, so there was never time to establish any type of friendship. All I know of him is what has been told to me.

"You said for me to come at the end of the day," Matias says.

Santiago looks between us, then up to the heavens. "Is there a reason she is here?"

From the hard edge of his eyes, I can see that he sees

nothing more than the person from the attack. The hostility feels like an itchy slime that spreads more and more until there isn't an inch of my skin free from it. It adds to the shame already covering me.

Matias looks at me and then back at Santiago. "I need to make sense of what happened to me, and I think she might be able to help."

The honest bluntness from Matias surprises me. I wondered if he planned on keeping secrets from the library keeper too, but it looks like yet one more person is going to be allowed into this messed up little group of my father's survivors. In a weird way, I think every person in this castle truly belongs to that group. Even if they choose to blame me, Brandon or the Fates instead.

The few people we walk past don't look up as we take a table off the far left side. I'm not surprised at the fact this specific table is hidden behind a bookshelf from the front door. I actually appreciate being out of sight.

There are more tables and chairs with similar setups down the wall of the bookshelf, but this one is the closest to the main library desk. Which is why we are here, since Santiago is on duty as long as the library doors are open.

"Okay, where do we start?" Santiago asks, settling into a seat across from me. His question is directed at Matias.

Matias turns to me. I hold his gaze as I try to think of something that can be helpful.

"Klause," I say to Santiago. "The cursed book is open. We can start there."

"The curse book talks about the movement looking to destroy the Red Book, not the powers of the Red Book when used against someone." His body shifts fully to Matias sitting between us. "What exactly do you want to know?" He taps the table with his index finger. "We need the question in order to find the right answer."

Matias hesitates for a second but then sighs. "Lord Duelo wanted to unseal my magic by using the Red Book's magic. It became clear he had no idea what he was doing because every attempt was different."

"What did he do exactly?" Santiago leans his forearms on the table.

Matias looks at me, then down at the table like he is about to unzip his skin and let us see everything he is.

"I was not the first of his test subjects, but I was the first that survived."

I lightly tap his arm with my finger. "Do you know what spell he used?"

If we can get an idea of the steps he took, we can narrow down the spell and see what influence the spell had on Matias.

"That's the thing. He didn't have one. He experimented with many," Matias says, fidgeting with his hands.

I share a look with Santiago.

"What part would the book play?" Santiago is looking at the table with grave focus now. I can see his brain compartmentalizing all the moving factors under a spell.

Matias looks confused and turns to me for clarification.

"How did he incorporate the Red Book?" I ask.

From what Jesse told me, Matias and Bianca have little knowledge of magic growing up in Fierno. She had a crash course while here, but Matias was asleep during that time. He wasn't here long before departing, then getting kidnapped.

"He used the book as a can opener to crack me open." He clears his throat. "The book is like a source of magic accessible to a wielder who taps into the power. That is the only way I can explain it."

"Does the book act as a form of stone or talisman under a spell?" Santiago asks.

In a spell, the talisman or magic stone would help power the spell by providing the strength needed to carry out the request. The remaining ingredients in the spell would be tailored for the desired results. My father was tapping into the magic of the Red Book.

Matias shrugs. Santiago rests his hand on Matias' for support.

It's starting to make sense. My father's plan wasn't to destroy the Red Book if doing so would uncap everyone's magic. He would never want to be at a disadvantage again. He wants to be more powerful than others. After all, he never liked competition.

"I think so," I agree. "He uses it as a part of a spell. But what spell?" I ask.

"He tried so many..." His words trail off, leaving behind room for interpretation.

"He was guessing." Santiago whispers. His eyes drop to his hands.

"Test subjects," I add. Finally, truly settling into the meaning behind those words. They were truly test subjects.

"The thing is..." Matia's words trail off, then as if finally getting enough courage, he looks up and meets my gaze, then Santiago's. "Something he did worked. The book gave me something."

The pause that follows is only because wrapping our minds around the news is a reach. My father actually accomplished part of his goal, yet he doesn't know.

"How?" Santiago whispers.

"I don't remember exactly which spell did it." Matias pulls at his hair.

"You never let him know." I'm in shock. The mirror expression on Santiago tells me I'm not the only one.

"I didn't want him to get what he wanted," Matias says, looking up at the ceiling as if eye contact is too hard to hold at the moment.. "He didn't uncap my magic but knowing something he did had a result could have only encouraged him."

"Instead, you subjected yourself to further torture." I lean back on my chair and look at him with new eyes.

This man didn't just endure, but continued enduring in order to not allow evil to prosper. Yeah, Matias and I are nothing alike. He is brave.

"I couldn't let him win. Whatever he had planned next would only be worse."

"Matias," his name falls from my lips in a soft tone.

Recalling the words he said while helping us escape, I ask, "In the cell you said the book wants revenge. What exactly did you mean?"

Santiago waves a hand between us, getting our attention. "Hold on, start from the beginning."

Matias leans back and takes a deep breath.

"I was picked up at the edges of the Black Castle soon after the attack. The first time Lord Duelo tried to uncap my magic, it didn't work, but I was still alive. Which hadn't happened with his other test subjects."

My heart aches for him.

Matias looks between us as if waiting for us to add anything. When we don't, he continues, "After surviving, they zeroed in on me. They no longer tested on the others, deeming me strong enough for the process. They just needed to find the right spell, and then on the sixth attempt something happened."

"What happened?" Santiago asks at the edge of his seat.

Matias looks down at his hands and this time he fists them

tight. "I heard a voice inside my head. That was the first time I heard it but not the last. I hear it at night. It makes it hard to sleep. Amy Bee gave me herbs that help quiet the voice."

"What does the voice say?" Santiago asks.

"At first, I only heard it while they attempted spells on me. Later on, I heard it even while alone in my cell. It started by encouraging me not to cave and give Lord Duelo what he wanted. It told me to hold on and fight the pain. The voice was angry, but not for what I was enduring..."

"Calaca called you its sire." I pause mulling over all the details and implications. "The magic that created it is in you. The voice is the Red Book," I say, concluding.

"I think it is," Matias says, tilting his head.

"Books don't talk." Santiago looks at us like we lost our minds. "Did the voice ever identify itself?"

Matias looks pensive, as if he is thinking back to those days. "It told me it wanted to fight back. It said that before long, Lord Duelo would lose his patience and begin finding ways to completely destroy it."

The book is right. I wouldn't put it past my father to get to that point sooner rather than later. If Matias was the only soldier that survived his attempts, taking him away would bring my father to the edge. Unknowingly, I took his only hope.

But the thing is, the book shouldn't be able to talk to him at such a long distance. "How does it still reach you if you are now so far away?"

"That's what I want to know," Matias says. His voice is stronger.

I recall his words to Amy Bee. He doesn't want Bianca or anyone else to know until he has an idea what it is and how to fix it.

I cross my arms. "Why don't you want Bianca and Brandon to know?"

Santiago leans back with a gasp. "Are you expecting me to keep something from my King?" His tone is stern.

Keeping things from his King and future Queen is not something he would willingly sign up for. I would've thought Matias made sure Santiago was on board first. Did they not talk about this before?

"I'm sick and tired of being a burden. I want to do it myself. Just let me figure it out first. I am not asking you to lie, just don't tell him until I can figure out what it is and how to fix it."

I relate all too well to that feeling. Matias and I are alike in the broken and beaten parts of our soul. They have been bruised black and blue.

"Lying by omission." Santiago shakes his head. "Also, you're not doing it alone. We are here." He gestures between us.

Santiago makes an obvious point. Even though he is not asking for aid from Bianca and Brandon, he is still asking for help.

"They're looking for the Red Book, which should be their focus. I don't want to distract them. I know the second Bianca learns of my problem, she will want to fix it. Brandon will drop everything else to do it to see her happy."

Then it hits me. He is keeping his distance from them, not because he doesn't feel like he belongs there or trusts them, it's because he fears they will figure out his problem. Then they will focus on fixing it. I don't know if Brandon would truly drop everything to help Matias. He is the King and has a duty to his people, but Matias was right about something. He would do anything for Bianca.

"Can I trust you two to help me?" Matias looks between Santiago and me.

Our gazes lock as we both nod.

"All these secrets are going to give me an ulcer." Santiago grunts dramatically.

"How can we know for certain if the Red Book is the voice I hear?" Matias asks, rolling the sleeves on his shirt.

"I now think you were right." Santiago gestures in my direction changing the topic of conversation. "Checking out the cursed book can't hurt. We need to cover all our bases."

"I think we should ask Calaca," I say to Matias' question.

"The thing that followed you two here?" Santiago's face pales at the thought.

"She's not that bad," Matias defends.

"It's not a girl." I roll my eyes. "Can you call it?" I ask Matias.

He nods in confirmation.

"Perhaps that is something we will do tomorrow, during daylight." Santiago clears his throat. "It's dark now and more than one guard will be alerted to our movements in the forest."

Matias appears ready to object when I add, "Brandon will be notified within minutes."

This revelation causes him to close his mouth.

"Tomorrow it is." I knock on the table with my fist and I get to my feet, intending to leave, but Santiago raises one hand, stopping me.

He goes to his desk and returns with something in his hands. "I guess we can start here." He pushes a black book in my direction.

I take the infamous cursed book I have been hearing so much about. The material feels so fragile. Easy to erase from existence. The notion that the information on these pages has been relentlessly pursued to a lethal degree is preposterous.

"What are you doing?" Santiago looks at my hands.

I flex them, letting go of the cover I had been bending. I open the book to the first page and trace my finger over the name written on the top. "Klause P." I look at Santiago. "Do you know what P stands for?"

"His last name?" Matias asks.

We both turn our heads and give him a perplexed look.

"I'm not sure what it stands for." Santiago looks through the pages of the journal, but we all know it's unlikely he spelled out his full name on a journal entry.

"I know this might not mean much, but If we find his family tree, we could find more information linked to their disappearance and the Red Book."

He nods. He gets up and gestures for us to follow him. We walk a few rolls down, then he leads the way into a tall bookshelf.

"This is all the information we got," Santiago says. "Perhaps looking into him while we wait to talk to the creature is what we should do."

"Calaca," Matias whispers behind me, but not loud enough for Santiago to hear. "Where do we start?" he asks, looking at the impossible number of texts on the shelf.

The description on the row reads 'autobiographies.'

I look at the shelf and think about all the moving pieces. We might not know exactly what we need, but learning as much information about the topic will only help clarify the image. If I have learned anything from my father, it is that learning all you can about your enemy is essential to know how they would act.

Klause is not our enemy, but the answers to a lot of our questions lie around him and the time he spent in Puerto Quinn.

"I think we should split into two tasks." I gesture to one section of the shelf containing the autobiographies. "People like Klause don't go through life unnoticed. His peers must have written about him. The time frame is between one hundred and fifty and two hundred years ago."

Santiago walks over to the autobiographies. "Anything between that fifty-year gap?"

I nod, and he turns to face the bookshelf. I turn in Matias' direction. "We should use the same time frame to look at family trees. If we find the full names of Klause's family, we will connect his research easier."

Matias looks up at the shelf with a sour expression. "This is going to take us weeks."

"I got it," Santiago says.

He gestures for us to move away and takes the spot in front of the bookshelf. He extends his hand forward and a blue light glows out of his palm towards the books. The glow grows as one by one more books join in the light. The light is not strong enough to grab the attention of the people in the main sitting area.

With one hand up, palm facing the shelf, Santiago uses his other hand to write the year gap we are searching. A section of books slides out of the bookshelf into mid air. It slowly floats down into the floor in front of Santiago.

"That's still a lot." Matias rubs his brows.

"We don't need to get through them tonight," I say, shoving him forward to help me carry the books to the table. We fill our arms and do a second trip to carry everything. "Let's do as much as we can, then pick up tomorrow."

Santiago carries his own pile of books to his side of the table. The stack he has is twice the size of ours and consists of various sized journals.

"We can switch between piles," I offer.

Santiago gives me the first side smile. "I would appreciate that."

Matias cracks his knuckles. "Let's do this."

The only tracker of time becomes the candlelight in the library. Every hour the flames flicker announcing the time change. Santiago has to get up and help people a few times, but other than that we power through a big chunk of books.

A whistling sound distracts me from my work ahead. I look around, trying to place the noise, but my eyes are tired and I feel disoriented.

"It's Matias," Santiago says between a yawn.

"What?" I look next to me at the man in question. "He's sleeping."

"For someone who needs tea to sleep, he sure seems to snooze hard."

The chuckle that bubbles out of my chest is loud in the quiet space. I shouldn't laugh. It's mean but ironic. Matias jumps up at the noise, which causes Santiago and me to burst into laughter.

"I think that is enough for tonight," Matias says, stretching. "Good work everyone."

Santiago and I share an amused look at the statement coming from the person who had been sleeping.

"Let's all meet tomorrow during lunch at the clearing." Matias gestures to the back of the castle over his shoulder.

Santiago's expression falls, and I fight the smirk on my face. He needs to get used to the idea of Calaca. I have a feeling it's not going anywhere. We all will see more of it with time.

CHAPTER SEVENTEEN

JESSE

My eyes alternate between looking at the clock on the wall and the closed door. The papers before me are long forgotten since Janelle didn't show up to bed at a reasonable hour. I didn't look for her in the dining hall, but her absence was noticed by a few guards at both lunch and dinner. She should be in her bed by now.

I saw Isabel during dinner and know they're certainly not tied up by some plant emergency. What am I thinking? The idea that there could be a plant emergency is stupid.

The echo of soft footsteps sound behind the door. I pick up a piece of paper and pretend to scan the list of names between sheets. The front door of the shared space creeks as it opens. I wait until it shuts to look up and meet Janelle's tired expression. I can't help but be glad to see that whatever she was doing wasn't fun. A very selfish part of me would have hated to see her walking in happy with laughter trailing after. It would've cut me.

"Long day?" I ask before I can stop myself.

She joins me in the sitting area, taking a seat across from me. "You are talking to me again," she says.

"Did I ever stop?"

Do you even care?

"I was at the library doing some research." She rolls her shoulders.

Her face is stone cold, as if waiting for me to question her further. Whatever she was doing, she obviously doesn't want to part with the details. I do the opposite.

"I didn't ask," I say.

I pretend not to see the twitch in her armor by looking at my papers once more.

"What you do with your free time it's your problem. You do have to find the Red Book again after all. Isn't that the only reason you are here, anyway?"

Her eyes sharpen at my words. "Yes, that is the only reason I'm here."

There's a gentle ringing in my ears that only I can hear.

"Getting your magic back is the goal. The sooner you find the Red Book, the sooner you will get it back and leave."

Her eyes don't blink despite every word hitting a nerve. "As always, the Lord of Wisdom has gotten it all right. I'm here only to get my magic back. Now, if you excuse me, I have a long day tomorrow." She stands up and heads into her bedroom.

I watch her walk away and shut the door behind her as the well-known melody of lies rings in my ears. Her lies give me air and with every inhale, it gets easier to breathe. She is here for something else and a small stupid part of me hopes that it's me.

I toss the papers on the table and head to my room. Tomorrow will indeed be a long day. I have to speak to a few trusted sources we have in the forest. Whether other forest creatures knew of the traitors amongst their kind is yet to be seen. Brandon is planning to have zero tolerance for those who've allied with Duelo, but we need to figure out if his allies are strays.

I make a pit stop at the library first thing in the morning. As I predicted, Santiago is sitting behind his desk. A plate of breakfast food sits beside him. Thinking of it, I haven't seen him in the dining hall in a while.

"Would it kill you to eat away from your desk?" I ask, crossing the distance between us.

He looks up from whatever he is reading and stands. He shuts the book and shoots me an odd expression. "The name Kitty Paws might need to be reassigned to you."

I roll my eyes at the taunt that once had Roman fuming in anger.

"I made no effort to conceal my presence." Gesturing to his untouched breakfast, I add, "I haven't seen you at the food hall in months."

"Yeah," he says while running his finger through his hair. "I don't know where to sit."

I first think the comment is a joke because Roman and I always sit at the same table. We have been for years. Then I realize Santiago has never sat with us. He has always been part of small gatherings at Brandon's, but when it comes to castle events, he always stood on the side with *Sofia*. Thinking back, the last time I saw him in the dining hall, it was the last time I saw her there.

He huffs out softly, self reprimanding. "It sounds juvenile but," he pauses, looking into space.

"It's not," I assure him. "Whenever you are ready, there will always be space next to Roman or me. You know that."

"I know." He nods. He clears his throat, then looks at me expectantly. "It's there something I can help you with?"

I nod. "As a matter of fact, I heard Janelle was seen leaving the library late at night." Admitting to waiting for her isn't something I'm willing to do. "Do you know what she was up to?"

His all-too-knowing gaze tells me I'm not fooling him. I didn't think I would, but I had to try.

"You have people watching her or something?"

His displeased tone will make my request more difficult than I thought.

"Are you offering?" I give him a teasing smile.

"Leave me out of it." Both of his palms go up in the air as he takes a step back. "What I can assure you is that Matias and Janelle are not doing anything that could harm anyone in the castle or disobeying the King."

I should've known Matias was with her, but he has better things to concern himself with. "Shouldn't he focus on figuring out his own problems?" My question is rhetorical, but the sharpness in my tone is evident.

Santiago takes a seat without looking away from me. "What do you really want to know, Jesse?"

There isn't a specific thing I want to know. I want to know what exactly she is searching for. I cannot ask her since I don't want her to know I care. Yet I want to make sure that if there's anything I can do, he needs to let me know.

I'm the juvenile one.

"Is there anything I can help with?" I finally ask.

"I need you to arrange a training session for Matias. He needs to learn to wield magic in self defense but not with all the soldiers. I don't need to tell you he is behind."

He trained with Roman for a bit before he departed to Fierno. From what my brother shared, Matias was worse than

Bianca when she first arrived. They blame it on the cursed book unbalancing him. I figure things could have only gotten worse now.

"Is that all?" I grunt more than ask.

"For now, If something changes I will let you know." Santiago's tone is chipper.

"I would appreciate that." I knock on the table before pushing away from the desk. "I will see you around."

With a teasing smile Santiago mocks-salutes me.

I fight the urge to flip him off over my shoulder. I've shown enough emotion on the subject. Giving him more ammunition will not help me. Instead, I begin my route to the training grounds. Releasing some steam on the training circles is all I need to feel better.

I'm not sure what I expected from Santiago, but not fessing up with what Janelle was up to was not it. Perhaps this is what I deserve. I need to stop thinking of her all together. He might be doing me a favor.

The training circles are packed with soldiers waiting their turn. Today is not a regular training day. Once every two weeks, people may take their sparring sessions to another level. It's a bit more aggressive than usual. This is used to sharpen senses and take off the safety net. Death is not allowed, but anything outside of mortal danger is encouraged.

I spot Roman on the edge of the circle first. He is giving his second in command orders before dismissing him and making his way to me. The trail of dirt on his elbow tells me exactly where he was this morning.

"Are you okay?" Roman asks after a minute of standing next to me. I don't answer with anything other than a head nod. "I hoped that after this mission you would be a little more yourself."

"I'm fine," I say, between clenched teeth.

My eyes find Resse across the circle. The old man once ran our best squad in the Royal Force. Instead of retiring, he has found himself a place running the training circles. He is the person running the order of sparring sessions taking place. Resse will find someone to duel me, saving me from finding someone to agree. The best part is that Resse always matches people to strength and ability, always keeping matches fair.

With a gesture, I catch Reese's attention. A head nod in confirmation later and my intentions are known.

"Blowing off steam is one way of dealing with your problems."

Roman chuckles and despite his remark, I can tell he doesn't disapprove of my choices. He has found himself one too many times in the circles.

Roman gestures to Resse too, making the old man grin devilishly. I scowl at my brother, knowing damn well if he is part of the roster, Resse will partner him up with me.

"What are you doing?" I ask

"Saving whatever poor bastard was going to be stuck with you."

I cross my arms. "You think you are funny?"

"What I think seems to not matter for a while. As a matter of fact, not a damn thing seems to matter, but your shit mood."

The current duel on the circle ceases and Resse steps forward. He gestures to Roman and me. "Go at it, boys!" He hoots with a wide grin.

I step up to the circle. The crowd erupts in cheers and laughter. It's not often that the brothers have matches against one another.

A soldier off to the side shouts, "Beat some sense into him, Roman!"

I follow the voice and narrow my eyes to the soldier that belongs to my brother's squad.

"What?" Esteban asks, smirking. "Finally ready to let out some anger over the redhead?"

"He can't help falling for her demonic tricks." Eve, a soldier I trained in the past, says shaking her head.

"He can get over her and move on." Esteban claps with the rest of the crowd. "I don't even blame him. If I was dog-walked by a dragon, I would walk around looking half guilty too."

His words hit too close to home. Have I truly been walking around looking half-guilty?

"Shut it," Liz, a fellow soldier and friend, tells the others.

Eve looks down at her shoes while Esteban scowls back at Liz, offended to receive an order from a soldier beneath him.

"Focus, Jesse." Liz says. Her eyes tell me to get my head on the tasks before me.

"Perhaps you're the one needing to be saved." Roman shakes his head. "I could've finished you in the time it took you to listen to those idiots."

I don't answer him as I toss my first punch in his direction. Roman doesn't take it easy on me. Before long, all thoughts regarding the soldiers' comments vanish. The lack of information coming from Santiago and the existence of Janelle somewhere in this castle fall to the back burner.

Staying on my feet becomes my only focus. None of the punches I throw ever connect. Roman skillfully blocks each successive attack. I grow tired and the fire inside me dies one breath at a time. After a bloody nose, my breath grows heavy, and it's not long before I'm on the floor tasting the dirt of the training circles. I land on my back and I let out a laugh that keeps me from getting up. Roman gives me his hand and I take it.

"That smile is worth the bruises," he says.

I take a closer look at him and realize I did manage to do

some damage. His ear is bloody and there are bruises on different parts of his face and arms. I pat his back.

"We didn't use magic," I say, finally realizing it.

Roman shrugs. "You wanted a physical release. Magic wouldn't have accomplished that."

"We can volunteer a girl next time," Esteban says with a wink.

This time my swing isn't blocked on time. It lands right on his jaw. The impact makes a smacking sound that catches the attention of most of those around the circle. Shocked and amused expressions are shared amongst those around.

"Walk it off," Resse tells Esteban while clapping. "Next two get in the center."

I walk off to the locker room. The fire inside me lit once again. The few people inside see the state of my face and rush out of the room. Roman is the only one to follow me inside and stay.

"That good humor was short-lived," He says, scratching his head.

"Fuck off," I yell in his direction.

"You are mad at someone, but it's not me. It's not even her. You cannot hate her, so you feel like a traitor."

I wipe the blood off my face and pace the floor. My chest is heaving as I breathe. "Do you think it's true?"

"What?" Roman takes a seat on a bench.

I point to the door. "What they're saying. That she played me all this time."

"They don't know anything. They make assumptions, that's all." He shrugs.

"She has done awful things," I say, trying to convince myself why I should stay away from her.

"Haven't we all?" He sits back and wipes his hands on a white cloth he picks from the ground. "I'm not saying any of us have the score she does, but perhaps when all people know about you is the most awful thing you have ever done, then it's easy to point fingers."

This is all messed up.

He stares at the wall as if it can show him the answer to all this. "We have known her since she was no bigger than three feet tall, climbing on the side of your window to spend the night listening to music and eating our snacks. You think we never caught on that she would eat my cream cookies?"

"You ate a lot of those growing up."

I recall the snacks that, despite my aversion to them, became part of my daily route to grab from the kitchen.

He rubs his chin. "I sure did, but the number of boxes doubled during the summer." He shakes his head. "That was not just me."

"What now?" I ask my older brother. I look up at him and for the first time in years, I'm searching my big brother's eyes for answers.

"If you have questions, have you tried," he pauses for effect, then adds, "to ask?"

What did I expect by asking a serious question to this tool?

His smart ass answer deserves the swing I throw his way. His defenses are down, which is why my blow lands. Roman bends over as the air leaves his stomach.

"Good one, brother," I say, patting his back. "I have somewhere to be now."

I head out of the training grounds towards my room with a beat on my step. The stress that had plagued me only hours ago seems to have mellowed. I can't say it's fully gone, but it doesn't overwhelm me to the same extent.

I look around my bedroom suite when I step inside but I know I won't find Janelle in here. It's far too early for her to be here already. I shouldn't seek her out but I know no matter how much I fight it I will end up waiting for her at night.

I make quick work of showering and changing to fresh clothes. Last night Brandon assigned me a task. At first I was annoyed at the request since it requires me to leave the castle for most of the day for the foreseeable future but I will be back every night.

After careful deliberation, Brandon decided not to ask leaders of different forest creatures directly about Duelo. I am hopeful that is the right decision. We know their nature, and their alliance to Duelo feels careless. Duelo knows I was at his keep the night of his meeting, but I doubt he told any of his allies about my presence.

Searching to see if these individuals are on their own won't be hard to find if we ask the right people. I'm glad Brandon gave me the job. It gives me something to occupy my thoughts outside the castle walls. It's time to go hunting.

CHAPTER EIGHTEEN

JANELLE

I hand Isabel Amy Bee's note and see her hesitation to even take the piece of paper. She reads it a few times, given the amount of time she stares at the words. There are not that many words altogether.

"I will have this ready by lunchtime. Do you mind dropping off the new basket?" She asks me in a soft tone.

I think that if I said no, she would cry. I nod instead and give her a reassuring smile. There are a lot of things to fear in this world, and Amy Bee doesn't seem to be one of them. I have no idea what Isabel has done to land on the medic's bad side, but a little part of me is glad I'm not the only one with problems. Even perfect little Isabel has them.

The morning goes by fast and soon enough, it's time to deliver the basket. Isabel has a system in which baskets only need to be delivered once a week. Since I delivered most yesterday, I only have Amy Bee's delivery today.

The clinic is quiet as I approach. The majority of the staff can be found in the dining hall at this time. I knock lightly on the entrance when I don't see Amy Bee right away. She sticks her head out of one of the observation rooms and gestures at me to wait for her at her desk. I do.

"Well, would you look at this," Pad says, entering the clinic behind me. "Two days in a row."

"How are you, Pad?" I smile at the old man.

He pats the sides of his stomach. "Not going hungry. That's for sure. Did you eat today?"

"About to." It's a half lie. I plan on finding food after I'm done with Matias and Santiago.

"Oh hey Pad," Amy Bee greets him, finally joining us.

She reaches for the basket and inspects all the different herbs inside. "Everything looks to be here."

"Is one of those for me?" Pad asks.

Amy Bee nods and gives him a smile. "How are your hands doing?"

"Well," he pulls his hand up and they are shaking. "The shakes are back. It makes cooking so much harder."

"What's wrong?" I ask as I take a closer look at his hands.

"Arthritis." He looks at his shaking hands like he is trying to will them to stop, but to no avail. "Magic can heal and cure only so much. The toll of the body is something out of the range of power." The laughter he lets out is hollow. "I suppose we would all live forever otherwise."

This is the first time I noticed the tightness in his eyes that wasn't there yesterday.

Amy Bee pulls one bag and hands it to him. "This will make you feel better instantly. I can't apologize enough for making you wait a single day longer."

She was furious with Isabel because she forgot the bags used for medical pain. Looking at the strain in Pad, it's no wonder why Amy Bee was so upset. She knew what the day would be for him without them.

"Thank you," Pad says as he takes the herbs in hand. He

kisses the bag and pulls it to his chest in a gesture of appreciation.

"Wait," I say without thinking.

I reach Pad and place my hand in his. I close my eyes and push the healing energy into him. It's unlikely that I'll be able to completely heal him. Oli has had a bad knee for years now. I've been able to soothe his pain to the point he feels as if nothing is wrong with him.

Pad gasps as we both watch as his hands stop shaking.

"It's gone, the pain is gone." His laughter is genuine this time.

"How?" Amy Bee asks in shock.

"It won't last forever, maybe a couple of days," I say.

I didn't have to soothe Oliver every day, but about once a week unless he had an especially hard day. I might have to add stopping at the kitchen as part of my routine before or after breakfast to make sure Pad is ready for the day.

"Can you cure chronic pain?" Amy Bee asks, trying to figure out what just happened.

"I can soothe it. I can heal only small things like cuts and scratches. But for big illnesses or internal injuries, I can soothe the pain away."

The look on Amy Bee's face is close to diabolical. It's a smile, but I've never seen something so wide and expressive on her face. I take a step back and regret ever saying she wasn't something to fear. Isabel has my condolences.

"Can you please be here by five tomorrow morning?"

"I don't think so. That's an unholy hour."

Who on earth gets that early to do anything requiring functioning?

"Janelle Duelo," Amy Bee says in a sweet sing-song voice. "Be here tomorrow by five in the morning or I will go find you."

Her smile drops and the tone of her voice does, too. "You don't want me to go find you."

"Fine," I spit out. "I'll be here tomorrow morning at five."

"I do not know what's happening, but I will be here too with breakfast for all of us," Pad says with a smile.

"That is very nice of you, Pad," Amy bee says in a cheerful tone once again.

I watch the little sociopath walk back to her desk in her cheerful mood.

"I will head out then." I look between them.

"See you tomorrow bright and early," Amy Bee waves with a smile, like she didn't just threaten me and forced my hand.

I roll my eyes and leave the clinic. Looking at a clock on the wall, I realize I spent longer than anticipated with that errand. I make my way to the forest behind the castle. The training circles seem almost deserted as the dining hall fills with hungry people.

My steps pause in the middle of the yard as pressure rises, slowing my pace. The current pressure of the atmosphere resembles the one of water. I take one step and the pull against it reminds me of walking in a pool.

"This is odd," I say.

I place my hand up and try to scan for magic when I recall my lack thereof. That is also when I recall the protection spell that encapsulates the Black Castle and its grounds. I push against the pressure and walk past it. Once the tension drops, I know I have crossed the barrier. I look back at the castle and admire how the few people that were visible by the gardens seconds ago are gone. The protection spell conceals anyone on the other side from sight.

I walk into the woods and find the first clearing and spot Matias and Santiago right away. They are sitting side by side on a boulder with a bag of snacks between them. I knew that planning to meet during lunch didn't mean either of them were planning on going hungry. I'm glad about it too.

"There you are!" Matias greets with a smile.

The bags under his eyes look smaller and the smile less heavy. Last night I was so tired. I slept like the dead and from the looks of it, so did Matias. I'm glad for it.

I only get a nod from Santiago, but I don't mind. That's a better greeting than I got yesterday.

"Let's not delay this any further." I turn to look into the vegetation. "Matias, can you call for it?"

"Already?" Santiago asks, looking into the woods. "Shouldn't we prepare what we plan to ask?"

"Are you scared?" Matias looks amused.

"Who? Me?" Santiago shakes his head.

"She will not hurt you. She listens to me. I often wonder if I will find her on the edges of the barrier, but she is never there." Matias taps his chest. "It's like I know she will only come if I ask."

"Then ask," I urge him and stop myself from reminding him once again that Calaca is not a girl.

Santiago is about to say something when movement from the bushes to our right alerts us. The skeletal figure draped in cream color fabric steps out of the darkness into view. No one says a word as it crosses the distance directly to Matias's side.

Santiago moves behind me. His hands grip to my shoulders tightly. "Don't worry, Janelle, I will protect us."

"Yeah," I say slowly. "By using me as a shield." I push his hands off me.

"I don't remember you being so tall." Matias looks up at Calaca with concerned eyes. "You can hear me when I call you in my head?"

Calaca nods its head slowly.

"Can you hear all my thoughts?" His tone is curious, not accusatory.

"I can only hear you when you call for me," it confirms.

Matias lowers his voice. "What about the other voice?"

"You hear others?" Calaca looks around as if someone else was around it would see them. It stops when its body turns to the castle. "You hear voices inside the Black Castle?"

"Sometimes," Matias says. "Well, one voice."

"I don't hear voices from here." It points at the castle. "I've got to get closer to the walls to hear what they whisper."

"No, I hear them here." Matias gestures to his temple.

Calaca moves its skeletal hand over Matias and takes a closer look.

"I don't hear anything inside your head but you."

"What do you see in Matias?" I ask, prompting. "You said Matias' magic is what you recognize as your sire, correct?"

Calaca nods. "I sense your magic, the one that created me."

"Yeah, about that." Matias scratches his head. "I don't think that magic is mine. I think it's the Red Book."

Calaca inclines its head to one side, then another.

"Is it?" I ask.

"Books can't talk," Santiago says, still hiding behind me. "The Red Book is not the voice inside your head. It has to be someone or something else."

Calaca looks between Santiago and Matias. "The magic that created me, it's not yours but bestowed to you to keep?" Calaca asks.

Matias shrugs one shoulder. "I think so."

"If that is the case, look inside you. The way you reached for me, reach for it and demand answers."

The order is so simple. Matias looks at me and a flash of apprehension crosses his eyes.

"What if, by letting it talk to me, it takes over?"

He hasn't talked to it or listened to what it has to say out of fear of losing control.

"It can't." Calaca reaches for him and places one hand on his shoulder. "The vessel is yours. It can't hurt you."

"It took control once." Matias steps away. His eyes find mine and I can see he is close to spiraling. "The day we escaped. It raised the dead to help us. I didn't do that. It took over."

"It did it to protect you." I step forward. I can feel Santiago reach for me to pull me back, but his hand isn't quick enough. "If it meant to do it again, I doubt there is much we can do to stop it."

"Nice pep talk," Santiago murmurs behind me.

I'm being realistic and I need Matias to be it, too. There's no time to waste.

Matias finally nods and closes his eyes. I know the second he hears the voice on his head as his whole body flinches.

"What does it say?" I ask after a minute.

Matias's eyes finally open and look around. He takes in his surroundings before looking down at his hands, then body. The slow inspection is odd at best. The stiff action makes me take a step back.

"Sire," Calaca drops to its knees.

It tricked him. Somehow, it knew that talking to the book would allow it to take over. What we are looking at is no longer Matias.

I stretch my right arm out beside me and call for my snake. The power I used to feel coursing through my veins and fingertips is gone.

Matias places a hand on Calaca's head, petting it lightly before turning to us. I continue to step back until my body hits Santiago's. His hands go back to my shoulders, and this time I don't push them away.

I look at the hollow eyes that minutes ago held so much fear and concern.

"You are not Matias." My voice carries disbelief.

"I am not." The words are delivered expressionless. "I will return his body to him after I deliver my message." He taps his ears and adds, "listen."

It takes a step closer to us and we take a step back. Our eyes trained on it.

"What do you want?" I ask.

"Return me to The Red Book to be whole again. I will leave the body only once I'm reunited with my other half."

"Yeah, you think we haven't tried to get the book back," Santiago says in a dry tone.

"Try harder!" it yells. "Speak to your King and tell him what I said. I will no longer allow the boy to keep me a secret. If he doesn't, then I will and this time I won't let the boy return."

Santiago and I nod in answer to the request. Matias's head inclines just before his body drops. A coughing fit follows until his breathing finally settles. I rush after him and kneel. I look for his pulse and breathe out in relief when I find it. He stirs and I rise. As Matias comes back to consciousness, I look up at the heavens and thank the Fates.

"What happened?" Matias asks.

I give him my hand and help him rise to his feet. "We can confirm the book is the one talking to you in your head. Part of the Red Book is in you."

"Did it say it wants to be reunited with the rest of the Red Book?"

I nod.

He rubs his head. "It told me that much before everything went fuzzy."

"We can't keep this from them." Santiago gestures back to the castle. "We have to tell Brandon now."

"Why?" Matias's question is confused and filled with apprehension.

"The book plans to tell them if you don't," I say.

There is no way around this.

"What if they lock me up?" Matias asks, nearly shaking.

"Why would they do that?" Santiago looks at me as if I can explain the odd question.

"I have that thing living inside me. Its magic can manifest in me and I don't know how to control it." There's a pitch of terror deep in his voice. "I can be considered a threat."

Despite that being the truth, I doubt it will take that little for Matias to become a threat to Brandon Oscuro. The King of Puerto Quinn might be the only person who has close to uncapped magic. But trying to explain that to Matias might not be the best thing. He is being irrational, and using logic won't make him understand.

"Matias." I take his hand in mine. "No one is going to lock you up again." The tremble of his hands doesn't stop but his hold tightens on me and I feel the urge to make it go away. "I won't allow it," I vow.

"I won't allow it," Calaca vows.

I look at the creature. Its expression is as neutral as ever but there is an assurance in there that tells me it means it.

"I got you out once. I will get you out again," I finish.

The sincerity must convey in my tone as Matias finally nods. A little of the panic leaves his body.

Santiago clears his throat. "What will it be, then?"

"I will tell them," Matias says.

Calaca moves to Matias and inclines its head.

"Now that you know it's not really me, will you be going?" Matias asks.

Calaca slowly shakes its head. "You still have my services. Sire finds you trustworthy enough to protect it inside you. I will do everything in my power to protect you."

Well, at least that stays. The need to find the Red Book only continues to grow. The stakes get higher and higher. My conversation with Jesse last night comes to mind. It serves as a reminder that I still got a job to do. If I want to see my magic back, I need to find the Red Book.

I gesture to Calaca and wait for it to turn in my direction. "Are you aware of my father's whereabouts?" I ask.

Calaca shakes its head. "I've been guarding the castle. I never left the forest."

I clear my throat. "Can you find him?"

"I can't leave my sire unguarded." The cloth covering its skeleton sways in the wind.

Matias makes eye contact with me and nods in understanding. "I will be safe in the Black Castle. Lord Duelo is my biggest threat."

Calaca stares at Matias but after a beat it nods in understanding. "I will find him and report back."

We stare as it walks into the woods. Once a few feet inside the heavy brush, it looks back. As if carried by the wind, Calaca melts into the greenery of the forest.

CHAPTER NINETEEN

JANELLE

I walk with Matias and Santiago to the dining hall. We find Jesse and Roman sitting down, having a friendly and relaxed conversation with a group of soldiers. Roman looks up as we approach their table and at meeting my eyes, he immediately knows something is up.

He rises to his feet and waits till we get close enough before asking, "What is it?"

Santiago takes the lead, addressing the brothers. "We need Brandon for this conversation."

Hunched over, Matias avoids eye contact and keeps his focus on the floor. I know he didn't want it to come to this, but there isn't much of a choice. Regardless, a little part inside me feels like I'm betraying him.

"He should be in his office," Jesse says. His eyes pour into mine like he is trying to read me with just one look.

I don't hold his gaze, choosing instead to look toward the hall. We have already attracted the attention of the fellow guards at their table. I notice Isabel is not here, which means she's probably already back at the nursery. I look for a clock on the wall and realize I'm late to return from lunch.

I know she will understand, but I don't want her to be stuck finishing the work for the day.

"We should hurry," I say.

We make our way to Brandon's office and find him with a few advisors in a heated conversation. Roman enters the room first, making eye contact with the King. That's all it takes for Brandon to ask everyone else to leave the room.

"I believe we should stay and hear whatever is so urgent," an advisor suggests.

I've never learned any of their names. They all look alike to me apart from the one woman who is currently absent and the young guy.

The young guy is laying back on a chair and clears his throat as he rises to his feet. "Let them be," he says.

"You would say that, Damien. We all know you just want to leave because you are hungover," a short man with a beard says.

Damien waves to the room with no care in the world. He inclines his head to the Oscuro brothers as he walks out of the door. His eyes skip me as he passes, choosing to look down at the ground instead. I see he belongs to the ones who cannot meet my eye.

The other advisors follow after him grunting about the dismissal. Every single one of them shooting a scowl my way. They belong firmly to the group that hates me. I expected nothing less.

Brandon rounds his desk and approaches us. "They think being glued to my side would be best for Puerto Quinn," he says with humor. "Made any progress?" His question is directed at me.

"It's Matias," I say.

Brandon looks at Matias, who is inspecting his own shoes, then looks back at me. "I figured it was about Matias. That's why you all met up in the library. What is the update?"

I look over at Santiago, who is sporting a look of confusion. He's not the one who told him about our gathering. Of course, King Oscuro knows what we have been up to.

"News travels fast," I say.

"The walls talk," Brandon says with a slight smirk on his face.

His eyes move to Jesse, who is watching the exchange with a frown. There's something there, but I can't begin to imagine what.

I clear my throat. "My father stole the Red Book to uncap his magic and become the most powerful wielder in Puerto Quinn, if not the world. To his despair, he doesn't know the right spell. He has been using test subjects to experiment and they've all died during his attempts."

I look at Matias, and despite him agreeing to tell Brandon, it feels wrong. I'm confessing to a room full of people the worst thing that ever happened to someone else. Clearing my throat, I glance back at Brandon.

"Matias survived my father's attempts to uncap his magic. During one of his attempts, the book spoke to Matias."

Brandon's eyes move to the boy who visibly shrinks at the mention of his name. I decide then and there that Brandon or anyone else doesn't need to know anything that isn't absolutely necessary. The details belong to Matias. Only he deserves to share it at his own pace. If the Red Book wants the King to know of its existence in Matias, it will have its wish, but nothing more. I don't forget that the Lord of Wisdom is standing just a few feet from me. So I choose my words carefully.

"The book fears my father would soon tire of trying to

uncap magic individually and would resort to destroying it altogether," I speak truthfully.

"The book can speak to you?" Brandon asks Matias.

A small nod in confirmation is all we get.

"This is great news." Brandon moves to his bookshelf in a hurry. "Can the book tell us where it is?" He pulls out an old text and searches through its pages. "A location spell might do the trick."

"Brandon," Santiago says. His voice is full of sorrow. The only clue that having this discussion has any effect on him. "The book left in Duelo's possession isn't the one talking to Matias."

Brandon looks at everyone in the room simultaneously. "Someone explain."

"The book concealed part of itself inside Matias. In the case my father destroys the other part, it can be restored." I cross my arms and prepare for the reaction I know my following words will have. "It spoke to us earlier today. It has a request for you, King Oscuro."

"Is that so?" Roman asks with empty humor.

His posture is defensive and protective. An outside force is demanding something of his King.

"The book wishes for you to retrieve the other half to be reunited. That is the only way for it to leave Matias' body." Santiago's tone is mocking.

They've been trying to get the Red Book for months now, yet somehow the stakes just tripled.

Brandon looks at his brothers, then out the window, digesting all the information we brought up.

"There is a part of the book living inside him," Brandon says.

It's not a question, but Santiago and I nod, nonetheless.

"I need to speak to Bianca," Brandon says.

At the mention of her, Matias finally looks up. Sensing his refusal, Brandon raises a hand.

"She has to know what is going on," Brandon tells him with a hint of defensiveness in his tone.

The King of Puerto Quinn misses nothing. Regardless, Matia's objection is fruitless, because as much as he wants things to be different, she is going to find out.

"I'm sure Bianca will love to hear her little brother is possessed by an ancient magic book." Roman drops to a chair. "Her favorite part will be how he told Janelle before anyone else."

"Technically, he told Santiago and I at the same time," I clarify.

"What do you think?" Brandon asks Jesse.

"They aren't lying," he says with a sour expression on his face.

"I didn't ask if you heard a lie in their words. I'm asking what you think about all this?"

Jesse doesn't react.

Brandon throws his arms in the air, a gesture nothing like the King he has been embodying lately. This is the old Brandon. The one who would join Jesse and me on our summer adventures.

"I used to always turn to you on any occasion and ask for your point of view. Bounce ideas back and forth. She is here. Can I get you back too?"

"What is going on?" Bianca asks from the doorway.

Her eyes look to Brandon but quickly after finds Matias. She walks to his side first. He shifts uncomfortably at her invasion of his space.

"Hey," she says carefully.

In one breath Matias turns to Bianca and says, "Lord Duelo used the book to uncap my magic, and while doing so, the book sealed a part inside me to protect itself from being destroyed." He taps his temple with trembling hands. "The Red Book talks to me here because it lives inside me."

"Attaboy," Roman barks out a laugh. "Rip it like a sticker."

"A sticker?" Jesse rounds on his brother.

Bianca's shock is momentary. She takes a step closer to Matias and continues talking to him in a soft voice.

"You know." Roman mimics with his hand the gesture of removing a bandaid. "Like that."

"That's not what it's called." Jesse looks around as if in confirmation this is truly happening.

The anxiety previously flooding the room takes a break and allows us all to breathe just a little lighter at the idiocy taking place.

"What's it called then?" Roman's tone carries disbelief.

I wouldn't be surprised if he thought Jesse was making this up.

"I refuse to tell you." Jesse mimics his brother.

Roman points at him. "Because you don't know."

"These men truly lead me?" Santiago asks, his hand touching his neck, appalled.

"No," Brandon says. "I lead you."

Brandon claps a few times, gathering everyone's attention. I can't help but think of my grade school teachers using the same tactic while trying to gather the attention of kids in a classroom. As the conversations go on, we are not far off from that scenario.

"We can't let that thing stay inside him," Bianca says with a tone that means business.

This is a side of her I've not seen other than the night of the attack. The determination in her eyes is something I admire.

"What choice is there?" Roman asks and I don't think he means it in a patronizing tone but a genuine inquiry.

What real choice do we have on what's happening?

"Mel," Bianca says, and before she is even done, Brandon is already shaking his head at her words. She continues, "he might not be able to retrieve the magic from him, but he might know what we're up against. The better informed we are, the better prepared we will be to face whatever is ahead."

I can't help but smile because she's Brandon's perfect match. Her reasoning cannot be topped. Whatever argument Brandon has at the tip of his tongue doesn't make it past his lips.

King Oscuro looks half defeated when he gestures for everyone to take a seat and moves to his desk. "I hate to say it, but I think Mel might have answers for us."

"Great." Bianca sits with her hands clasped on her lap. "When do we depart for the underworld?"

"We?" Roman asks, moving next to Brandon behind the desk.

Brandon looks around the room. He gestures in my direction. "Janelle and Santiago can stay. There is no need for them there."

"Yeah, too many people might attract attention while traveling," Roman adds.

Brandon pads his back. "Exactly why you will stay behind."

"Hey," Roman rounds on his brother. "Why do I always have to stay behind?"

"Your job is to lead the Royal Force," Jesse reminds him. Causing Roman to begin bickering.

"Enough," Brandon interjects. "Bianca, Jesse and, of course, Matias will go to the underworld. But we can't simply show up. I will send word to Gabriel to meet us at Fierno. His brother is difficult to deal with. I'm hoping that in exchange for a visit with his brother, he'll be more willing to share with us."

"That being said." Santiago rises to his feet. "We should get going."

Santiago stops at my chair and gestures for me to join him. I don't say anything to the people gathered around as I follow him out of the room. Right before shutting the door, I hear the beginning of Roman arguing his point for joining. Unlike Bianca's, he has no basis for winning.

"I will walk you to the nursery," Santiago says.

I look at him and realize this might be the only time he has spoken to me, unless absolutely necessary. His tone even sounds friendly and warm. I heard it before when he spoke to others, but never directed at me.

"You don't have to do that," I say.

"I don't mind paying Isabel a visit. I haven't seen her in days."

I don't care if he walks in the same direction that I do, so I don't argue with him further. We arrive at the nursery and join Isabel. I go straight to work and leave them to have a social visit.

Before Santiago departs, he finds me watering plants.

"If you want to come to the library for dinner, I will continue my research." He looks around uncomfortably. "We are still doing that, right?"

"Yeah," I say. "I need to look for the family tree."

"I will see you there."

With one last look around, he leaves.

CHAPTER TWENTY

JESSE

Lies hide the truth, but with every lie that falls from her lips, I learn of her intentions. My hope gets stronger with each deceit she utters and I breathe easier. My gift allows me an insight no one else has. The ring in my ears is a light in my darkness telling me to hold on.

I can't help but daydream about what would happen if I ask a different question. Would she keep lying?

"Jesse." Brandon waves a hand in front of my face. "Are you listening?"

I nod, but I've definitely checked out.

Matias' revelation about the Red Book being inside his head is not easy to digest. I look at a clock on the wall and see that it has been a few hours since the news. We are all inside Brandon's library with Lexi Blue, trying to see if there is something here that can help Matias. Nothing here is even close to the date of the Red Book. In other words, there are hardly any texts older than it. Its magic pioneers ours. There is no way to understand its creation.

We leave the small library none the wiser.

"How did she take the news?" I ask, referring to Bianca.

Brandon doesn't ask me to elaborate. He walks towards the window and looks down at someone. "She is currently digesting the information in the gardens."

I nod not knowing what else to say. She seems to do better in her thoughts out there.

"He is all she has. I can see in her eyes the fear of losing him," Brandon says.

I can only imagine what she might be feeling. Bianca was a child when her parents died. She found Matias and in him a family. Now his fate is uncertain.

"She is not alone. She's an Oscuro for what matters." I clear my throat. "So is Isabel, Lexi, Alejandra and Matias. We are a mixed match bunch," I say.

"A family that makes the weight of our responsibilities worth it." Brandon smiles my way and I realize this is the first real smile he directs at me in a while.

"Is there anything I can help with meanwhile?" I ask, changing the conversation.

He moves away from the window. "We received word from Gabriel an hour ago. We are departing in two days." He tosses a piece of paper across his desk in my direction. "I need you to pick a handful of guards to join us."

"Why me and not Roman?" He is consistently involved in this part of every trip.

"He is still sulking about not going." Brandon rolls his eyes.

I nod, understanding Brandon wants this done as quickly as possible. "Consider it done. I'll have a list by tomorrow morning," I say.

He touches his chest. "You almost sound like the old you."

"I don't think any of us are the same after the attack. The castle itself changed."

I can see it now more than ever. It started with the vacancies. Those who departed in fear of war have no inclination to return after the danger has passed. The safety that once ran the halls is now gone. The way people look at Janelle is another. Despite her lack of magic, they look at her like a risk.

"That's true," Brandon admits.

He rises to his feet and walks back to the window. With the expression on his face, I have a very good guess who has captured his attention.

He clears his throat. "There is no shame in admitting we all need our person to feel whole. You were missing yours, that is all."

"Could it be that she is my person, but I'm not hers?" I look down at my hands. I can't ignore that once upon a time Janelle was destined to another. Her soul was tied to another man. A man, the Fates chose for her. "I think Janelle is just fine without me while I'm lost without her."

Just like that, the reality of my situation comes out.

Brandon has a way of allowing the surrounding space to feel safe. Safe enough to witness the most vulnerable pieces of me. Thinking back, it might be his openness to let anyone see how much he cares for Bianca and his kingdom. His openness is wielded like strength. How have I ever seen it to be anything else?

"Janelle is a skilled liar." He finally breaks the silence. A glint in his eyes.

I think of all the lies she has told me recently. Every time the ringing echoes in my ears. How each time that tone registers, a leap of hope spreads in my chest.

"Do you hear it?" Brandon asks.

I nod in confirmation.

He chuckles loudly. "I bet you are holding onto that hope for dear life."

"You have no idea," I say with a hollow smile.

"She is trying Jesse. I can see it." He holds my gaze.

"It's never going to be enough I fear." I run my fingers through my hair.

He tilts his head. "Enough for who?"

I start to say something but stop. I don't know the answer. Enough for me? I am fighting the urge to reach for her every time I see her. Even when she isn't in my space, I have to keep myself from thinking of her. That leaves the people she hurt inside the castle, and I know that there is nothing she can do to make it up to them. Even her *gift* cannot heal that pain.

But she is trying. She has taken her time to help Matias instead of focusing all her energy on finding her father. If getting her magic back was truly the only reason she was here, today wouldn't have happened.

Brandon nods at the silence. I don't have to tell him my conflicting emotions and thoughts. He can see right through me. Does the color of my soul tell him as much, or is he looking deeper, trying to piece together what is wrong with me? And therefore, how he can help me.

"Then stop. If you're asking for permission, you have it. If you are waiting for them to approve of her, they never will."

We have come to the same realization.

"This was never meant to be easy, huh?" I ask my wise, all-knowing, little brother who knows more than anyone the value of love and freedom don't come hand in hand.

I should have known that all the years of sneaking around, stolen glances, and secret smiles would end this way. The shared moments as children and troubles as adults pointed towards a never-ending problematic relationship. Yet, not once did I imagine myself with anyone else.

Brandon chuckles and looks out the window once again.

"It can be, but not with her. Would you rather have it easy with someone else?"

Never.

CHAPTER TWENTY-ONE

JANELLE

Isabel and I focus on work for the remainder of the afternoon. As on the day prior, there isn't any conversation between us. Instead, we work in a comfortable silence that is almost therapeutic. All the questions I have regarding the upcoming events are organized in my mind. As the minutes tick by, I get more eager to go into the library and search for answers.

As we begin cleaning up for the day, I hear the front doors opening and no other than Roman walks inside, this time alone. His expression seems solemn until his eyes find Isabel outside the small office, locking up for the day.

"Did you secure a spot in the departing party?" I ask as he reaches me.

His good humor drops as he shakes his head. "I always miss all the fun."

"What fun?" Isabel asks with furrowed brows.

Roman leans over and places a gentle kiss on her forehead. "I will fill you in during dinner." He turns in my direction and nods. "Janelle," he says.

Isabel plants her feet on the ground and pulls back on Roman's hand. She turns to me with a soft smile. "No more baskets tonight."

"Great." I put two thumbs up before gathering my things to depart.

"You can come and have dinner with us. Would you like to?" Isabel asks.

A pitty invite to eat with them in the dining hall. I've hit rock bottom.

Her expecting eyes are the complete opposite from Roman's bored gaze. He doesn't think this is such a great idea. As a matter of fact, neither do I. The last thing the brothers need is to be seen as giving me any type of friendship after everything.

"I have plans," I tell her.

She thinks I'm lying. It's obvious from her expression. Her eyes don't shift, as if waiting for me to change my mind.

"I'm meeting Santiago." Not a lie. "I told him I would eat dinner with him already."

I give them an apologetic smile. That's only half a lie. I did tell him I would go during this time, but not for that reason.

"That's nice of you," Roman says, then pulls Isabel after him.

She waves me goodnight as she is rushed out of the room.

I make my way down to the library and wonder if I should stop at Pad's first, but decide against it. I will see him tomorrow morning with Amy Bee. There's a grunt stuck in my throat when I think about her. I shake my head and focus on my task ahead. If Santiago mentioned dinner, I imagine there would be food involved.

The library is dead silent when I walk in. The small wooden desks that are often filled with people hunching over papers are now empty.

"There you are," Matias says with a smile. His hands are full with a big tray of food items. "I got enough for everyone."

"About time," Santiago says, coming from somewhere in the back of the library.

"Oh, you are here," he says to me, disinterested.

I cross my arms. "You told me to come."

Santiago helps Matias lower the tray to the same table we occupied the night prior.

"Oh, you're sensitive today, huh?" He mocks me, then tosses a piece of bread my way. "Come eat, you are obviously hungry."

I take a bite out of the bread I caught and join them on the table. Hunger has finally caught up with me. When I'm full, there's still a bit of food left on the tray. Thanks to the boys it doesn't last there much after.

"How are you?" I ask Matias.

He gives me a look while still chewing.

"I will take that as an answer."

"No, it's not bad," he says after swallowing. "Bianca and I spoke. I think not having secrets between us is better. We feel better, you know."

I don't, but I nod like I do. I never had a close relationship with my siblings the way Matias and Bianca do.

"Alright, let's start looking at some of these books so we can free up some space." Santiago leads the way by pushing his plate of food to the side and picking up a book.

I'm certain that the clutter annoys him more than anything. It might be why I was invited tonight. I open a book and begin going through a family tree. Matias does the same with one hand on a book and the other on his spoon.

The light in the room dims, announcing the sun setting outside. Other than a few coming in and out of the library asking for Santiago's help, nothing interesting happens. My eyes grow tired and my yawning grows in frequency.

A gasp from Matias has me rising to attention.

"What?" I ask.

He turns the book in front of him to me and slides it across the table. Careful not to toss some of the other books that clutter the space, I pick it up.

The page features the family tree of a witch family. I look closely at the faces of each and every person who is shown but no one jumps at me.

Santiago moves behind me, too impatient to wait for me to be done.

"Pazduelo." Santiago points over my shoulder at the family name. "Why does it sound familiar?"

"There is no room for fear here." Matias taps his chest with a close fist. "I recognize her." He points at a photo at the bottom of the page.

"Olivia Pazduelo. The infamous witch who was forced to marry a prince from hell," I say remembering all the times I heard her story.

Santiago shakes his head. "I've seen it somewhere else."

"Doesn't look like she or any of her sisters continue the family line." Matias gestures to the blank section of the book.

"Or the book doesn't know to add the names." I shrug.

"I know it was somewhere important." Santiago looks up to the ceiling deep in thought.

"How do these family trees get recorded into paper?" Matias asks.

"Magic," Santiago and I say at the same time.

Matias gives the book a grimace and I can't help but laugh.

Santiago shakes his head. "It's not like The Red Book. This magic is old and only cares to keep records. We have records of all influential families. Even the families in the human lands."

Santiago pauses staring into mid air. Without any explanation he rises and then disappears into a bookshelf. His footsteps are hurried.

"Where is he going?" Matias stares at his retreating figure.

I shrug, but I know whatever he just thought of is going to be good. There is no point in making guesses. I lean back, leaving my book aside and wait for Santiago. It's not long before we hear a hoot of cheer as the hurried steps grow closer.

He almost falls back into his chair, an excited smile playing on his lips. He taps an enormous book he places on the table. "I once read the history of Paz." He shrugs. "I was bored, believe it or not, but there are periods where there's nothing to do around here." He gestures to the space around us.

He opens the book in his hands and looks for one specific chapter at the front of the book. When he finds it, his grin widens.

"King Maxxon renamed the kingdom to Paz in honor of his wife Mia Pazduelo on her thirtieth birthday. They both passed peacefully in their sleep at 99. The crown was then taken by their eldest daughter, whose line continues to rule." He points down at the book. "These events are dated before the creation of the Red Book. Only a few years after the gates to the underworld were opened."

"A whole kingdom. What a gift," Matias says, looking over Santiago's shoulder.

"Mia Pazduelo." I point at the name on the family tree.

There are a total of three sisters on that tree branch. Next to Olivia Pazduelo and Mia Pazdulo is another woman named Maite Pazduelo.

"One married a prince from hell, and the other the King of the Human Lands. I wonder what happened to the third sister," Matias says.

"Have we unknowingly discovered a connection between a

witch family, the kingdom of the human lands and a prince from hell?" Santiago asks us with furrowed brows.

If this family is linked to the royal families in Paz it's not common knowledge. The ruling of Queen Mia Pazduelo was also so long ago that it's possible her name got lost in the marriages that followed.

"As curious as I am about it, there are more pressing matters at the moment. We don't have time to add another topic to our research." I point at Matias. "We haven't even addressed his magic and how he needs to learn to control it."

I control my expression and fight the shudder I feel every time I think of what Matias did at my fathers keep. It has only been a few days but we don't need Matias going off the deep end and resurrecting people.

"Already taken care of." Santiago looks almost proud that he's ahead. "He can begin tomorrow with Lexi Blue and Alejandra."

This seems to be news to Matias from the look of shock on his face. There is also a tint that colors his cheeks.

"Lexi and Alejandra?" he asks in a whisper.

Who is he nervous to be around? I wonder. Before I can ask any questions he yawns loudly.

"I feel like today was a total waste of time," Matias says.

I look over at the number of books we got through. We definitely have not gotten any closer to learning how The Red Book works but we did learn something valuable.

"At least we know that if the royal bloodline in Paz has magic, it very well means Klause could be there," I point out.

Santiago clears his throat. "Why don't we ask your friend to look for him when it returns from checking on Lord Duelo?"

"Good idea," I say.

Having Calaca look for Klause could lead us to more answers, but I do have my doubts about what it can accomplish. If Paz allows magic, a creature like Klause who is purposely trying to stay hidden will be impossible to find. But if there is something that can find him, it will be Calaca.

"I think it's time to go to bed." I get up and do a long stretch.

Santiago rises too. "Are we picking up where we left off tomorrow?"

"When will you be leaving for Fierno?" I ask Matias.

"Two days."

"Then we need to make every day count." Santiago reaches for the books we have already looked at and discarded. "I will put these back. Oh no, don't worry about it. I insist."

I roll my eyes at his mocking tone.

"How is rooming with Jesse?" Matias pushes his chair to the table and steps back to walk out of the library.

"What about Jesse?" Santiago asks.

I give him a side eye but don't answer.

"Do you wish things were different between you two?" Santiago follows us.

Looking back now, I regret many things, but Jesse will always be the biggest one. If I had stayed away when my father ordered me, he would've never known me and wouldn't have been hurt by my betrayal.

The day I left town, I made a promise to never repeat the mistakes of my past. I will never let anyone control me, and I will never betray anyone I love again. I will fight.

My eyes ache, but I fight the urge to rub them. "I love him," I confess. "I love him enough to want what is best for him, and that isn't me. Even if I wished for our friendship to be back. It never will, and that is for the best."

"That is selfless," Santiago says. A hint of something in his tone.

"Well, I do love surprising people."

"You never know what the future might have in store for you." Santiago gestures to the wood walls of the hallways. "I would be careful what I say out in the open like this. The walls talk and the whispers of your love might carry out to him."

There is no one in sight but us three.

"It's not a secret," Matias laughs and I give him a scowl that shuts him up.

"If we are done talking about me, goodnight," I say and part at the end of the hall to the right.

Matias is staying with Bianca in Brandon's suite, so I know he needs to go left, and I have no clue where Santiago stays, but he waves bye and returns to the library. His room might be on the other side of the castle with the rest of the staff.

When I finally make it to the room, I stop just before I open the door. My hand holds the handle lightly. I don't know if I'm hoping I will find Jesse in the shared space or not, but my heartbeat rises at the idea. Not even ten minutes ago, I admitted to my feelings for him. My skin crawls at the thought that he somehow heard. Stupid Santiago, putting ideas in my head about walls whispering.

Nothing is going to happen when I open this door. Then why am I so hesitant to push it open?

CHAPTER TWENTY-TWO

JESSE

When Janelle enters the suite, it's the first time in the past few days that I'm actually working. The list of soldiers who are able to accompany us on the trip is long. I have narrowed my search to a few names. I plan on paying them each a visit tomorrow morning to deliver the news.

"Hey there," I say, fidgeting with the papers.

She eyes me. I'm ready to rise and say anything that would prolong her from going into her room, but she joins me instead.

"You're here early," I say.

I wonder if it's obvious to her how hard I am trying to make conversation. Before she can say anything someone enters the suite. Alejandra opens the door and stares between us. This might be the first time I've seen her near Janelle since she arrived. That is certainly not a coincidence.

I expected an exchange of words, or perhaps some sneers, but Alejandra promptly shuts the door behind her and walks to where we are sitting.

"It's no secret that I oppose you staying in the Black

Castle," Alejandra says while crossing her arms. "But do you know why?"

I've dreaded even the idea of this conversation. The memory still brings me guilt. The lovely, energetic sing-song creature that would walk through the halls of this castle stopped the night of the attack.

"It's.." I try to say but pause.

"My sister." Alejandra says cutting me off. Her glare tells me she isn't talking to me. "The same sister who crossed paths with your snake the night of the attack."

Her expression is pensive. The anger and disgust she once did not bother concealing now looks soften. Not completely gone. The frown is there, but the hatred is somewhat mellow.

"Sofia loved Pad. She would've loved to know that he no longer lives in so much pain." She shifts in place, looking uncomfortable. "You should try that healing gift of yours on Matias. His mental discomfort might lessen."

That's actually a great idea. Janelle's expression tells me she hadn't thought of it before.

"Goodnight," Alejandra whispers in my direction and retreats, exiting the suite to her own room down the hallway.

I hardly have time to process what just happened when the door slams shut. Not aggressively, but in a rush.

"I think she likes him." Janelle looks at the shut door for a second before turning in my direction. "I saw them talking in the gardens."

"We all like Matias," I say.

There were a few conversations we had about welcoming him and helping him acclimate to the castle. His attitude towards us has held off any plans and his current predicament isn't helping.

"You don't like him like that." Janelle does a thing with her brows.

"What are you suggesting?" I cross my arms. There's a chance my question is coming off as obtuse, but it's not on purpose.

"I should get to bed," Janelle says and rises. "Goodnight."

"Wait." I call but she's already at her door.

I run after her and slip inside before she can close it.

"Jesse." She gasps and takes a step back.

She's looking at me like being inside her bedroom is scandalous and forbidden. The idea is incredulous. We've spent endless nights side by side watching the rays of the sun creep on the skyline.

"You shouldn't be here," she says between clenched teeth. "You need to go." She points at the door.

Rejection hits me square in the chest. It bleeds into anger. I feel it vividly under my skin.

"What the hell are you so scared of?" I ask. "Your dad isn't here to tell you to stay away. But if that's what you want you need to tell me."

"Nothing good will come of you being here." She points out to the hall again. "There we can have civilized conversations with minimal interaction. But here." Her head drops. "Jesse, stop making this so hard."

My anger bubbles higher with every word as the lack of a ringing in my ears tells me she truly believes this.

What I say will only matter as much as she will hear me out. If I don't say it now, I will always wonder why I didn't. I think of a way to lead the conversation there, but I don't think I have time. I'm one word from being tossed out. It's now or never

"I just want to talk." I raise both hands in surrender.

Realistically, I can approach her any other day, but I will be gone in two days and the idea I will carry this with me for much longer is excruciating.

218

"Janelle." I reach for her hand and she lets me.

Her hand is warm in mine. I don't remember the last time I did this, but I remember how much I miss it.

"This is not how things were supposed to be between us." I shake my head.

We have never called what we have anything other than friendship. As much as we both knew, it was so much more. We never said it. We never admitted to it out loud. Doing so now feels so fragile and raw. There's so much I'm not ready to say, but I think I have put it away for far too long.

"The night of the attack changed it and there is no going back," she says and her eyes don't meet mine.

There is a truth there. The remainder of what is here cannot fit in the mold we used to have. We would have outgrown it, anyway. At one point or another this feels unavoidable.

"Perhaps not back, but forward. A new version of what we were once supposed to be." My eyes plead, but her gaze is firmly downward.

"What do you want from me?" She fidgets with her hands.

"Everything."

The palms of her hands bear the marks of her time in the nursery, but they've become significantly more capable than they were a year ago.

"I have nothing to offer. Even then, in all my riches and glory behind a golden cage, I could've offered you nothing, nothing but a death sentence at the very least."

I take mock offense. "You wound me for thinking me so vulnerable to your father." I sober my expression. "I would've saved you."

If only I knew the extent.

"I'm not the damsel in distress guys like you come to save." A tear trails down her cheek, and I catch it with my thumb. "I didn't love myself enough to stand up for me, Jesse. How could I have ever been able to love you right?"

The one tear turns into many. They trail a path down her face. I know objectively Janelle is an ugly crier, but I find her the most beautiful when she's open and vulnerable like this.

"Is that your only objection?" I ask, my heart leaping.

"I don't get a happy ending. Don't you get that?" She hiccups.

"Who says that?" I search her face and this time her eyes meet mine.

She shrugs. Her expression is defeated, and I see the fight leaving her.

"Janelle," I whisper, taking a step into her space.

"Yes," she says, out of breath.

"Shut up."

I seal my lips to hers and let the worries of the world fade away. This is the closest I've been to heaven. Who would've imagined I would find it strictly in the proximity of the fire spitting angel in my arms?

I pull away long enough for us to catch our breaths.

"I have always loved you, Janelle. I have loved you longer than I have done anything else in my life. My choice has always been and will always be you."

There is no other way for me to live. Brandon was right. There are many other choices that would be easier, but they wouldn't be her, and therefore wouldn't be for me.

The gleam in her eyes is full of something I missed seeing. I've taken it for granted for years. I never noticed it until the day it was gone.

"We will talk tomorrow." I kiss her forehead and force myself to walk out of that room.

Leaving her with her thoughts is the first step. Janelle has always been one to do better in her own thoughts.

As I lay awake in bed, I trace my lips. A smile spreads wide as the memory of my first time kissing those very lips comes back to mind. How could I ever forget? It was the first time I was kissed.

15 years ago

I watch her from a bench in the garden for about fifteen minutes before I make my way inside. She is still wearing her flowy red gown. Her hair is no longer in the elaborate swirl at the back of her head, but I love it this way, all over her shoulders, spilling like delicate flames showcasing under the party's lights.

Everyone has finally gone home. The event was hosted to celebrate Mrs. Duelos' 50th birthday. The first ball Janelle has been allowed to attend.

I saw her seconds after she entered the room. I witnessed how, for the first time, the rest of Puerto Quinn's high society finally realized the incredible beauty Janelle Duelo is. Dangerously so.

I take a bottle of champagne I managed to steal from the back kitchen and enter the room. She spots me as soon as I walk inside. Aside from a few staff members cleaning up for the night, we are the only two left. Janelle doesn't stop swirling in place. Her hair and dress swing with the motion, making her look wild and free. Her smile is contagious and rare to see in the open.

I chuckle to myself as I catch up. "What do we have here?" I set the bottle on the floor and put my hands on my waist, watching her.

"Tonight was the best night." She doesn't stop dancing.

I grab onto her hand and pull her to my chest. Once together, I swirl her in place. We continue her dance across the ball room. The music is no longer playing, and the tables are now put away, but the light is low, and the energy is in the air.

She wasn't allowed to dance much when the party was happening. Part of me wants to ask her why, but I know her relationship with her family is complicated and completely different from mine. The Duelo family has invisible rules they must follow without ques-

tion. Their family lives in a different town and practices a different culture. I don't understand all of it.

We hear voices approaching from the double doors. We both stop dancing, gasping for air with the adrenaline running through our veins.

"Don't let them find us just yet." She makes a run for the garden.

I don't hesitate to run after her, stopping just to grab the bottle of champagne from the floor. The garden lights are a few and far in between. We make our way to the gazebo hidden behind a line of trees on pure muscle memory. We can't really see our way there and don't use magic to illuminate the way. Once the solid wood of the gazebo comes into view under the beams of moonlight, we burst into laughter. We are too far from any house windows, so we don't hold back.

We let our backs hit the ground side by side. Our hands grace each other as our breathing gets back under control. The chill of the night cools down my heated skin.

"Have you ever been kissed before?"

Her question is out of left field. It makes my laughter stop for a second, and then it starts again at the absurd idea.

"I think not," I say, out of breath. A playful tone to my words from both the acceleration of the night and the wine. "I have done my fair share of kissing, but I have never been kissed."

Without hesitation, Janelle leans over to me and places the sweetest kiss on my lips. "You now have been kissed, Jesse Oscuro."

My brain short circuits.

Her hand is still on my cheek but has moved her face back. I don't know exactly what comes over me, but I close the distance between us. My fingers sink into her hair as my lips trace hers. I cup her face with my palms and marvel at how soft her skin is compared to the roughness of my hands.

Janelle Duelo is the farthest thing from soft or delicate I have ever known, yet at this moment, in my arms, she is. And what a privilege it is to be the one who witnesses it.

"Why?" I ask once we finally break away.

"I may not have control over many things in my life, but I get to control this." Her eyes pour into mine. "I decide, and my choice is you."

CHAPTER TWENTY-THREE

JANELLE

I'm certain the Fates are not awake this early in the morning. It's immoral and almost disrespectful to start before the sun is out. The view from my window is pitch black.

It's not beyond me to admit that I'm more than likely being dramatic. I love early mornings, but on my own terms. Being compelled to wake up early for work is something I don't enjoy. Whatever Amy Bee has in store for me is work-related. Certainly something to do with my healing gift.

As I approach the clinic, I hear a crowd of people. When I enter, I'm not surprised to see a gathering of about twenty just inside the doors.

"It's five fifteen. I was about to go get you," Amy Bee says with a chirpy voice.

The room is full of the senior citizen staff from the looks of it. I never noticed how many of them have canes. The selection of canes is impressive. Some are the standard black or wood, but others have fancy decoration wrapping.

"I'm here," I groan.

"As I was telling everyone, Janelle has a very special gift

that helps alleviate chronic pain." Amy Bee gestures to Pad. He's sitting on one of the chairs set in the middle of the room. "Pad, can attest that getting help with this gift was better than the herbs."

Pad rises to his feet and does a little shake. "I feel brand new."

I know he's exaggerating. At the very most, he feels himself soothe off pain. What I don't get is why they have to sell the idea to these people. Living in pain and only having herbs to alleviate some of the symptoms should make my gift sound like a gift to them. No pun intended.

"I'm not letting that fire breathing demon touch me," a woman in the back yells. She is wearing big thick glasses that cover most of her face.

I almost forgot who I was to these people. It's not about accepting help. It's about accepting help from me. Allowing my blood-stained hands to help them is no simple thing.

"Alright," Amy Bee says as she reaches for the basket on her desk filled with herbs. She takes a bag and hands it to the woman in the back. "You can take your herbs and suffer in silence. As for the rest of you. If you wish to relive the old glory days where you walked pain-free, please make a line." She gestures to the side. "Janelle will see you in that room."

Inside the room, I find there is one observation chair and a stool. I take the stool and sit. For some reason, I pull on the sleeves of my shirt and wonder how many people are actually going to stay.

"Are you ready?" Amy Bee asks.

I give her a double thumbs up.

An old man enters the room. His cane is a deep green color. He says nothing as he hops onto the examination chair. I move to crack the door closed. I can't help but peek at the number of people who have lined up like Amy Bee told them to.

"Martha always has to make a fuss about nothing." He clears something from the back of his throat. "I didn't fear your kind back in the day, and I sure won't do it now."

I smile at the old man. Regardless of telling me I don't scare him, he's looking at me like I'm a person. He's also right that the old lady, Martha, is just making a fuss over nothing. Most of the people seem to stay.

"Back in my day, they called your kind coals," the old man says.

"Is that so?" I ask, taking a seat back on the stool. "I've never heard of that. Is it the name for my family or the city of Ignis?"

When people say "your kind", they usually refer to one or the other. I used to be able to tell which one by the topic but lately it has been hard to tell.

"The city, of course. Your kind are known to sustain fire far more than any other. The name went out of fashion and dragons came to be."

That name I've been called all throughout my life.

"Do you know about what year that was?" I ask.

"With my memory, I hardly remember to complete all my daily duties and I do them every day!"

Of course. I reach the old man and place my hand on his arm. I close my eyes and send healing energy to him. When I'm done, I open my eyes and find him staring at me with wide eyes.

"I hope that helps," I say genuinely.

"About fifty to sixty years ago." His words come out in awe. He touches his head and the smile on his face is bright. "I was in my twenties, so it must have been around that time."

"Thank you," I say.

The man takes my hand and grips it tightly. "Thank you."

I walk the old man to the doorway and let the next person

inside. Amy Bee supervises the whole time but tends to her usual tasks of the day simultaneously.

I finish in the clinic before I'm expected to be in the nursery and I decide to stop by the library. Santiago wouldn't be himself if he didn't at least research something regarding yesterday's newly gained information. If he's anything like I think he is, he is probably already at it. I can't deny I am curious.

The halls are quiet this early in the morning. Only a few guards are walking their perimeters as I cross the castle. When I arrive, I notice that the library doors are slightly ajar.

"You're lying." Jesse crosses his arms.

"Why would I do that?" Santiago waves his hands in the air. "I have no idea where she is, and if I did, you would hear my lies."

When I cross the threshold, his eyes snap in my direction. A curve at the edge of his lips kicks up.

"Why do you even need to know where she is, anyway?" he asks Jesse.

"That is not your business," Jesse shoots back.

Santiago rolls his eyes, then turns to me. "Hey Janelle, where have you been?" He leans over the desk and holds his face in his fist. "The masses want to know. What could you possibly be doing so early?"

I look between the boys. "I was at the clinic."

"Are you sick?" Jesse looks me over.

"No."

Santiago goes around the desk and takes my arm in his. "You can fill us in during breakfast. We are getting food." He looks over his shoulder to Jesse. "Are you coming?"

CHAPTER TWENTY-FOUR

JESSE

I walk behind Santiago and Janelle as we make our way to the dining hall. The breakfast crowd isn't as big now as it is during lunch and dinner. Since most of the castle staff begin their mornings at different times, there is a flux of activity.

Following a few steps behind, I witness for the first time how people look at Janelle. There are some who avert their gazes as she walks by, but others make a point of sending scowls her way. I can't seem to help my returning one as their eyes move from her to me close behind. They're quick to change their expressions when I meet their gaze.

I knew coming here with her would bring mixed emotions. The events from the past few months have been hard on everyone. I have found it hard to come to terms with what I feel for Janelle because of that but I can't stop the anger at witnessing her treatment.

If being with her would turn those scowls my way I know I am ready to receive them. I am more than prepared to take the accusations and betrayed expressions. I know there is no way to fully avoid them. I have made a choice and living with it is what I must do. I could have never chosen any other way.

Santiago wastes no time directing us to the food as soon as we walk inside. I watch as he takes a plate and piles a reasonable amount of food for a growing boy. I follow suit but notice Janelle isn't partaking.

"Why aren't you getting food?" I ask Janelle looking at her empty hands.

"I had something already," she says over her shoulder.

"Where?" I raise a brow.

"The clinic," she says. Then turns to fully face me. "Pad send some there for everyone."

Well, that is nice of him. I had no idea Amy Bee had that kind of arrangement with Pad.

I finish getting my food items with Santigo and lead the way to the same table I have been sitting at for years. I can feel more than see Santiago hesitate before following me and taking a seat. Janelle chooses to sit next to him and across from me.

I try to avoid looking around because I know I will be getting odd looks from people around us. It's not their fault that they are curious but I can't scowl at every resident of the castle. It isn't on my agenda for today. Soon enough the sight of Janelle and I eating and walking side by side will be old news. Nothing to gossip about.

Perhaps that is just wishful thinking on my part.

"Well hey there," a guard says while he sits beside me.

However, the greeting is directed at Janelle. For his sake, she doesn't answer him. Just gives him a blank stare that fills me with some type of ridiculous pride.

I feel like a child ready to jump up and scream, "see she won't talk to you, but she talks to me."

"What? I thought after everything that happened we needed to stay away from the dragon, but she is here helping the elderly and supplying the castle with herbs." He holds his face with his fits and looks at her with the same puppy eyes I've seen him used on others.

I don't even bother telling him to stop. With those cheap tactics, he will bury himself. There is no way she will fall for them. Wait.

"Helping the elderly?" I turned my question to her.

"Please tell us more," Santiago says between bites.

Looks like I am not the only one who hasn't heard of this. The past couple of days, I've tried to not think of Janelle or follow in any of her footsteps. I've not been very successful, but I tried.

"Earlier today at the clinic," she says to me, then turns to West on my side. "How did you hear about it? It's only been a few hours."

West takes a bite from his apple. "The walls talk," he says between chews.

Janelle looks at the clock on the wall then at Santiago.

"I have to go," she says.

She picks up her plate and takes it to the trash.

"Wait." I chase after her.

I take her plate out of her hands. I move to the trash and empty it out for her. The act is so casual and so much like we used to be.

"Jesse, do you know what you are doing?" she asks, looking around anxiously.

I take a step closer into her space. "Definitely." I trace her lips with mine then take a step back. "Go on. I will find you later," I say.

Her eyes are open wide and if it wasn't for the slight tint of pink on her cheeks I would worry she was in shock. She turns to the hallway doors and swiftly leaves. I don't have to look around to know every eye is on me.

"That was subtle," Santiago grins in my direction.

What can I say, I can't help it. I could have never been able to.

CHAPTER TWENTY-FIVE

JANELLE

"Stop whining, it's your job," Matias says.

The large number of people coming in and out of the library is truly testing Santiago's patience right now. Lined up one by one in front of the help desk, they all patiently wait for him. Santiago rolls his eyes as yet someone else joins the line. He paints a fake pleasant smile on his face and goes up to help them. It's an awfully busy day at the library for lunch time. During meals it's usually when the halls are emptier, but that is not the case today.

Isabel and I finish early at the nursery. She is in a hurry to get back to Brandon. As their trip to Fierno nears, she needs to do a lot of the planning for them.

"Found anything?" Matias asks me.

I shut a book with a bang. "No."

Pad catches my attention as he looks around the library as if searching for someone. When his eyes land on me, he waves. He dashes through the crowd, stopping when he finally reaches my table.

"I need your healing magic," he says.

Getting straight to the point. I appreciate the lack of fake pleasantries.

I tilt my head. "Do you feel bad?" I healed him a couple of days ago and from his walking speed, he can't be in too much pain.

I reach my hand to him, but he waves me off.

"I need you to come with me." He clears his throat. "I'm afraid this person can't come to you."

I give Matias a look and he gestures for me to go ahead. I follow Pad out of the library, giving Santiago a wave and gesture that I will be right back. The sour look on his face might have more to do with the line starting to reform in front of his desk.

We walk down to the tower that houses most of the people who live in the Black Castle. We stop when we see a cluster of people outside of a door.

"My good old friend is in a lot of pain today. Do you think you can take some of that away?" Pad asks in a hush tone.

We reach the door and the people standing outside all turn to look our way. The first thing I see inside is a young woman hugging a distraught older woman. Amy Bee exits the room and greets Pad and me.

"What is she doing here?" the girl asks with disdain.

She looks familiar at first glance but I can't place her. Her bloodshot eyes and tear streaked cheeks pain her so differently from the times I have seen her walking in the halls. I remember her wearing the Royal Force uniform, she is one of Romans soldiers.

"She's here to help Martha, Liz." Amy Bee takes the hand of the older woman holding onto Liz. "There is no reason for your mother to be in such pain. She will recover from her surgery, but she needs her heart to rest. The pain poses too much stress."

The woman nods with tears trailing down her face. "Whatever she needs."

Amy Bee opens the door of the room and gestures for me to follow her. Pad is right behind me like a guarding shield to all the unfriendly faces. Most of the people in the room shoot me suspicious looks, but that is about it.

We go into an adjacent room from the living space and pause at the doorway. The woman on the bed is paper thin and pale. The moment her eyes focus on me, she trashes from side to side.

"No. Do not touch me, dragon!" she yells.

"Go ahead Janelle," Amy Bee encourages me.

The smell in the room is strong. There isn't a window to open and let the air circulate. I hold my breath as I take a step closer and realize this is the woman who refused my help earlier. She looks so bad I almost don't recognize her. Her hair is sweaty, plaster across her thin face.

"Stop, do not touch me." She looks around for help. "She will burn me. Don't let the dragon burn me!"

I don't think she is fully coherent. Her rambling sounds like a fever dream. Her medications must be creating hallucinations. I'm no stranger to this scene. I could count in my hands the number of times my mother was in this same position. Delirious on pain medication, healing from yet another injury caused by her condition.

"Janelle," Amy Bee says with a forceful tone.

I take the remaining steps to the bed and place my hand on the top of hers. She tries to fight me off her with her other hand, but she is too weak. I tighten my grip. I close my eyes and allow my gift to flow.

My focus falters for a second as her sharp nails pierce my skin. Small moon shapes of blood paint my hand as the healing light flows from me into her. Her strong, tight grip loosens as the pain in her fades. I can see the edges of her eyes go from strained to relaxed.

Her hand holding mine drops to her chest and I take a step back. My job here is done. Martha's daughter rushes to the bed and hugs her. Liz stays by the doorway, watching me in awe. Tears gather in her eyes and they fall one by one.

I don't expect her to say anything, but she surprises me as she follows me out of Martha's room.

"That is my grandmother. She was terrified the night of the attack. She lost many friends who couldn't outrun the fire." Wiping tears off her face, she continues, "What I'm trying to say is thank you."

"I hope she feels better," I say and mean it.

She might fear me, but she has a good reason. I know healing her today won't make everything better, but I hope it helps.

"Healing huh," Liz points toward my hands. "Who would've thought the dragon had something left?"

"The healing dragon." Pad saddles up to us. "I like it."

As I make my way out of the room Jesse steps inside. I first think he is here for me but the surprise in his expression tells me otherwise. He wasn't expecting to find me here.

"Janelle," Jesse says with furrowed brows and follows me out. "Amy Bee brought you to help?"

His guess is spot on. There really isn't another reason for my presence.

I nod.

"I am here paying a friend a visit. If you want to wait, I won't take long." He stops talking and picks up my hand for a close inspection. "You are bleeding."

The small nail shape indentations only have a little blood on them.

"It's nothing." I pull my hands away.

Pad, along with a few others, have stepped into the hall and are watching the exchange I'm having with Jesse. I feel like I am under a microscope.

"You can't heal yourself," he says.

I roll my eyes because I, more than anyone, know that to be true. The reminder isn't necessary.

"I need to go back to work." I give Pad a wave and head out. My job here is done.

Jesse doesn't follow when I move to leave but his eyes stay fixed on me until I round the corner. His expression is determined and I know he isn't done with me. At least not for today.

I make it back to the library and see that Santiago has helped all the people in his line. He is now with Matias, looking over a book.

"Did I miss anything?"

Both boys shake their heads. I don't let that discourage me. I sit back down and dive into the next book in my pile. The number of books scattered around seem to have increased but I know that isn't true.

We have been looking for days and a hint of Klause or the creation of the Red Book is nowhere in sight. It feels like just when we think we make a discovery, even more questions arise. My focus is on any text written around the time Klause wrote his journal to see if they happen to mention any of his movements. While Matias is searching for family trees that could give us direct links to people who were around Klause. Santiago is focusing on old text that guesses on the magic behind the Red Book.

"It would have been nice if you told me you would be here," Jesse says as he takes the empty seat at our table. "I thought you were working at the nursery."

"I usually am," I say, only looking away from my book for a second. "But I got out a little earlier today."

"Because?" he asks.

"Does she need to report her every move to you?" Matias asks. "I missed that rule."

The harsh tone has Santiago and me turning to look at him. I would characterize Matias as a funny, bubbly guy. Hard tone and daggers for eyes isn't like him, yet that is exactly what he is doing now. All directed at Jesse.

"He hasn't had lunch," Santiago interjects before Jesse can respond. He rises to his feet. "Let's get some. I'm starving." He pulls on Matias's sleeve until he rises too and follows him.

"I wanted to find you to give you this." Jesse puts a small jar between us.

I stare at it but make no move to take it. Sighing, he picks it up and takes off the lid, then scoops a small amount of ointment into his index finger. He takes my injured hand and applies the ointment to the marks. They are no longer bleeding, but the ointment soothes the small sting.

"Can we talk?" he asks.

"I'm busy." I open another book and start looking.

It's a book from Matias's pile, not mine but I don't want to admit I took the wrong one. I scan the page and search for Klause's name amongst many names on a family tree.

"You can't talk because you are busy?" He looks at the packed table. "Looking for what, exactly?"

I roll my eyes but put my book down long enough to say, "I'm looking for Klause's family tree." I open my book again and begin going down the names on the page before me.

Jesse picks up a book and opens it to the first page. His eyes run down the page slowly.

I close my book. "What are you doing?"

He doesn't look away from his book. "Helping you."

"I don't need help." I sound like a petulant child.

"I wish to speak to you about what happened yesterday,

and you said you're too busy, so I'm helping you finish here so we can talk." He taps the open page. "If you don't mind, I'm trying to read."

I can't fight the curve at the edge of my lips. I want to touch the path he traced while kissing me.

Shaking my head, I refocus on the book before me. I can't keep looking at the same page for too long before he notices I'm daydreaming. Turning the page without looking could cost the cause greatly.

"Oh, you're still here." Matias hands me a plate of food while giving Jesse a disapproving expression. "We didn't bring you food."

"I did." Santiago drops a plate in front of Jesse.

The 'traitor' expression Matias shoots Santiago is comical.

"I'm not here to give her a hard time," Jesse tells him.

"Sure." Matias crosses his arms.

"Grr," Santiago mocks. "You two are adorable." He gestures between Jesse and Matias.

A blank expression takes over Matias. His arms drop to his sides. At first I think his reaction is because of Santiago's comment, but as seconds pass, a shock of awareness fills me.

Something is going on and I would bet it has something to do with the entity living inside him. Jesse is staring at him too, his book long forgotten. Santiago, on the other hand, is deep into his food plate.

"What is happening?" I ask, slowly reaching for his hand.

The second my hand touches his, Matias gasps loudly. His breathing is erratic and eyes are wild. I'm on my feet and rounding the table to his side. Jesse is next to me instantly.

"Are you okay?" Santiago asks, finally clued into the situation at hand.

Matias looks between us, then to the door.

"Calaca," he whispers. "It's back and wants to speak to us."

He gets up and takes a shaky step forward. Jesse reaches for him and offers him his shoulder. Matias leans on him as they make their way out of the room.

"Calaca?" Jesse asks me.

"Yeah, it has a way of talking to him in his head. We sent it after my father."

Maybe it found him. I look over my shoulder to find Santiago following us with his plate of food in hand.

"Santiago," I say in disbelief.

He stops chewing long enough to ask, "What?"

I shake my head. Am I even surprised?

I make quick work of taking the cursed book with me. If my plan works this might be exactly what we need to get all the answers we have been searching for. It doesn't hurt to take a shot in the dark.

CHAPTER TWENTY-SIX

JANELLE

We avoid taking the hallways that lead to the dining hall. They are the busiest at this time of the day. A few groups of soldiers send us curious looks, but nothing too alarming about the fact that we are all walking into the forest together.

When we reach the edge of the border, we all slow down. Just like last time, every step feels like it's underwater. The full force pushing against us is not enough to stop us, but enough to weigh us down. After we make it through, the air feels freer. The load on our limbs goes back to normal.

"I can walk now," Matias says and steps out of Jesse's hold. "I was just caught off guard and I felt dizzy, but I'm fine now."

"Are you sure?" I ask him.

He shoots me a scowl. I raise both hands in the air. He is being testy.

"Calaca?" Matias calls.

The clearing is empty, and the forest is quiet. The thought that this could be a trap crosses my mind a second before Calaca steps out of the treeline.

At the sight of the creature closing in on us, Jesse moves to my side. His hand takes mine and I don't fight it. I don't fear Calaca and I doubt he does, but it feels nice to know he is here.

I don't need magic to feel powerful when he is by my side.

"I come with news," Calaca tells us in a deep voice.

I look around to make sure we don't have an unsuspecting onlooker near enough to listen.

"Santiago," I say, looking back at the castle.

He is standing about twenty feet back.

"I'm listening from here," he says with obvious dread.

"He's afraid?" Jesse asks with a chuckle.

I shake my head in disbelief. He's still holding on to his lunch plate, scooping the remaining content with his spoon.

"I have found Lord Duelo. He has not relocated from where you departed."

"What?" Jesse looks between me and Matias. "There's no way."

"He must be scouting out the next hideout," I say.

I try to think of all the other possibilities. He should've done that by now, but I don't know what he has been up to. It's been nearly a week since we departed.

I look at Jesse. "That or he really doesn't think we would go for him there."

Jesse shakes his head. "We are. Brandon wanted to pay a visit on our way back from Fierno. We expected to find the place empty."

"He is waiting for us to take the fight to him," I say.

"I need to talk to Brandon. We're departing tomorrow for Fierno. We're going to have to take a bigger set of soldiers and pay Duelo a visit." Jesse runs his hands through his hair.

Matias looks at me with apprehension.

I can't help but try to reassure him. "Brandon knows you are not trained in combat. No one expects you to use your magic and join them. You and Bianca will more likely be asked to sit back. ”

After all I have seen these past couple of days, Brandon will do everything in his power to talk Bianca out of joining as well. Reminding her that someone needs to keep an eye on Matias might do the trick.

Jesse takes in Matias' expression.

“Yeah.” His tone is not too convincing.

I know he is thinking that Brandon will try, but whether or not Bianca follows directions is not truly up to him.

“I'll keep you safe,” Calaca vows.

Matias gulps, but I can see how the creature gives him some kind of reassurance. I wonder if it's the Red Book that creates some type of connection between them. It definitely comforts him.

“Calaca.” I step forward. “We need you to find someone else. This person might be impossible to find, but we want you to at least try.”

“No one can hide from me,” it says.

“This individual has gone unnoticed for so long that we have completely forgotten about their existence,” Santiago says, still standing near the shield.

“An old being?” Calaca turns my way.

“Klause. P.” I give the cursed journal to Calaca.

Calaca sniffs the book and turns it on its bony hands slowly.

“Ahh,” Calaca makes a noise of familiarity.

“You know him?” Matias asks with wide eyes.

“I don't forget a thing.” It turns to me. “An old creature indeed.”

“Creature is one way of describing it.” Jesse crosses his arms. “We will depart for Fierno tomorrow. After Fierno, we will visit Duelo at his hideout. If you find Klause, you can meet us on the way."

Calaca turns to Matias. "I will not be long."

Matias nods.

Jesse turns in my direction. "We'll talk tonight."

Before I can say anything he is jogging towards the forest. I watch him go, realizing the only thing in that direction is the Fates temple. Brandon must be there paying them a visit.

Santiago waits for me and Matias to make it to the edge of the shield before turning back to the castle.

"I told Alejandra I would take you to train with her and Lexi Blue today," Santiago says.

Matias looks between us with a sour expression. "Will you stay with me?"

"Yeah of course we will." Santiago gives him a gentle smile. In a hush tone he says to me, "His separation anxiety is getting worse."

Matias obviously hears him and shoots him a glare over his shoulder.

"Lexi Blue is going to bring a couple of volumes from her personal collection for us to go through. Hopefully we can find something there."

Instead of going directly inside the castle we walk to the training circles where a group of cadets are sparring.

"I hope to start training again once we are back from this trip," Matias says with enthusiasm.

I look over at Santiago who mirrors my expression. It's probably not the best idea to have Matias train with anyone until we get that book out of him. Even simple sparring might be dangerous to whichever cadet finds themselves facing him.

We find Lexi Blue and Alejandra setting up a table with chairs and books off to the side from the training circles. We are situated on the other side of the locker rooms keeping us out of sight from where the cadets are sparring but anyone coming in and out of the locker room can easily spot us.

"Why are you so stiff?" I ask Matias.

I noticed the posture and tension on his shoulders. He was not like this a couple of minutes ago.

"Hi," Alejandra says to Matias in a soft tone. Her eyes move from me to Santiago. We don't get a greeting. It's more like a murmur under her breath.

"Lovely to see you too," Santiago says with a frown. He ignores her and moves to Lexi Blue. "I brought him here as promised. Now where are the books?"

She gestures to a brown box under the table.

Lexi Blue moves towards Matias, not bothering to greet me or Santiago with more than just a head nod. She leans closer to him and says something I can't hear from where I stand. If it was even possible, Matias becomes even more tense.

"Let's go easy on him Lexi," Alejandra says, then steps back at the sharp look directed her way. "Lexi Blue." She clears her throat. "He's not comfortable tapping into his magic until he can differentiate his from the book's."

It's evident that Matias and Alejandra have talked about this before. Lexi Blue looks from Alejandra to Matias then waits until he nods.

"I can help you with that." She takes his hand in hers and closes her eyes. "There it is. The dark smokey one has to be The Red Book's magic. Yours is the other one. The silver color one."

Matias' eyes are open wide and staring at Lexi Blue like she grew another head.

When he doesn't react she opens her eyes. "Can't you see it?" she asks.

He shakes his head. Lexi Blue lets out a huff of impatience.

"Let's try this." She gestures for him to extend his arms and allow magic to flow.

"We can get through these while they do that," Santiago says, lifting a couple of books from the box to the table.

I nod and take one from his hands. I force my eyes to focus on the page and not turn to see how Matias is doing. A few cadets find us and stick around at the edges to see what is happening. A glare from Alejandra is enough to send a few of them scurrying away but not everyone.

They attempt for a few hours to make the magic flow, but other than a few shows of power Matias isn't very fluent. However, the attempts at tapping into his magic leaves him exhausted.

Santiago closes the last book of the small pile and sighs. "We tried," he says.

We didn't find anything useful, but I don't think either of us thought we would. Lexi Blue is known for her brilliance and if there was anything worth finding she would have already.

"Why isn't she helping us go through text in the library?" I ask, gesturing to Lexi Blue.

"She is in her own way." Santiago points at Matias quickly approaching us and begins to pack up. "She is fascinated by the powers of the Red Book and has spent the last few days taking books from the library to dissect."

I don't have to know she hasn't been able to find anything. It's in the low cast and tiredness written all over Santiago.

"We just got started. It's been only a few days. Maybe Mel will give us something on our visit that will lead us the right way," Matias says with optimism.

I am not sure the answer lies with a creature of the underworld, but Brandon must know what he is doing. No stone needs to be left unturned.

"Let's grab dinner then keep searching in the stacks we

have at the library." Santiago leads the way out of the training grounds.

We spent more hours in the library, and the only difference made is the number of books left on the table. Even after my eyes grow tired, I push myself. Once I realize my eyes can't focus, I call it a night. The boys are more than happy to stop.

I don't miss how Matias goes to the gardens instead of his wing of the castle. His sneaking glances tell me exactly who he is planning on seeing and why Santiago and I didn't get invited.

"Does he think he is fooling anyone?" Santiago asks, staring after Matias.

I chuckle. "How do you know?"

"Oh, I followed him." At my stunned face, Santiago chuckles. "I can't help my curiosity." He shrugs unapologetically.

He sneakily walks after Matias into the gardens. I shake my head but move to the closest window that looks out into the gardens. I watch in awe at how Santiago walks straight to Matias and Alejandra and sits between them. He taps their knees playfully.

The cerise shade Matias turns into tells me everything I need to know about what Santiago could be saying. Poor thing.

The idea of going to my room and talking to Jesse makes me restless. I feel like I have said it all already. What else can I possibly add?

I could dive deeper into that feeling and acknowledge that the fear of finally accepting something between Jesse and me isn't what scares me, but the outcome. The hope of what motivated me to keep going for so many years. The disappointment of failure is too great.

Instead of dissecting that trail of thoughts, I decide to keep myself busy by making a few visits. I stop at the kitchens first. I find Pad running through recipes for the upcoming week. His presence is soothing and comfortable to be around.

Afterwards, I go by the clinic. The uncomfortable back and forth I have with Amy Bee is enough to send me straight to my bedroom. She didn't see a need for me to place any form of social call and I honestly should've known better.

I pace back and forth in my room. My eyes stray to the clock. I refuse to acknowledge just how long I've been doing this.

An opening and shutting of a door followed by footsteps give me pause. There's a knock on my door before the knob slowly turns.

"Jesse," I say as he stands on the doorway.

My heart rate rises with every step he takes my way. I want to run and hide, but from what, I'm not sure. He is a foot away from me and I am all consumed by him.

"I..." I want to say I can't and I won't, but the objection dies on my lips. "The thought of things going wrong scares me. I've lost so much and you are by far the best part left of me."

The truth has been spoken, but I feel less free. That's the thing. If I'm honest with myself, there is a part inside me that clings on to the notion of Jesse as part of me.

"I have no clue what this would look like, Janelle." His eyes pour into mine and suddenly I feel light as a feather. "I will see to it with you. Together, we will figure it out. One step at a time. All you have to do is stay."

I close my eyes and picture it. For the first time, the image that conjures in my mind isn't one of impossibility. It's an image so close to my reality that if I stretch my hand out, I can touch it.

Will the fear of the burn stop me from reaching?

"I can only push so far. What would it be?" he asks in a whisper.

There has always been only one choice, and I made it a long time ago in a gazebo under the night sky drunk on champagne and dreams. Just like that night, I take a leap.

I take the fabric on his shirt in my hands and fist it tight. There is no going back after this. I pull him down to me and this time it's me who dips in first.

To his lips I say, "my choice is you."

CHAPTER TWENTY-SEVEN

JANELLE

"Where are you going so early?" Jesse asks in a groggy voice.

This man can wake up at the entrance of a fly. I'm making a conscious effort to be quiet and even took extra precautions when getting out of bed.

"The clinic," I say, pulling pants on and throwing a shirt over my head.

A groan comes from him before he tosses the sheets aside and sits up.

"Fine, but you owe me."

"No," I say slowly. "You don't need to come."

"Don't be ridiculous. Why wouldn't I go where you go?"

Ridiculous, right?

"I will be leaving today." He pulls me to stand between his open legs. "I just got you and I'm leaving. It feels wrong."

It truly does, but I'm glad for the space. I need to think, and being around Jesse makes it hard. My thoughts get cloudy and hazy. It's hard to have a straight thought around this man.

"You will be back soon enough." I lean down and kiss the tip of his nose.

There are only a few people already waiting for me at the clinic. As always, Pad sends breakfast and Jesse makes quick work on scarfing down a big portion of it. Amy Bee gives him a scowl when she realizes the food is almost gone. Jesse can't do anything but smile at her sheepishly.

"I was hoping that would save me from making a trip down to the dining hall."

Amy Bee has the best disapproving scowl I have ever seen. I have the urge to apologize and it's not even directed at me.

"Sorry," Jesse says, but from the gratified expression on his face, I know he is not.

Amy Bee knows it too. The forced, pleasant expression on her face looks ready to snap.

"If you'll be here every morning, I'll tell Pad to send more over from now on."

I have the urge to tell her no, but Jesse beats me to it.

"Once we are back from the trip." He confirms with a nod.

"Speaking of the trip." Amy Bee moves to a side closet and pulls a bag. She hands it to me. "I heard Isabel was looking for this."

I open the bag and find a set of first aid kit items.

"It wouldn't hurt." Amy Bee smiles.

I don't mention the fact she could give her this herself. Being their messenger is feeling like a part of the job.

"I'll deliver," I assure her.

I heal the few people in the clinic and, just as quickly, I'm on my way to the nursery.

"You don't need to walk me there," I say.

I'm holding Jesse's hand in mine and the action feels so natural. We cross paths with a few guards, but none of them spare us anything more than a nod.

The smell of dirt at the start of my day has grown on me. I associate it with peace and quiet. It doesn't feel that way when I spot Alejandra at the entrance of the nursery. She's in conversation with Isabel but it ceases when I'm spotted. I try to let go of Jesse's hand, but he doesn't let me.

Alejandra looks between us with a blanked expression. "Your presence is required at the King's office," she says in my direction.

"For what reason?" Jesse asks, but Alejandra just shrugs.

"You both will find out sooner the faster you make it there."

I expect her to go on her way after that, but she accompanies us to Brandon's office. When we reach the hallway that leads to his office, we hear a trail of voices coming from behind his closed door. The echoes of arguments carry through the open space. I can't make out the words and voices. However, they all sound familiar.

When we stand just outside the doors, the words finally become more clear.

"Well, isn't that naïve!" someone shouts from inside. "The choice to hold back will only cause further distress on their people."

"There is no reason to get loud," Brandon says. His tone is not angry, but drained.

"Don't you look at me that way. Before you were King, I changed your diapers!" That is the unmistakable voice of Dorty.

The young woman is a daughter of a royal house. Her family resides in Petra, better known as the City of Stone. They were the second stop in Brandon's tour earlier this year. I don't know her as much as I know of her. The few and far interactions we had were always in passing.

Alejandra opens the double wood doors and Jesse and I follow her inside.

Brandon frowns at Dorty. "So you say, but you aren't that much older. I always doubted your claims."

"The woman of the hour," Bianca says with a tight smile.

I look around me and see a large party of what I can only call royal offsprings standing there. I've met every single one of them multiple times growing up, but despite their faces being familiar, I never did much socializing past pleasantries. The Oscuro brothers are far closer to them, as they often gather in groups during events.

"Well, at least she looks good," James says.

That comment earns him an elbow to the rib by his oldest brother, Jill. The brothers belong to the Aether family from Helios. Their city is the farthest one from the Black Castle and the border. I know only one thing about the brothers and that's that the brothers are trouble.

"James is second in line for the Aether title. Let him at least try his luck for the Duelo royal line." Sabrina fans herself from a couch across the room. "Or has Jesse finally gotten himself out of the friend zone?" She searches my face for two blinks before laughing. "I guess not."

She's the only daughter of the Hue family. Her family resides in Gallalo, known as the City of Light. Their home was the first stop on the royal tour due to its distance to the Black Castle. Sabrina's attitude has always been as sharp as her tongue, yet she has always been good at staying under the radar.

I stared at the faces in the group. "What is this about?"

"The news of your return to the Black Castle has made its way through Puerto Quinn." Brandon walks to his desk and takes a seat. "There's outrage about the way your treatment here is being described."

"Outrage is one way of saying it. They are rioting for her return," Jill adds in with a smirk on his face. "The city of Ignis takes the mistreatment of their royal family seriously."

"Rioting?" I ask, looking at Brandon.

"Your father was not a Duelo by blood. The city of Ignis has denied him altogether. They deny his claims and his title in relation to their city. They have declared you their only living representative."

Brandon has chosen the words thoughtfully. A subtle reminder to everyone in this room. Regardless of relations and social power, that is all our royal titles carry. No one would dare say it out loud, but our social influence in our cities is far more dangerous than Brandon would like to admit. My father didn't turn on Brandon with the backing of Ignis because he knew they would never follow him. They never truly accepted him, regardless of how much he tried. My father married to become a Duelo. The city would never see him and one born a Duelo as equals. They all awaited the day one of my brothers would take over and rule. The day never came to pass, and it was all because of him. I can only guess how they all took that.

"You are the only living Duelo and they want you back," Jill says.

"My mother is still alive."

I don't know why I say it, but I can't help it. Ruling was never part of my path. I never truly dreamed of something farther than my freedom.

Sabrina laughs from her place on the couch. "She might as well be dead for all they care."

"They're not quiet about it. Riots, protest, you name it. They're not happy with the decision for the crown to punish you." Dorty reaches for me and places a hand on mine. "They want you to be forgiven. To them, punishing you is punishing them for something neither of you could have helped."

"Why would Ignis want me as their representative after everything?" I ask.

"You are royal, Janelle." Dorty's expression is serious and as sincere as I've ever seen it. "You have a name to live up to and the majority in this room can attest that it comes with a lot of sacrifice. We've watched you be molded into your father's puppet. How could any of us blame you for performing?"

"It happened to you, but it could've just as easily happened to us," James says.

"We have failed you." Dorty drops her hand from mine. "As a matter of fact, any of us could have ended up in your position."

"Ignis deserves better than me. I'm not worthy anymore. I don't think I ever was." Looking down at the floor, I gulp. "Perhaps it is time for another family to take over the royal title."

"Being perfect isn't what makes someone worthy of a title," Sabrina says.

"We cannot return her to Ignis just yet." Brandon leans over the table.

Dorty turns to Brandon and stares him down. "Don't you get sassy with me, King Oscuro. You cannot deny we're saying anything but the truth."

Brandon shakes his head. "The Duelo house is in shambles. They want her back, but she is not ready to take on her duties as the head of that family while her father is not found. There's too much room for him to sneak his way back."

"Give her to us. We will give her refuge." James nods at his brother for support.

"I think we have heard enough from your mouth." Jesse scowls at the youngest Aether brother.

James's lips spread to a wicked smile, delighted to have gotten on Jesse's nerves.

"Thank you," I say, out of words.

"Well, that's far more than I expected from her." Dorty points in my direction. "She has been reformed."

I step forward and look between Jesse and Brandon. Roman has now joined the impromptu meeting but is standing lazily by the door. There is zero concern in his expression. The tilt of his lip might indicate a level of amusement at the scene.

"I'm not done here. I appreciate all of you," I say as I turn about the room, making eye contact with every visitor who has traveled this far for me. "I wish to stay and finish what I've started. This way I will earn my magic and my title back. I want to bring honor back to my royal name. That would be the only right way I can accept my title."

"Novel," Jill says, and nods. He has always been short of temper and valued self-sufficiency the most.

"Now if you don't mind," Brandon opens his office door. "You're all welcome to stay, but we will depart soon for a pre-planned trip."

"Don't worry about us," Dorty says, leading the way out. "We have plans anyway."

"Yeah," James says with a smirk. He stops before Jesse and extends his hand. "No hard feelings?"

Jesse takes his hand and shakes it with a scowl firmly in place.

I try to catch his eyes after James steps aside, but he doesn't meet my eye. I can't help but feel like Jesse is upset at me for something.

"Janelle?" Brandon is still holding the office door, and I take it as my cue to leave.

"I will get back to my duties." I incline my head and turn to exit.

"They're right." I stop and turn back to Brandon. "Your rightful place is something I can't deny you. The Fates decided your title and birthright."

I want to convey my doubts about the Fates and what they have in store for me. It's understandable that I feel this way considering the challenges I faced as a child. But I say no such thing. Instead, I incline my head and retire back to my daily duties.

Trying to understand what has already been written by the stars is pointless. All the pieces haven't been played yet, and until then, making assumptions will only lead to questions.

CHAPTER TWENTY-EIGHT

JANELLE

I don't hear from Jesse or any of the Oscuro boys for the remainder of the day. My worry over the earlier interaction upsetting Jesse only grows when I don't hear from him by lunchtime. I skip lunch in favor of finishing my tasks early. I monitor the door, expecting him to show up any minute to check in, but he never does. Other than Isabel coming in and out, that door remains closed.

I walk into the library and find it more empty than usual for late afternoon. We still have a few hours until dinner, but I finished all the tasks ahead of time. As I always do with any spare time, I go to the library.

"Is Matias getting ready for the trip?" I ask, wondering why he isn't here.

"They already left." Santiago looks up from a paper to a clock, then back at me. "A few hours ago, actually."

"What?" I sit down and look at my hands.

Perhaps things are worse than I imagine. I can't even think of what exactly could've been the trigger. Leaving without a word isn't like Jesse. My eyes focus on a bit of dirt under my nails. I'm often diligent to clean it all out before I leave, but in my hurry today, there's still some left.

"Jesse didn't tell you? Trouble in paradise already?" Santiago asks.

I don't want to show that the comment hurts my feelings, so I push it aside.

"Did you hear about the impromptu visitors?"

He chuckles. "Who didn't? Royals can be such spectacles. There are actual fan clubs for them. Did you know?"

Now that is ridiculous. I give Santiago a side glance and he meets my eyes. A belly full of laughter erupts out of him.

"Do you want to know if you have a fan club?"

"Absolutely not." I get to my feet. "Actually, there is something I've been meaning to do."

Now feels like the best time to do it. For the past couple of days, I have been circling questions that have no answer. At least I have no answer for them. But the answers might be closer to me and I just need to reach for them.

The last time I went in, I was asking something of them. This might not be exactly the same scenario, but I'm seeking something. I don't want to get my hopes up, but I lose nothing by trying. After all, a small part of me just wishes to know if they would allow me in.

I make my way to the Fates temple. As I approach, the stone structure appears enchanting. The trees and leaves provide a contrasting green backdrop to the gray granite walls, only partially covered. The chirping of the birds blends into the magic of this place.

I close my eyes and remind myself I'm no longer the girl who once came here seeking help. Seeking freedom. The tightness that once shackled my wrist together felt like it would sink me in the waters of my reality. Now it all feels so vain.

From where I am standing, the problems that once made it hard to breathe seem like nothing.

Stepping inside, I ponder if I will be denied entry. I don't realize my eyes are closed for a second. The fear of rejection is just as bad as the fear of not knowing. I take a step forward and cross the threshold. The low glow of three figures above a small pool greets me. My feet are frozen in place. I have wanted to come here for so long, but now that I'm here, I can't seem to move forward.

"Seek what you wish to find, but ignorance is bliss for the feeble," the blue looking fairy says.

Her sisters don't look my way, choosing to stare at the water instead.

Goading me is exactly what I needed to move. I sit on a stone bench across the water fountain and take in my surroundings.

As soon as I realized my stay at the Black Castle was going to be longer than expected, I knew I had to make a visit. I once pleaded with the Fates to alter my future. I'm not sure exactly what I expect or hope to get from them, but if I'm making amends and turning things back around, I need to make this request.

"I'm trying this new thing where I make things right." A wave of shame passes through me. "I asked you once to change my fate. Would it be possible to change it back?"

"She is asking twice." The pink looks up from the water.

"Just to fix things," I hurry to say.

The gold floating creature moves closer to me. Its face is not human-like, but almost enough for me to make out an expression of comfort. "What is meant to be will be. Fate has a way of finding a way. One wrong choice does not alter the ending."

The words hit me like a punch to the gut. I am scared but

those words give me so much hope. I'm winded as tears gather in my eyes. The emotions floating are high. It's like everything I've pushed and compacted into my chest cracks open and is freely out for them to see. There's no point in hiding.

"I want to be worthy." A tear runs down my cheek and I wipe it with my palm. "I want to make up for all I have done."

The visit of the other royal offspring has reminded me there's a chance. I haven't been all bad. There is room for redemption and something to go back to. Not to mention Jesse.

"You have come here to ask us to make you worthy?" Their three faces, free of expression, close in on me. "You must not ask for something only you can do for yourself."

"I want the opportunity to make the right choice."

"You get that every day you draw a breath," they say in unison.

There's a chance for me to make it. The realization of this makes my chest lighter. Lately I've felt like I'm swimming against the current. My arms are getting tired and every time I look up to see my progress, it's not enough. There's so much more to do. I'm behind despite not taking a day off. I'm tired.

"What about Ray?" I ask, looking from one to another. "My soul was bonded to him. He became my soul bond after I asked for my fate to change. Can that be undone?"

There is a giggle shared amongst them. I wish more than anything to be in on the joke right now.

"You severed that the second your hand wielded the blade that ended him."

"Regardless," The pink one peers up. "You never meant to bond with him or anyone else. Not in this life."

"This life," I follow.

They giggle again.

"We may not meddle on bonds created in other lives. But

it's always fun to see them find each other in every life they live."

"Interesting," I say carefully. "Are you all telling me I've found my way to a bond I had in another life?"

Could this explain this unavoidable connection I've had with Jesse since childhood? Why we've always been magnetically pulled to each other.

"We cannot say." The pink one giggles again. "Go on and face the situations presented to you. The opportunities to do what is right will be plenty. It's up to you to bear through it or cower from it."

With that positive message, they all turn back to the water fountain. They point at different things displayed on the water and whisper amongst each other. I don't wish to overstay my welcome and make my way out the back door.

I cover my eyes from the sun as I take a step outside the temple. There is only one entrance and one exit on the opposite side, leaving me with a longer walk back to the castle. I start my journey feeling lighter than before. The sun is high up and I can feel the rays beating at my skin.

A noise that doesn't belong to the forest stops me in my tracks. I freeze and my senses are suddenly on overdrive. I strain to listen closely and catch a grunt and huff. I hear it again.

I'm not alone.

I hear it a couple more times. Whoever is making the noise is not trying hard to conceal themselves. I debate if I should go investigate or rush back to the castle. The bushes and tree tops hide it from sight, adding to my nerves.

I didn't tell anyone I would come out here. The decision felt safe, but I never counted on being hunted. Stupid thinking for someone with so many enemies.

Movement from a bush alerts me I'm too late for an escape.

A body flops down clumsily. An older man struggles to get to his knees. His clothes are dirty and bloody. He's clasping a hand to his stomach. His hair is plastered across his forehead, drenched in sweat. When he rises to his feet again, I realize it's Oli.

I run and kneel next to his body. There is a wound on his belly that profusely continues to bleed. I press my hands down on the wound to stop the bleeding. I close my eyes and push the healing magic against it. The continuous flow of blood tells me it's not working.

"The wound is too deep." I lean over closer to his face. "Oli, what happened?"

His eyes don't focus on me. I need to get him help soon. He has already bled so much. The hand I have on his belly isn't doing anything. I can feel a pulsing flow under my skin.

"There isn't much time," he says in a painful whisper. "He is coming for you, my girl. I had to warn you."

"Hold on," I say, getting to my feet. "I'm going to get you help."

I'm still a few miles away from the castle, but I need to get there as soon as possible. Running there and coming back with help isn't an option. It would take too long. I've never felt more powerless to not have magic. This is the time it would be vital.

I stand behind him and hook my arms under his. I lift up as much as I can then walk backwards in the castle's direction. If I had my magic, I would've been able to pick him up as light as a feather. With a single spell, I could have crossed the distance between us and the clinic. But there's no point in dwelling on the what ifs.

Oli is a big man, easily four times my size. Every few steps, I run out of breath.

"They are coming soon," he says between heavy breaths. "You need to leave. Go far away."

"Dammit, stop talking, Oli," I yell. "Save every breath to fight for your life."

Please.

His body begins to feel limp in my arms, but I refuse to think about anything other than pushing forward. I don't look down at him as I keep going. The burn in my calves intensifies as my breaths become shorter.

I can see the castle walls through the tree branches. The clinic must have something to fix him. Out of all the herbs that I transported and helped grow with my own hands, one of them is damned to help him stay alive.

My shoes slip on the muddy ground, and I fall backwards. I grunt at the impact but get up in the same breath. I resume my position and begin pulling again.

Please. I plead with the Fates. *Don't take him away.*

This forsaken forest in the middle of nowhere is not where Oliver will find his end.

The grunting coming from Oliver gets softer and softer until only a few murmurs remain. The Black Castle comes into full view, but far too slowly.

"*Please!*" I yell to the sky, the Fates, to the unfair strings that have paved the road for this.

I look down at his chest. Oliver has started to bleed from his mouth. Every time he spoke, more and more blood spread across his chin and down his shirt. I'm running out of time. His breathing becomes more shallow to the point I no longer see the rise and fall of his chest.

"No!"

No, please, not him.

I finally stop and kneel at his side.

"They are coming soon," he breathes.

"Let them come."

I hunch over Oli's chest and hold him as his lungs push

quick shallow gasps. I lay there with my ear pressed to his chest and count every shallow breath. *One, two, three, four, five...*

My tears fall when the sixth never comes.

I wait for it. I couldn't move even if I tried. My limbs are glued to the ground, frozen in place, holding on. The moment I look at him I would have to accept the fact that I'm in a world where Oli no longer exists.

I don't know how long I stay there, but the sun sets between the trees and the forest floor grows dark. After my skin chills, the only thing left to do is to make sure he doesn't spend the night alone here in the open. I can't think of him being cold while his skin is still warm to the touch.

I get up with little to no sensation in my arms and legs. My mind is tucked in somewhere deep and my body is going through the motions. I hook Oli's arms over mine and start pulling again. Every step feels like a heavy stone dropping. I don't look behind me, instead I just follow the path. My mind disconnects from the actions.

My limbs finally collapse when my body reaches the shield around the castle. The additional tension and weight of the shield is almost too much. I crawl to Oli's side once again and hold him.

"Oli," I try to say, but all that comes out is a whine between sobs.

Soldiers walk out of the shield and surround us on all sides. They're not facing us, instead their eyes are trained on the forest as if waiting for whatever lurks there.

"We need to prepare for a burial," Roman says somewhere behind me.

Footsteps announce even more people joining in.

"Janelle." Roman reaches his hand to me, but one glare

from me stops him in place. "We need to transport him inside the shield."

"I will do it," I say, wiping at my face.

"You don't have to do it alone." Roman stretches his hand to me.

I push it away. "I don't want nor do I care for your sympathy." The words come with venom. "I will bury him on my own."

It's the least I can do to him after I failed him. Oh, how I failed him. Oli deserved so much better than this.

"You think I'm going to give Oliver a burial because of you?" Sorrow fills his eyes as he looks at the man in my arms. The recognition is evident.

"You knew him." It's not a question.

"Oliver was born and raised in the Black Castle. His family has been here for generations. His cousin works in the kitchen to this day."

I never saw or heard of a friendship between Oliver and anyone outside of my father's men. Looking back, he was never friendly to my father's men. My father trusted him mostly around me, but that might also be because my father never noticed any nefarious intentions in him.

"He never said he knew any of you." I look up at Roman.

"He left a long time ago and never came back. He told Jesse in your father's hide out that he couldn't leave you. "

"Me?" I sit back, but I feel as if gravity is dragging me down.

"He stuck by you, Janelle. He was your shadow in that house of horrors. Oliver was loyal to the crown, but he was more loyal to your wellbeing."

I let my head lead forward and fall on Oli. How stupidly selfless. He always had a place to escape to. I imagined he stayed with my father because he had nowhere to go. I doubt he knew about the attack any sooner than me, but I will never know. He can't tell me now.

"There is only one person guilty here, Janelle. That's your father."

"He is coming," I say, looking down at Oli. "Oli said he is coming."

Olis' death is a personal attack on me. My father wanted to hurt me. The wound is supposed to weaken me for the fight. He will come for me next.

Roman calls for a soldier. "Send word to King Oscuro. The Black Castle will be under attack by nightfall."

He looks up at the sky as if asking the sun if it would stay up longer to buy us time. There isn't much light left. The castle is filled with powerful people, but there are far more vulnerable innocents. If rumors in the halls are to be believed, Brandon took even more soldiers when he added paying my father's hide out a visit to his agenda.

The ones gone to the underworld might be our undoing. There is no coincidence about it.

"Attacks at nightfall." Roman shakes his head. "What a cliché asshole your father is."

Oli is put on a stretcher and carried to the clinic's castle.

"We will get him ready for the funeral ceremony. He is one of us and deserves to be sent off like it." Amy Bee gives me a gentle smile I saw her give to her patients.

In a way, it soothes the ache in my heart. As if the pain I feel isn't unique to me. I'm not alone. But only I can do what needs to be done next. Is this what the Fates had referred to as opportunities to do what is right?

Amy Bee gestures to Roman, getting his attention. "I have a way of contacting someone at Fierno. This person might get to Brandon quicker than a messenger."

"Please do so," he says, then turns to me. "If only you had

your magic. It would be fitting for your father to meet his end with it."

Amy Bee clears her throat. "I will be back with something."

I watch the sun slowly hide behind the mountain peaks. I know two things for certain. One, my father will come tonight and I will be here to receive him. Second, only one of us will live to see tomorrow.

CHAPTER TWENTY-NINE

JESSE

Regardless of the number of times I've visited Fierno, there is always something that manages to surprise me. This time it's a festival for the dead. Colorful decorations are covering every available surface. Abandoned and nearly burned down buildings are not spared. Every light post has a crown of yellow and orange flowers and paper cut out banners connecting them from one to the other.

"Who pays for all of this?" I ask.

The place still looks half inhabited and full of rubbish, but festive.

"One of the crime families. I believe their name is Robles," Bianca says with a pleased expression. "I love the streets during this time of the year."

"Why?" Brandon and I say at the same time, referring to the reason the crime family does all this.

I've come in contact with the Robles family in my search for the Duelos and they have little care for the people at Fierno.

"It's a cultural tradition for that family. The celebration is to honor their dead. For a place like this that sees death much too often, the holiday was quickly adopted." Bianca shrugs.

That's an interesting holiday to partake in. I look over at Brandon, who is watching Bianca intently, and I wouldn't be surprised if soon enough we join in on the holiday. I think of my grandpa and how having a holiday to remember him on would be great.

A tall figure crosses the clusters of people walking about the center of Fierno. I've met Gabriel only at social functions, but it's hard to mistake him for anyone else. He is evidently in a hurry as his eyes frantically look around. Once he spots Brandon, he picks up his pace, coming to us.

"I cannot stay," Gabriel rushes to say. "I'm needed in Luzes to handle an urgent matter, but I'll return as soon as possible. Get started, I won't be long."

"Wait." Brandon tries to follow Gabriel, but he can only raise his hand before the angel calls for his wings and shoots up into the sky.

"That was quick," I say, looking towards the darkening sky. I lose track of him almost instantly.

"How are we supposed to summon Mel?" Matias asks.

I look at my brother. "You are the King of Puerto Quinn. If someone can summon anyone in the underworld, it has to be you."

Brandon doesn't seem concerned. "I think I have an idea."

The gates of the underworld are concealed. The building we approach appears deserted, but the door, in contrast, has a polished new handle that suggests there is something behind it. Upbeat dance music blasting from the speakers is very unconventional. The young woman behind the front desk smiles wide and waves as we cross the front door.

"Welcome, welcome, come on in. Gosh, y'all are like the

first people to come here in a week." The young girl gets up and rounds her desk. "My name is Rory."

"Hi, Rory," Bianca says tentatively.

"I'm sorry if I come off too strong. I haven't socialized in days. To say I'm eager for interaction is an understatement. I didn't realize this job would be so boring. One would think working minding the gates would be more exciting." She sighs in obvious disappointment. "They mind themselves."

Her word vomit is met with silence and blank stares. The absurd amount of energy gives us pause until her outfit registers. Rory is dressed in business casual, with black dress pants and a white button-down shirt. Her shoes are sparkling sneakers that shine like a disco ball. Her hair is also black with strips of pink. She looks like a mismatch of badass and girly.

"Sick style." I tell her, trying to fill in the silence.

"Thanks, but I'm taken." She fans her face.

"I wasn't," I try to say.

"I'm flattered, though. You're cute." She looks at Brandon. "Is this your brother?" She gives him a once over.

"Also taken," Bianca hurries to say. She takes a step closer to my brother.

"Okay, I see. Grr," Rory growls at them, then winks.

"You aren't human," Matias says, pointing out the obvious.

Few humans choose to live in Fierno and even fewer would venture to places like this where being in the vicinity of demons is part of the job.

"You're not a full witch either." Brandon points out, looking at the girl between furrow brows.

I take a closer look and realize he's right. There's definitely magic in her presence, but not in the way it feels with us. Brandon must be able to see way more with his soul reading gift.

"That's right." Rory rounds the desk and plumps down on her chair.

"What are you?" I ask, hoping my own gift will help me figure out if she lies.

"I already told you I'm not available." She turns to Bianca, covering her face from my sight. "Is he always this bad at taking rejection?"

To my utter surprise, Bianca laughs. The traitor.

Matias leans on the desk with one of his charming smiles. He's good at those.

"You're good at avoiding questions, huh?" he asks.

"Fine," she says with her hands up. "If you insist, you can pick me up tomorrow for dinner. I get off at ten. Bring me flowers and open the doors. That's all I require."

"You said you were taken," I remind her.

"To you." She looks over at Matias. "For you, on the other hand, I'm single. I like blonde curls." She winks at him.

While Rory entertains us, Brandon walks over to the wall and plucks a piece of paper from the complaints section. He jots something, but instead of dropping it on one of the trash baskets below the different signs, he walks over to Rory's desk.

"We would like to have this message delivered to General Mel." Brandon hands Rory the piece of paper.

"Are you sure?" She opens the note. "He is quite the sour puss. You would think the man's sense of humor died along with his soul."

If there was any room to believe she's a simple witch, it died right there. Not even the most brave of our kind would dare speak of general Mel in that way. She is either crazy and has zero self preservation or is far more capable of facing a predator like Mel.

She takes a second to read the note before turning back to my brother. "Should I even bother asking?"

"No," Brandon says.

"Perhaps you two are more alike." She pouts. "Go," she says with a wave dismissing us.

Brandon leads the way to a room to the side. The glow of the gates illuminates a connecting room covered in vegetation. The walls are covered in moss and leaves.

I take the note from Brandon, curiosity beating me. "Melly's custody request to Puerto Quinn," I read out loud. "What does that mean?"

Matias looks at the note over my shoulder. "Who is Melly?"

"You will see." Brandon walks over to the gates and pushes a red button on the side.

A loud ring blurts through the room. It's only minutes later before we hear a loud beating of wings before a creature lands on the edge of the gates, just on the other side of the doors. It stares at each of us intensely.

"Message for general Mel." My brother hands the creature the piece of paper.

The creature opens the paper. After a glance, he bursts into full belly laughter. His laughter trails as he flies off the gate and disappears into the mist of the other side.

"Now?" Matias asks.

"We wait," Bianca says.

She takes his hand in hers and walks to the other open room. There's a picnic table in the middle with benches. We sit in silence with only Rory's music blasting through from the reception filling in the space. Until the creaking of metal gates announces the entrance of someone from the underworld.

General Mel looks exactly as I imagined. He is a tall, menacing looking creature with little patience and a dangerous air. There's no doubt in my mind that he is as ruthless as he looks. His eyes don't miss a thing as he scans the room.

"What do we have here?" His statement comes out somewhere between disapproval and disappointment.

"Where is Melly?" Matias asks, looking behind Mel like he would see the requested creature from the message.

"Where she will stay." Mel frowns deeper.

"What exactly is a Melly?" I ask.

"A very requested headache." Mel turns to Bianca. "Is my brother here?"

"He was," Bianca explains. "But he was called urgently somewhere. He told us to go ahead and call for you and he would be here soon."

"Pathetic," Mel says, leaning against the arch of the entryway.

Despite his discontent, he doesn't appear to have any intention of leaving.

"Perhaps we can talk to you about why we are here, and when Gabriel arrives, you can have his full attention," Bianca suggests.

From her outside demeanor, anyone would think she's feeling incredibly confident, but I've gotten to know her lately. The slight shake of her thumbs tells me she feels anything but that.

"I'm glad to see there's someone with brains around here. It restores my faith in the future of Puerto Quinn."

I can almost feel the restraint my brother is showing to not bite on Mel's antagonistic comments. Successfully, he swallows his detours and begins explaining our reason to be there. I can see the moment Mel's interest in Matias sparks. The demon's eyes narrow, not in suspicion, but in close inspection.

"Well," Mel says and closes the distance to Matias. "Let's see if it's true."

With one finger, Mel pokes Matias' head, then a light of sparks like a zap of electricity ignites.

"That looks about right." Mel confirms with a nod.

"What just happened?" Brandon asks, looking between the two.

"My advice is to restore it to the book." The demon returns to the wall and leans against it.

"Obviously." Bianca rises to her feet. "You've told us nothing new."

"Wrong. I gave you confirmation that your assumption was correct." Mel shrugs. "I wouldn't call that nothing."

"We had confirmation when the book spoke to us directly," I say.

Mel ignores me. "The electric shock was a warning for me to stay away. I think that's a brilliant suggestion. I'll take it." He glares at Bianca. "What, did you expect me to have some bizarre insight into the magic inside your forsaken kingdom?"

Before Bianca or Brandon can respond, a series of shouts erupts from the reception area.

"Hey there lady, you can't just," Rory shouts, then trails off.

Seconds later, a tall woman burst into the room in a rush. Her hair is winded and her eyes are wild with fear. I've never seen her before. She has an angelic face and air to match. It can only mean one thing.

"LeeAnn, what's wrong?" Bianca hurries to ask.

"The Black Castle is under attack."

The air leaves my lungs as if struck by a blow.

"Who said this?" Mel asks her with scrutinizing eyes.

LeeAnn turns to Matias. "One of the plants you brought me is called the whispering leaf because if synced to a sister plant, they can whisper to each other."

"Its sister plant is at the castle's clinic." Matias concludes.

"Amy Bee and I quickly figured it out when conversations from each other's clinic would suddenly be whispered. She urged me to find you here and tell you to come home as soon as possible. They are outnumbered."

"Amy Bee told you this. What else did she say?" Brandon steps into her space, seeking the truth from her soul.

"Don't kill the messenger." Mel steps between them. "She's an angel." He gestures over his shoulder. "Hardly her fault for your problems."

"We need to go now," Brandon says, and we're all already on our feet. As if the air suddenly deflates him, his face falls. "We'll never get there on time. The soldiers waiting for us outside the city will not make it any sooner."

"I'll join you," LeeAnn says. Her face is fearless and full of determination. "I can fly there, but I can only carry one of you with me." She looks at Brandon. "I can get you there in a matter of minutes."

"Not your fight, sweetheart." Mel gestures for her to step aside.

"These are my friends." LeeAnn gestures to Bianca and Matias. "I know some angels that will go with me. I will call them now. We might be able to get some of you there sooner."

"Fine." Mel rolls his eyes and turns to Brandon. "I will aid you with reinforcements in your time of need. That's what my brother would've wanted me to do, anyway." He points at Bianca. "At a price, of course, but we shall discuss that later. I can get there quicker than the angels, but cannot provide a ride." He turns to LeeAnn. "By the time I see you there, the problem will be resolved. You might as well stay."

She crosses her arms and raises a brow. "The enemy isn't only Lord Duelo and his loyal soldiers. He has allies of other magical capabilities."

Mel shrugs. "Like it makes a difference. I'll see you there then."

"Wait," I rush after Mel. His steps do not falter, but his pace slows enough for me to catch up. "Lord Duelo is going after his daughter."

"So," he says.

"I will give you anything for her safety." The words do not fully register before they leave my lips, but they are true, as my existence without her is unimaginable. "My soul is yours if you keep her safe."

"Do you really think I want that thing?" He stops to fully face me. He looks at my chest as if he could see the very soul he shudders at. "All pure intentions and loving emotions, disgusting." He shakes his head and continues walking to the gates, leaving me looking after him.

Brandon places his hand on my shoulder. The act is meant to be comforting, but it feels too much like condolences. I shake him off me, but don't move away.

"LeeAnn will take me." Brandon turns to leave. "There is one other angel outside. If you wish to beat Bianca to him, I suggest you hurry."

I run for my life.

CHAPTER THIRTY

JANELLE

The hot water of the shower beats at my skin until it turns red. The burning sensation of the heat feels good. It helps pause my thoughts and the images of earlier. I don't look down for a while, worried I would see Oli's blood going down the drain. I wash it all off and tell my mind to focus on what is coming.

I'm quick to change into the same training gear I wore the day of the attack. I've kept it all this time because the fabric and fit have proven versatile. My fingers move across it and wonder if its true purpose for staying in my possession was to be used when I made things right.

My father will come here again, but this time I will not aid him. I will also not allow him to leave. There is no world where he gets to live while Oli doesn't. I'll make sure of that.

The ring of an alarm blasts through the castle, then flashing lights quickly follow. I finish dressing and make my way down to the dining hall. The chatter that normally flows through the halls ceases to a dead silence, only making the alarm noise seem louder. No shouts are heard, but people share comforting words as they move to the prearranged hiding spots.

I walk to the window and look out at the back of the castle. The people outside are motionless, their heads facing the edge of the forest. Then I see them.

The sight of movement causes my heart rate to speed up. Dozens of small duendes descend upon the castle's protective barrier. Their speed makes a mere flash of movement before they slam into the invisible shield. The protective barrier doesn't seem to startle them. They climb on top of each other, covering a section of the shield.

I rush into the dining hall where the majority have checked in for marching orders. Roman is arguing with a few of his soldiers as I cross the distance. I'm making my way to him when Santiago appears out of nowhere and takes my arm.

"Any news?" I ask. Referring to the evidently missing King, Bianca and Jesse. "Was the word sent?"

"Not sure it matters. They went to the underworld. There's no way they'll get back on time." Santiago looks over the crowd at the barrier.

The duendes have climbed seven feet up in the air and began punching the barrier with their magic. The shield doesn't give in, but a blue glow illuminates the spots being hit.

"It won't give out, right?" A young woman next to me asks no one in particular.

A huff comes from somewhere behind us. "Of course it will not."

I'm not as confident as them and from the pacing and Roman's face, I can see he isn't either. I push forward toward the Royal Force guard, but I'm once again pulled back by Santiago.

"I can help," I say.

We all know who is behind this and what he wants.

"Without magic? They don't want your help, Janelle." He takes a step close until our noses touch. "They will sacrifice you to gain time." He looks around him, but no one is paying attention to us at the moment. "Roman can't save you if Brandon isn't here."

I rest my palm on his cheek and say, "I never needed anyone to save me, Santiago. I have always saved myself. It's time I save others."

His eyes take me in with a new expression. He hesitates but concludes on something as his stiff fingers finally let me go and reluctantly steps back.

No soldier gets in my way as I cross to Roman. Nearby, Isabel sits with Lexi Blue, both of them wearing tense expressions.

Roman doesn't stop his pacing as he spots me. But a thundering noise outside has us both running for the garden doors. We stop just inside the threshold. The grounds are now empty of people other than those outside the barrier.

Unusual dark clouds hover on the other side of the shield. The clouds rotate and shift from side to side in a way I've never seen before, then lightning strikes. The blue glow intensifies to cracking spider webs that spread quickly. This level of magic is beyond my father. Roman and I know that.

"It won't last," I say.

"Line up, soldiers!" Roman shouts behind us.

A group of men and women rush past us. They line up side by side, standing as a second shield between the castle and the enemy.

The lighting stops along with the pounding from the duendes and they climb off one another and return to the forest edge. A second later, the shield drops.

It breaks apart into dust particles falling down like sand. As it clears out, we see no other but my father, standing in the middle of the clearing with a victorious grin on his face. As if it was even possible, he looks far stronger and bigger than I remember him.

My first thought is that he has done it. He managed to uncap his magic with The Red Book. But if he had done that, he wouldn't be here the moment Brandon left. He would not fear the King if his magic was one that could match his.

The only other answer is that he once again took from my mother. I wonder if she is dead. If he drained her of life once and for all. My heart aches for the last piece left of her. She was always too weak to stand up to him, and I've only ever been strong enough to walk away. That all ends today.

My father's cocky expression is mocking. "I have come for what is mine." His eyes narrow on me before turning to the crowd. "Your King is not here, so I'll make the request to you and your people. It's simple really, my daughter, in exchange for your lives."

Not a single soldier standing between my father and I flinch at the offer. I close my eyes, expecting the murmurs of fear from the people inside the dining hall to turn into demands of my return. None come.

"You have one chance to hand over my daughter!" My father shouts over the silent crowd.

"And you will hand over the Red Book?" Roman asks in a mocking tone. His previous concern is now masked behind a confident shield of his own making.

My father's laugh is hollow. "Oh, no."

"Why do you even want her back?" A soldier shouts from the sidelines. "She isn't that good of a fighter."

I'm actually a great fighter despite my lack of magic, but this is not the time to get offended.

"She is not a good maid." A woman in uniform chips in.

"There are always wrinkles in the laundry she does." She shakes her head in disappointment. "Sad really."

I'm out of words because not once have I ever done any laundry that was not my own. I look down at my shirt and see no wrinkles.

"She isn't even a good cook!" Pad shouts from the crowd. "Burns all she touches. One would think she had her magic back."

The crowd bursts into laughter.

They're not turning me in to buy us time. They're distracting him by mocking his request with irrational excuses. I feel tears gather in my eyes and do everything to hold them back.

"I want the traitorous witch back to face her fate," my father says, breaking through the humor.

The laughter of the crowd dies. Despite the coldness in his words, I don't shiver. I'm not hurt. I chose my path and for once I feel like I'm standing on the right side.

I turn to Roman with determination. "I can do it." My best chance is to get close to him. I doubt he means to kill me here. "I will end him and all this will be over. People don't have to die. With him gone, his army will be easier to destroy."

"Without magic?" He looks at me like I'm crazy. "We'll be offering you like dead meat."

"I am offended you think so little of me." I fake a pout.

Amy Bee rushes towards us, out of breath. "I hid it so well I almost lost it. Brandon gave me this a while back." She opens her palm between us and shows us a red round ruby.

I have seen it only once before, but even if my eyes were closed, I would feel it. My magic calls to me like a part of my soul standing outside my body.

"Good old friend," I whisper.

"This is not how she was supposed to get her magic back,"

Roman says with hesitation and forgetting that this was his idea initially.

"He's not counting on me to have it. What better than the element of surprise?"

Roman pulls at his hair in frustration. "I already called for them. They will find a way to get here soon. I know it."

"We don't know that. We're sitting ducks in a building full of scared people." Amy Bee looks back at the crowd. "Brandon entrusted me and I would like to say it is due to my judgment. I say we do it. He will understand why."

Roman gives me a pleading look, but it's not enough to change the events about to happen.

"These people have been through enough. Allow me to do right by them." I step closer to Amy Bee. "I got it from here."

I open my palm and she drops it there. I feel the restraint of power behind the glass like it knows who is holding it. The magic sealed inside can't wait to get home. I close my fist tighter until the glass breaks in my palm and the power slips into my bloodstream through the cuts in my hands.

The shock of power snaps goosebumps on my skin and spreads within seconds. My vision sharpens, my surroundings slow, and my breathing settles as the familiar all-vivid weight under my skin seeking freedom reaches my fingertips, waiting for release.

"Did it work?" Roman stares at my bloody hand.

I grin up at him and that is all the confirmation he needs. My gaze shifts to the waiting faces inside the dining hall. I memorize as many as my eyes can find. I know I won't find Oli, Jesse, Matias, Bianca or Brandon, but as I turn around, I count them into my total reasons for doing this.

"Janelle, I know you got this, but a little help can't hurt." Roman hands me a sword from his baldric. "Remind him that the Duelo dragons are born, not bonded."

Despite however much my father would like to believe he's the Lord Duelo, he would only be as close as marriage would allow him. The blood running through his veins is not blended with fire. His magic can never conjure what my brother's and mine can.

"Don't go soft on me now." I take the sword in hand and pass it from hand to hand, registering the weight of it. For its size and vibration of magic, it's surprisingly light.

I relish on the blessing of being able to feel magic again. A thing I never thought of twice.

"I am ready," I say.

Roman leans closer to my ear and whispers, "I'm glad to have become someone you deem worthy of saving."

"I'm glad I get the opportunity to do things right," I whisper back.

I look ahead and match my father's impatient frown.

"What is this?" He gestures in my direction as I close the distance.

The guards standing in line break formation to let me pass. Nods of respect in my direction are the only sign that they know what is happening. The blood trailing down my hand into the sword at my side must make a delightful sight.

"Let me make you a deal, old man," Roman shouts from his post "If you can take her, then you can have her."

I cross past where the shield once stood. My father stares me down from his place at the front of his dark legion of traitors. His disapproving gaze moves from my sword to my face.

"I know you did not come all the way here just for me," I say as I take my place a few feet before him.

I gesture to the men behind him. This attack must have been in the works long before I showed up at his keep. Requesting for me to face him must be a distraction or the beginning of his actual plan. Regardless, I know my father enjoys boasting about his successes and, from the smirk on his face, this is going according to his plans.

His eyes trace every step I take, and every move I make.

"You might have something right about that." He looks behind him and smiles like a shared joke among friends. "But your survival has caused a lot more trouble than anticipated. It needs to stop."

The realization of his words hit me, and I almost lost my footing. The appearance of the royal offspring with the news of Ignis calling for me was just earlier today, but the outrage of the city has been happening for longer.

"My survival?" I ask, inclining my head.

"Do I truly need to say it?" My father looks bored. "I should've expected that your connection with the Oscuro boy would prove troublesome. It has always been that. But I never expected Brandon Oscuro to let you live. Kings don't forgive traitors."

His plan was always to have us all die the night of the attack. My brothers and I were never meant to walk out. The lack of anger at losing his two oldest children finally makes sense. It was at his own hand.

"Why?" I can't help the word slip from my lips.

I know the answer, but the child inside me seeks a reasoning that does not point at her father sacrificing her for his greed.

"Ignis needed to back me, but I knew they never would turn on their King unless he killed their precious leaders. You think I don't know they never truly accepted me? The second your brother was born, they counted the days for his ascension."

I add my brother's names to my list of reasons. Their only sin is being born to this man.

"Ignis answers to the Oscuros only because the Duelo

family allows it. Once you're gone, they will have no choice but to answer to me."

His logic is so flawed I can't say anything. Reason has left him.

"I would've let you live, Janelle. But you brought that boy and escaped with my only opportunity at uncapping magic."

"Jesse," I say. "His name has always been Jesse. And your opportunity at uncapping magic is named Matias."

"They are nobody!" he shouts.

"You will be nobody. All your schemes will amount to nothing," I say. Fury consuming my body. "Your name will fade to nothing."

I feel the moment his lips breath out a spell to compress my body. The contradiction I breathe out keeps my limbs mobile, but I don't make it known. Instead, I wait for him to cross the distance between us. I watch, unmoving until he is inches from me.

"You could've been so much. You, my obedient daughter, are the most like me."

Obedient. Not loving, precious, or any other endearing name. His care for me was always under the condition of me following his every command.

"I'm nothing like you, coward."

I swing the sword over my head and down on him. My father is fast, but he's not accounting for my magically enhanced speed. He isn't fast enough. The sword makes contact with his face from the top of his forehead down his nose and upper lip. The cut is shallow, but I've marked the man who counted himself untouchable.

His expression of shock is only momentarily. A small sheen of blood covers the cut down his face. My father doesn't wipe it off. He smiles wide and lets out a low chuckle.

A blast of wind pushes against me, but I counteract, then

hold up a shield in front of me. Blow after blow, my father screams as he attempts to push me back and tear me down. I don't move an inch. He pauses for a moment to catch his breath and reassesses.

I take the opening to open my palm wide to the floor. I call to the creature my fire forms and, like an eager puppy ready to play, it answers me. The fire erupts with a fierce greediness to meet freedom once again.

The snake I've called Dexter in my mind takes form and spreads all around us. It circles my father and me, cutting us both off from the outside world, then lets out a loud growl to the sky. There is no aid coming for either of us. I've yet to meet a creature that can cross Dexter.

My father's eyes widen at the realization that my magic is fully back.

"Kill them all!" he shouts to his men, blood dripping from his lips. His eyes narrow on me with a glint of victory. "You really think it will end with me?"

Above the crackling flames of Dexter's fire, the battle cry of creatures marching to the Black Castle fills the air.

"No," I say as I cross to him with the sword up and ready. "But *you* will end with me."

I cross the distance towards him and swing the sword in his direction. I've enveloped it on fire now and the blazing steel cuts through the air like lightning. My father is ready for my moves now, so it's hard to make contact but not impossible. It becomes a game of cat and mouse. I go in the defense, then in the offense. Blow after blow, I don't hold back and neither does he.

The more spells I block from my father, the more I realize how ill-prepared he is for battle. His skills have always been only talk and today I'm witnessing the extent of this mirage. His worst soldiers would hold their own against him.

I need to end this, and I know I'm able. The knowledge of what will happen next is what keeps me in this loop. He loses his footing and I toss a fire orb that hits the center of his chest. The air leaves his lungs, and he recoils to himself. I step up to him and raise my sword to his temple. This is it. One swing of the steel will end it all, but I freeze.

No magic is holding me in place, but the little voice in my head telling me there will be no turning back. This is one of those things I will have to live with. All the work I've put into turning a new leaf suddenly feels in jeopardy.

I lower my sword.

"Am I any better than you if I do this?" I say, kneeling on the floor. "I will only become another version of you."

My father laughs from his place on the floor. His chuckles are interrupted by coughing as he hunches over to his side with one hand holding his stomach.

A swirl of black smoke bleeds through the ground up and spreads until a person materializes and walks through the smoke. A tall man with a dark air takes in the scene. The creature looks at Dexter with curiosity.

"Mel?" my father asks with wide eyes. "Have you come to take me to the underworld?"

"I'm afraid even the underworld has standards you do not meet," Mel says with a grunt.

I've never met the demon in person, but his name and reputation describe him perfectly. His golden gaze falls to me and a look of disappointment passes through him.

"You can still do it. It's not too late." His expression doesn't change when I don't move. "Your soul is just as disgusting as your boyfriends," Mel says.

"What?"

Mel doesn't answer me. He turns to my father and extends his hand. Nothing physical or visual happens, but the connection is made known as my father's screams echo in the forest.

"Wait," I yell. Mel doesn't pay me any attention. I turn to my father. "Where is it? Where is the Red Book?"

My father doesn't move, but his eyes turn in my direction. His lips curve at the edges. The expression chills my skin despite the wall of fire surrounding us.

"You'll never find it on time. The Oscuros will never get it back. Not without war." He coughs. "The moment my soldiers and I don't return, someone will take it to the King of Paz. He will finally have the thing he needs to destroy Puerto Quinn. My death will be avenged."

I step back, staring at the hateful eyes of a man who'd rather see the world burn down to ashes than admit defeat. The King of the Human Lands will finally get an upper hand on *all* magic kind, not just Brandon. My father has doomed us all.

CHAPTER THIRTY-ONE

JESSE

The abrupt landing throws me off balance as soon as Pedro releases his hold on me. I find myself on my back, observing the sky as it moves for a full minute. I close my eyes and breathe in deeply.

We covered the distance between Fierno and the Black Castle in minutes instead of hours. Angels are speedily fliers.

"I puked after my first fly," Pedro says and pats me in the back like I did a good job.

I never thought I'd say this.

"Flying via angel is far too personal and my least preferred form of transportation."

"No hurt feelings," Pedro says.

Flashes of light thunder down from the sky. Dozens of bright white wings cover kneeling angels as they land one by one. Their presence shocks all, as the fight ceases for a breath. That's all the time it takes for the angelic creatures to rise to their seven feet. Then they defend the Black Castle.

Swirls of black smoke bleed out of the ground, forming terrifying figures out of nightmares. The demonic creatures join in with the angels and castle guards as they exterminate the enemy in the most gruesome way I've ever seen.

The guards are holding their posts well, not being backed into the castle walls. The angels reinforce their lines while the dark creatures pluck out enemy soldiers out of thin air.

I make a quick and count that every single body littering the ground belongs to the enemy lines.

A rain of black mist engulfs two groups of duendes. Simultaneously, a dozen of them fall to their knees. The mist slips into their bodies, then quickly to follow are agonizing screams. Their bodies drop like flies seconds later. Cloaked in dark mist, Brandon lands like a warrior ready for combat. LeeAnn makes quick work of stepping aside as my brother joins angels and demons alike.

He doesn't stand back with the line of guards. He lands in front of them and stands there, moving his mist from foe to foe. The screams of agony are the only signal of where he has hit his target.

"There you are!" Roman shouts. The adrenaline-high is clear in his voice.

He is currently battling a giant in formation with a few of his soldiers. Blow after blow, they attack in a coordinated effort until the giant falls. They make quick work of subduing him. No one is being spared. They came here with clear intentions of war and that's what they're getting.

A wall of fire off by the clearing shifts in an organized flow, catching my attention. The wall moves further, revealing the fire snake we've all seen more than once. It's as tall and wide as I remember it.

Dexter has been Janelle's biggest weapon and show of power. She has never openly labeled him, but I've caught her speaking to him under her breath more than once. It may not be considered a gift, but since only Duelos can summon a fire creature, it seems fitting to call it that.

"Her magic is back," Brandon says, then looks around as if in search of someone but gives up quickly after.

As the wall of fire clears, three figures come into view. Mel is standing just behind Janelle. They are both standing in front of the body of Lord Duelo sprawled on the ground.

I look at Janelle but find nothing in her expression but fury. No guilt has had time to slip in, but I know it's unavoidable. Taking her father's life is damned to leave a mark on her soul.

Mel is beside her, looking at the body on the ground with growing disinterest. He leans over to her and says something in her ear. Then he crosses the distance to Brandon and me.

"She's a lost cause," Mel tells me, then turns to look at her. "What a shame. She would've made a wonderful addition to my ranks."

Dexter lets out a long growl before rushing forward and picking up Lord Duelo. He tosses the once leader of Ignis into the air and catches him in his mouth. Dexter's body is made of flames, making him partly transparent. We watch the body slowly disintegrate, consumed by the fire until he is nothing but ashes.

Janelle wields air to pick up the ashes and carries them high in the air until they are long out of sight.

"I don't want your soul." Mel stares at Janelle with something close to pride. "I want hers."

"Her soul isn't for sale," I say.

"You boys, with your delusional state of thinking you make choices for them. It may not be for sale now but the day might come." His voice trails off as LeeAnn joins us.

The fight has ended. Angels move around the guards, offering congratulations and checking on all the injured. Their healing magic will have everyone back to normal in a couple of hours. However, LeeAnn's face is filled with worry. She walks straight to Mel, but once a foot away, she looks down at her hands.

"Where is my brother?" Mel asks with a blank expression.

"He was called away," LeeAnn says. She pushes her shoulders back and locks eyes with one of the most notorious creatures in the underworld. "Mel, I think he is in trouble."

"What do you mean?" he asks in a low, hardly contained tone.

"I don't know much but..."

LeeAnn's eyes fill with tears. Her hands tremble and her breathing becomes shallow. I take a step back and realize she is having a panic attack.

"LeeAnn, breathe please." Brandon moves to take her arm, but stops at Mel's block.

I know my brother doesn't mean to cause her harm. He likely believes that she requires a sense of stability in order to lower her heart rate. But Mel takes his proximity as a threat.

Mel pulls LeeAnn to his chest as swirls of black smoke from the ground envelops them.

"Hey!" Someone shouts.

A group of angels rush over at Mel. The smoke disappears and with it, has the demon and angel who stood there.

"Where's he taking her?" Pedro asks me.

"She wasn't feeling well. He's taking her back home." Brandon lies so easily and convincingly I wonder if I missed something for a second.

"She doesn't fly often since she always stays at Fierno," Pedro says, more to himself than to us. "She must've gotten sick."

The look he gives me implies I should feel more at ease about falling sick after my first flight. Other angels murmur things about why a demon shouldn't have been the one to help her home. But no one else asks us anything else. They move to leave as they continue to discuss amongst themselves.

"You lied," I say.

Brandon steps to my side, looking at the aftermath. "One problem at a time. Regardless, I truly believe he means her no harm. The way he acts around her makes me wonder if he suspects they have something in common."

"What do you mean?"

Brandon looks around as if to make sure no one is listening. "Mel isn't supposed to have a soul. He has made remarks about not having one. But when I look at him, I see a color. The same color is there when I look at LeeAnn."

I stand there in stunned silence.

The idea that a demon from the underworld could've the same color soul as an angel is preposterous. However, I believe Brandon when he tells me what he saw. There are too many unknowns.

It seemed as if they just met today in front of us. For all we know, that was the first time they met in *this* lifetime.

CHAPTER THIRTY-TWO

JANELLE

Each limp hurts as I walk across the yard. Soldiers are finishing clearing the grounds of those who didn't make it. Thankfully, the enemies never made it inside the castle, leaving behind only a few injured who were quickly healed by angels.

"Janelle," Roman gestures to the pile of enemies on the far left side of the yard. "Do you mind doing the honors?"

I nod and order Dexter to do his thing. The pile is in flames in seconds and in a matter of minutes it will be nothing but ashes. I extend my hand, and with a familiar wave, I call Dexter back. He falls into small sparks that return to my palms.

"Janelle!" Jesse rushes to my side and picks me up in a hug.

I hold him tight and breathe him in. The idea of him being here with me settles in. I got to see him again. I really didn't think I would.

"Are you okay?" Jesse looks me over as he is going to make sure whatever I say matches with his inspection.

"I'm great. Glad that it's partly over."

Despite the dismantling of the rebellion, the Red Book is

yet to be found. If my father spoke the truth, it's going to be taken to the king of the Human lands if it's not there already. Once in his possession, there's no telling what the future might hold.

May the Fates protect us.

The enemy just got hold of the one weapon that could destroy our world.

"You did what you had to do." Jesse's eyes are full of forgiveness.

"I didn't kill him." I look down at my hands, trying hard not to judge myself for the lack of will to see it through. "Mel did it. I only disposed of him."

"Is that so?" Brandon moves to stand between us. "What else did I miss?"

"My father didn't bring the book," I say.

Brandon nods as he expected as much. I share everything that was said during the battle. Including my father's threat about having someone deliver the book to the human King. I would like to think whoever was instructed with the mission would see the dangers of following that plan but his followers have always been blind to sense.

The King of Puerto Quinn takes everything in with a pensive expression.

"We got it from here." He takes my shoulder in hand. "It's time for you to return to Ignis. I need you to make sure those in the city stay strong in case the Human Lands declare war. I need each city to be ready."

"Brandon," Jesse says with furrowed brows.

"I will need someone to help her." Brandon smiles at his brother. "I would trust no one else more than my most loyal advisor. You'll be missed here, but you're needed there more."

"Thank you," Jesse whispers so low I almost miss it.

The brothers hug tightly. Roman sees the exchange from

across the yard and sprints in their direction. He joins in the embrace, probably completely at a loss for the reason behind it. Roman doesn't truly need a reason after all, does he?

I feel like an intruder at witnessing such a tender moment. I excuse myself and head back inside to look for one person I wish more than anything could hear the news of my return to Ignis. A big hug from him would cure the ache left in my soul, but I know his absence is the cause of it.

I walk into the clinic and find Pad standing by Oliver's bed. His hands aren't touching Olis, but the slight twitch of his fist tells me he's debating it. From my place by the doorway, I take a closer look at Pad. The similarities between them are now impossible to miss. I don't know how I didn't see them before.

"You are his cousin." I walk deeper into the room.

"He felt like my brother. We grew up together our whole lives. He never cared to leave until he met her. His wife."

I nod. "I don't remember her much. She died when I was a child."

He smiles fondly. "Timid, quiet woman with a gentle temper. He loved her."

I wish I would've had the chance to meet the woman he loved enough to leave the Black Castle for. I also wish I would become someone worthy of him staying behind for. There is no doubt in my mind that Oli remained behind for me. He even forsake his vow to the King for me.

"Thank you for bringing him home," Pad says.

Oliver's home is the Black Castle. He made it home. I was fated to fulfill my promise without knowing. This is not how I wanted things to go, but it's how they happened.

"It was the least I could do for him. Now, I vow to become someone worthy of all his sacrifices. To keep his memory alive."

"He was right about you, you know." Pad clears his throat. "You're just like Rosa."

"How so?" I ask, eager to learn anything I can. "Wait, he talked about me?"

I never got an inclination to believe Pad knew me before we met at the kitchens, but his kindness always felt deeper than the time.

"He mentioned you here and there. Rosa was an unstoppable force of nature with a strong will. She was also very caring of only those she deemed hers to protect."

I look down at my hands then back at Pad. "She sounds more like the person I should become than the person I am."

"We all have room for improvement." He pats his stomach in good humor.

I laugh and cross the distance toward Oliver. "I wish things were different."

"That makes two of us." Pad takes my hand in his and leads me out of the clinic. "It's time for some comfort food."

"I don't think I can eat right now, Pad."

"His favorite was stew."

I laugh and tears fill my eyes. "I know."

I recall the times Oli would visit my room during the nights my father would send me to bed without dinner. Olis idea of dinner was mostly crackers of different kinds or stew. It didn't take long for me to realize that he would be the one to make the stew.

One night I refused to eat it and he left it in my room in case I changed my mind. The next morning, my maid commented on the soup. My fear of getting Oli in trouble made it so I would never leave it again.

"Janelle!"

My name comes from the end of the hall. Matias and

Santiago sprint to us with a book in their hands and wide smiles on their faces.

"We found him." Matias pushes the book to my face. "We got him."

"Who?"

I take the book in hand and look at the already open page. My eyes find the name in a second, as if they already knew where to look. The name we have been searching for is finally spelled out before me and I cannot believe it.

Klause Pazduelo. His last name, at last. Pazduelo.

The connection cannot be coincidence. I no longer believe in those. Everything is a part of something. Nothing is a singular speck in this spiderweb called life.

"Look who his father is," Santiago says, almost shaking in anticipation.

My eyes climb one person up in the family tree.

"Knox," I say, the gasp I let out is audible.

My hands tighten on the book. His father is no other but a prince from hell. All the comments about his magic being ancient and not like ours suddenly make sense. His magic is demon-like. I look at the woman beside Knox. The infamous witch that married a prince from hell, Olivia Pazduelo. It looks like more than one of the Pazduelo sisters produced offspring after all.

"Olivia Pazduelo," I say, as if everything now makes sense.

Pad looks over our shoulders to the book. "Pazduelo is an old witch's name. Once known as the most powerful witches in existence."

Matias gestures down at the page and points at a woman in the same row as Klause. Under a different prince of hell.

"Rory," he says with a laugh. "We just met her at the gates to the underworld. She works there."

"We found his cousins." Santiago runs his hands through his hair.

The boys and I look at each other like we hit gold. We are a step closer to this person who has been at the center of it all.

Rory has a brother and his picture and name are stated beside her. The face of Ulysses stares back at me from the page. The young man I befriended against my will in the forest near my cabin. No wonder he was so intrigued by me. If his father is also a demon and mother a witch, he must have been able to tell that I'm a magic wielding creature living in hiding. His interest was out of curiosity.

"There are a total of four of them," Santiago says, pointing at the page. "Klause, Ulysses, Rory and Leo."

Klause is the only one whose mother appears in name and picture. The story of her arrival in the underworld is legendary. She is known as the only princess of the underworld. None of the others must've married their partners and moved to the underworld.

"You think Calaca will find him?" Matias asks me.

She has not returned yet, but I'm not worried.

"Calaca might be the only one who can and I can't say Klause would be too happy about it," I say.

After all, he has been in hiding for years now. Long enough to erase his kind from our common knowledge, but by Calaca finding him, his existence will once again come to light.

CHAPTER THIRTY-THREE

JESSE

I look down at the map on Brandon's desk. Much of what lies on the other side of Fierno is a mystery to us. We have old maps that describe the Human Lands, but there is only guessing on whether or not they are correct. After all, none of us have ever been there.

It has been only a day since we learned of the fate of the Red Book. Guards were sent to chase down different routes, but there is no way to find it when we have no idea how it's being transported. A needle in a haystack is the best analogy for how hard finding one book across border lines is.

"Once inside the Human Lands, we have no way of chasing it." Roman crosses his arms. "Not for long, at least."

The ban on magic beings inside Paz goes beyond being a mere preference. It's a law of the land. Magic doesn't function once a person crosses into their land. The power it takes to make that happen is impressive. But there are no records of how the human King shielded his land.

Janelle didn't have magic in her body, which allowed her to remain inside the Human Lands. But when I visited, I knew my presence was only allowed for a finite amount of time. How it happens is not common knowledge, but if I were to remain, my presence would've been made known to the authorities. It would've been a matter of days before I would've been chased out.

"Janelle could stay in the Human Lands because you took her magic," I say, looking between my brothers. "Perhaps doing that again will be the only way to get men inside."

The front door of the office opens and in walks a man I've never met before. The stride and swagger in which he enters the space speaks of confidence and far too much familiarity. I look over at Brandon, who is staring at the man with the same confused expression I'm wearing.

"I have come here to save your day." The stranger gives us a brief nod and gestures for us to react in one way or another. At the lack of reaction, he clears his throat. "Let me start over. My name is Klause Pazduelo. I heard you have a book of mine and that you are missing a very important book of yours."

At the mention of the name, we jump to attention. All we learned about Klause is fairly new. After all the things that have come to pass due to this man's words, it's hard to believe that he's here in the flesh. He doesn't look ancient or old at all. The man is tall and thin with curly brown hair and fair skin.

"What do you want?" Brandon asks with his king voice firmly in place.

Klause takes in my brother from head to toe. Sizing up the enemy is not the right way to describe it. It's more like Klause is assessing if he's the person whom he should bother with.

"King Oscuro," I tell Klause, taking a step forward, "has asked you to state your purpose for being here."

"Testy," Klause says to me before turning back to my brother. "I have come to make you a deal. I will bring you the

Red Book from wherever it may be and in return, I would like a favor."

"A favor of what kind?" Bianca asks from the doorway.

She closes the door behind her and makes her way to Brandon's side. She must've been listening in because she is looking at Klause with a similar disbelief to mine. It's a little starstruck.

When Klause's eyes land on her, his expression mirrors hers for a second before it quickly turns to a taunting mock. "A favor of any kind, cousin." He turns back to Brandon. "I have no current plans to cash it, but I'm sure I'll find something when the time comes."

"You think you can get us the Red Book?" Brandon's tone is distrustful.

"I know I can." Klause smirks.

"We have reason to believe that it's somewhere in the Human Lands," Brandon says in a challenge.

Klause shrugs. "Close to my home."

"You live in Paz?" I ask.

No wonder why his existence is something we've so easily been in the dark about.

Before he can reply I ask, "How can you bypass the magic that doesn't allow those who wield magic to stay?"

"What magic do you think created such a shield for an entire reign?" He pauses and taps his lips. "I didn't mean to say as much. Keep it to yourself."

I'm stunned. My gaze finds Bianca and a smirk paints her face. This is not at all who we imagined Klause to be.

"How long would it take you to bring it back?" Brandon asks.

Klause assesses my brother's question like a puzzle. His eyes look up at the sky like he is calculating something as his index finger taps his chin.

"Three months."

Brandon turns to us, giving Klause his back. "There's no time to call a meeting. What do you guys think?"

"I don't see how this can affect us negatively. We can conduct our own research in case he fails," Roman says.

"I do not fail," Klause says as he inspects a bookshelf.

Bianca looks over her shoulder. "Mel said that about you."

"Mel, the demon?" Klause nods. "Nice fellow."

I'm now completely sure that Klause is insane.

"I think you might be the only person who would say something like that." Brandon raises a brow. "Shows a lack of sanity."

"How sane can I truly be after so many years of being alive?"

Bianca shrugs. "He is self-aware."

My brother crosses the distance between them and extends his hand. "In three months, I want the Red Book, and you can have a favor in return within reason." His eyes are determined.

Klause's smile is wide and slightly scheming. "Deal. Now, where's my journal?"

CHAPTER THIRTY-FOUR

KLAUSE

There is no room for fear here.

The words are carved into an arch that leads to the back of the Black Castle. I stop only long enough to read it and roll my eyes.

I want to laugh at how much those words haunt me. They remind me of my childhood and despite all the fond memories of my mother, those words are not one of them.

Unbeknownst to my mother, the words would haunt her. She spoke them to herself. The noisy onlooker caught the words right off her lips by chance. They all echo them like it symbolizes some type of heroic act. Little did they know, my mother had no trepidation about what awaited her in the underworld. Her descent was more than willing, she chose to marry my father and follow him there.

I doubt she would have ever spoken the words if she knew the way they would live on for as long as her. On that note, I should definitely pay her a visit. I'm certain my visit to Puerto Quinn will make its way back to her in the underworld. She'll not forgive me lightly for not stopping on my way.

I give the castle one last glance. I spot a red head pop from the edge of the forest. The young woman captures my notice instantly. It's not her superficial beauty that attracts my attention. My eyes are looking beyond that to her inner core. I cannot see it in the literal form of the word, but I can sense it. Like two siblings feeling kinship despite distance.

She makes her way towards the building and I can't help but watch in fascination. She isn't alone for long. One of the Oscuro brothers meets her halfway and pulls her into his arms. I believe his name is Jesse, the second oldest. They share a tender kiss.

I look back at the quote on the arch and laugh to myself. There is not one, but two. What a funny play by the Fates. I wonder if the Oscuro brothers know they have two of my descendants in their home. I presume that's a negative. It's uncertain whether the two girls are aware of it themselves.

This is yet another reason I should pay my mother a visit. She would be delighted to know this bit of information. After all, we are all family.

ACKNOWLEDGMENTS

And the story continues... I cannot wait to wrap up this series and clue you all into the inner workings that have consumed my thoughts for the past year. I hope you are ready for the ride.

First and foremost, I want to thank God for the opportunities and blessings that have made this book possible. This year has been full of them, and I'm beyond grateful.

To my editor and beta readers, thank you. Your hard work, sharp eyes, and honest feedback brought this story to life in ways I couldn't have done alone.

To my husband, who has been at the center of the editing, troubleshooting, map-making, and emotional support process, you are truly everything. I love you.

To the amazing readers who supported The Fifth Soul and came back for more, thank you. Your support means more than I could ever put into words.

And finally, to you, the reader holding this book. I hope you found a piece of yourself in these pages. Thank you for giving my story a home.

:)

ABOUT THE AUTHOR

Diana Denisse is a writer of high fantasy novels and avid romance book reader who puts the magical world living in her head onto paper. She spends her free time hiking and exploring national parks across the country, seeking the magic at our fingertips.

To learn more about future books, please follow the social media links below.

instagram.com/AuthorDianaDenisse

tiktok.com/@AuthorDianadenisse

amazon.com/stores/Diana-Denisse/author